Rusty *LOVERS*

LEADING LADIES BOOK 1

LILAH NICHOLS

ISBM 978-1-7330546-1-4

For everyone who might
catch a glimpse of themself
in this novel.

Chapter One

Elizabeth leaned back in her chair and looked down the length of the ballroom of the downtown Marriott. The event had a good turn out tonight, slightly better than the previous three Silver and Gold meet and greets that she'd attended in the past. The ballroom almost looked like a romantic restaurant, with white tablecloths on small tables that were not so artfully arranged in two straight rows up and down the length of the room. Instead of waiters and bottles of wine, the hotel staff hovered near the refreshment table, probably watching phones hidden behind their ever-present clipboards.

Maybe they didn't realize the glow from their phones shone extra bright in the hotel's effort at ambiance. The lights were dimmed, and each table had an electric candle on it, adding a soft glow to the daters. The hotel was making an effort to have it be romantic, she supposed, but they probably would have had more success getting the singles who turned up to leave as couples if the refreshments had included a glass of wine, and the little tables had included an assortment of cheese and crackers.

There was always a bit of excitement at the start of the event, the women sizing each other up and the men trying to get a better look at the pool of speed daters before the lights dimmed. Eliza rarely had a chance to speak to the other ladies. They ranged in age from forty-five to almost eighty, although old Mrs. Sparkins insisted she was only seventy-five.

Eliza had encountered her one evening at the coat check, and stifled a laugh when the sweet older woman teased about how she was on the prowl for a younger man. It would be obvious to anyone that the late forties, early fifties crowd that frequented the live-action speed dating events were more the age of her son that she spoke of so glowingly.

Actually, it was amazing any hotel still had speed dating events anymore. The world of dating had been taken over by eHarmony and Ourtime.com. Eliza glanced up and down the room, and while it wasn't truly all silver and gold, it certainly did look like the anti-technology crowd. The ones who didn't want to swipe left and right or send out flirts and little greetings to find companionship in a world of pixels.

Eliza always felt she could get a better read on whether or not a man had the right kind of potential by meeting him in person. Something about reading bios and the pictures at the online dating sites, they never quite told the whole truth. And half those sites were thrown up by someone with little experience and an interest in making profits, not matchmaking.

The man sitting opposite her picked up her hand, drawing her attention back to him. He looked well enough, mid-forties, slightly graying, and devilishly handsome, but the problem was he knew it. He never seemed to stop talking.

"Been working there for 25 years, been having HR work on my retirement numbers. So I had to sell the condo downtown, the judge wanted me to give it to my ex." He barely paused for breath, and Eliza tugged slightly, almost succeeding in slipping out of his grasp. "And my summer house, oh, you would have loved that. All the ladies do, my last girlfriend wanted to replace all the furniture, but I like the old charm, and I didn't keep it out of my ex's hands just to let another woman overhaul it!"

She couldn't take it anymore. She managed a slight cough and yanked her hand free. She looked down the line of tables and saw more of the same. All the same speed daters who had been at the hotel last month. A few of the ladies looked out of a by-gone era, wrapped up in wool sweaters and brightly-colored silk scarves, the look completed with their fanciest charm bracelets and their best clip-on earrings.

Her impression of the men was slightly different, finding them frequently to be workaholics, people who turned up in work clothes and might be returning to work following the event. She might be standing there in one of her work outfits, but she left the office at five, if not sooner.

She liked the idea of this kind of dating, spending a few minutes and then moving on to the next table. Shaking hands and reading body language seemed an immense improvement over swiping left and right, even if it was just as ineffective. She groaned inwardly, kicking herself once again for letting her children put her up to this. "Go, mom. Try it." Jenny had said. "You have to get your feet wet sometime."

This wasn't so much getting her feet wet, as dipping a toe into the pool. It was less of a meet and greet every time and more of a job interview. Paul, or Bryan, or whatever his name was, kept right on talking. Eliza closed her eyes and counted heartbeats. She wondered why finding love a second time around had to be so hard.

The bell was still a few minutes away. If she excused herself, she might be able to fetch her coat and escape before the next date change. She worked up another polite cough, and stood. "Please excuse me, Philip," Cough, cough. "I really do need a drink." She did her best to make her voice sound scratchy and apologetic, and hurried over to the refreshment table, grateful he didn't follow.

She poured herself a Solo cup of ice water and scanned down the tables again. The ladies were the ones shifting every 8 minutes tonight, and as she peered around she saw faces she knew. Men who turned up, month after month and mostly spent their time talking about their legal victories over their ex-wives or their stuff. She sort of felt like it was coffee hour after church, only without the coffee and donuts.

Eliza drank the last of her water and waved to Philip. "Bye-bye, Philip," she muttered to herself. "Hope you find a maid, or a doormat, or arm candy. Whatever you are looking for here."

She used both palms to smooth down her trousers. She had worn her confidence outfit tonight. Black pants that smoothed out her generous curves, a perfectly draped top that showed off her long neck and showed just a hint of cleavage, and a gray knit jacket. She'd twisted her dark hair up in a bun, but tendrils escaped and framed her face. She knew she didn't look young anymore, but she wasn't about to resort to creams, needles or surgery to look young enough to satisfy a man ten years older than she was who wanted her to look twenty-nine.

Nope, it was either a man who wanted to share his later years with a middle-aged lady, or nothing.

She cast one last glance around the room so she could tell her daughter that yes, she'd tried, and no, there were no interesting gentlemen there. With a resigned sigh, she set her cup down on the table and headed across to the foyer. One quick stop for her coat and she'd make a run for home.

And then she heard it. A voice. It was low and smooth. Very intriguing. She turned back towards the other side of the ballroom, scanning. She checked her phone. It was almost time for the bell, and soon her window to escape would be gone. On impulse, she wound her way through the tables, trying not to look obvious, waiting for the voice to start again.

She stood still, feeling a little silly, searching the faces, but some instinct inside was insistent, demanding she find the face that went with that voice. As her gaze skimmed over the couples, many were familiar. Her brain had nicknamed most of them: Legalese, who spoke as if he were delivering a closing argument, and Bad Hair Day, only it seemed every day was a bad hair day. Eliza smiled as she looked them all over. It wouldn't be hard to match them up with each other, if any of them could get past what they wanted and get on with what they needed.

These hopefuls turned up and did this dance every month, meeting to speak for a few minutes, trying to find a connection. Some of the daters were pitched forward, clasping hands, and others were already checking their watches and packing up for the next switch. Every week the short conversations were nowhere near enough time to get past anything but the niceties. Any minute now the bell would ring and it would be the commotion of the change would begin.

Eliza scanned the far row of tables, and her patience paid off. There was a lull in the low conversation. The voice washed over her again, and she spotted him. She paused and observed him. He wasn't what she expected. Instead, he looked uncomfortable. Older than she was, well, maybe only slightly older. Graying, clean-shaven, sitting politely at the table. His date was gathering up her things, preparing to move on to the next chap.

She peered through the dim light, taking in the white button-down shirt, paisley tie and tweed jacket. Real tweed, the kind you could slide a pencil through. And unless she missed her guess, leather patches at the elbows. Not a look she normally went for, not since she'd had a crush on her Shakespeare teacher in high school, but it suited him.

His date stood and departed as the bell rang. The lady was tall, carrying her trench coat folded over her arm. The soft lighting illuminated her short, pale gray bob. She dipped her head one last time and darted off towards the refreshment table. Eliza let his voice wash over her as he said farewell. "Such a pleasure making your acquaintance," he said.

There was a flurry of activity as the ladies all stood and progressed to their next date. Eliza regarded him, looking towards the table where his next date would arrive from. But that lady was lingering, still leaning down onto the table, resting her alligator purse on the white linen cloth. She was dressed to perfection, every short blond curl perfectly in place, as she tried to prolong the previous date, hoping the fellow would want her number, perhaps.

You snooze, you lose, Eliza thought, and stepped up to the mystery man's table. "Hi there." She caught his attention and smiled.

He looked up, and warm brown eyes met hers. He pushed back his chair and rose to his feet. He was on the tall side, and the smile that broke over his features was genuine. He buttoned his coat and faced her.

Eliza couldn't help smiling back. His hair was neatly combed, and he smelled faintly of aftershave. Like he had taken time to get dressed up for tonight.

"Is there some kind of change in the agenda for tonight?" he asked, sounding a little confused.

Eliza held out her hand, "I'm sorry to interrupt. I'm Eliza Hamilton." He took her hand, not quite a shake, but instead he lifted it slightly and inclined himself forward the teeniest bit, just the slightest hint of a bow. He rested his left hand over the back of hers, enclosing her hand in the warmth between his.

Heat unfurled inside her, and a giggle almost escaped her lips. Oh my, oh my! She was impressed by his manners.

She saw his intended date finally getting urged over in their direction, and made up her mind quickly. "I know this isn't the way it's supposed to be done. But I was wondering, would you care to get a cup of coffee with me? Right now? There's a little shop across the street. They stay open late when there are singles events here."

He looked around, obviously uncomfortable with the idea of walking out on an expectant lady. And for a moment she thought he might refuse. Eliza realized he was still holding her hand, and she gave it a squeeze. "It's all right. It happens all the time, when a couple decides to speak privately, they disappear."

"Oh," he said simply. "I'm Frank, by the way, Frank Sutherland. It is a pleasure to meet you, Eliza." His voice was still warm, like Cognac, sliding over her skin. He finally let her hand drop, and stepped away from the table, moving behind his chair and using two hands to lift it back into place.

He had found the itinerary for the evening simple. The ladies came and went, and his only difficulty had been trying to recollect their names and features. It would have been easier with a notepad, they all seemed to run together after a while.

The offer of coffee was tempting, and Eliza seemed well versed in the event's protocol, so he chose to follow her lead. A casual chat in a coffee shop sounded appealing.

Eliza flipped the switch on the electric candle and made up a little fib. "That's how you signal it, that you've met someone and are out." She couldn't stop smiling. Finally. Finally, she'd met someone who made her feel butterflies again. It had been almost five years since she'd lost her husband, Jim to a drunk driver. He had been there one day and gone the next, and his loss left a gaping hole in her world. She hadn't expected to be alone for so much of her life. Maybe it just took time to find the magic again. Or a Silver and Gold speed dating event.

Frank followed her quietly to the coatroom and stood behind her while the attendant found her jacket. He stepped around her and slipped the woman a dollar, taking her coat and holding it up for her to shrug into. Eliza relaxed and enjoyed his assistance. He was polite, caring, and made being considerate of her feel as natural as breathing, eliminating any chance she'd look awkward with the sore shoulder or her sleeves riding up.

He paused with his hands on her shoulders as the coat settled into place, just lay his hands there for a moment, and then smoothed the fabric down. Eliza fought the urge to lean back against him. She didn't want to scare him off. But damn. Everything felt so right!

She inhaled, wondering what scent that was she found so intriguing about him. She hadn't given men's cologne a thought in years, but she was trying to make a memory of this one so she could describe it later. It was subtle, like vanilla and... *Sandalwood, maybe*?

She smiled over her shoulder, getting a better look at him in the brighter light of the lobby. He was tall, a great deal taller than her five feet four, even in heels. Trim, well built in a professor kind of way. The one from Gilligan's Island. Same stature and build, except slightly older. He wore it all comfortably, like he wore a jacket and tie every day of his life. But she was ready to bet money he wasn't in the business world.

He was too warm, too old fashioned. She led the way down the marble and glass lobby and out onto a side street. The night air was wet, like it must have rained while they were inside. She trotted across the street, avoiding puddles. There were cars parked up and down either side of the lane, and she made her way around them, not wanting to turn sideways to slip through them and end up getting rainwater all over her slacks.

It was eerily quiet. The traffic light down the street changed, adding a greenish tint to everything. "This seems so surreal, " she blurted. "I have never had that happen before, met someone at the Marriott and been inspired to walk up and ask them out for coffee." She hesitated outside the door to the bakery, and he leaned past her, getting the door and holding it for her.

"I'm glad you did," came his reassuring reply. "I felt so out of place. Like everyone knew everyone, except me." She'd felt the same way on her first night there four months ago. And now, she just wished she didn't know everyone there. So many of them had been soured by infidelity, legal battles and financial struggles. Like Phillip. He was probably a nice guy underneath it all, however all he seemed able to focus on at the moment was himself.

"Sometimes knowing everyone there is not a good thing," she confided. "It means you've met them all before and none of them are a good fit." Frank nodded, still standing close. Now that they were away from the dimly lit ballroom, he studied her. Her unruly hair framed her pretty face, and her dark eyes met his easily, like they were old friends.

They studied the placard over the bins of baked goods, and then each ordered a coffee before adding their cream and sugar at a side counter. They sat at a small table in the front window making small talk. "Was that your first time at a Silver and Gold meet and greet?" Eliza queried. She already knew the answer, it was so obvious, but it seemed a safe topic to start with.

He cleared his throat and took a sip of his still steaming coffee. "It was. I had no idea what it would be like. My ex, well, my soon to be ex, packed up and left one day. My son, Ben, had been out on his own for a couple of years. And when his mom filed for divorce and started dividing up our things, he said, "Dad, you can't let it get you down, you gotta get back out there."

Eliza smiled, thinking about how her own children had pushed her to do the same thing. Trust a couple of twenty-somethings to believe it's as easy as walking into a singles bar or wine tasting to meet up with the right gentleman.

Because the older she got, the more she knew what she wanted, and what she didn't want. Eliza wanted a man who was mature, not the euphemism 'mature' meaning older, but mature, as in able to handle himself. Someone who wanted to be a partner and a companion. Someone adventurous in the right way. Not sky diving, but wanting to get out and explore.

She had no trouble conversing with Frank, drawing out the details. His hurt that his wife of almost thirty years was leaving him. "I knew things were bad... hell, it seemed everyone we knew was struggling, working more, being home less. She got more and more distant, we shared the same house and the same bed, but not really the same space."

Eliza nodded her understanding. "The same emotional space?"

"I figured we still had it good. The bills were paid, our retirement was on track, our kid was turning out all right, but she was distant. There was nothing left of *us*. There hadn't been any intimacy for a long time. She said life with me was humdrum, and then one day she just decided she didn't want humdrum anymore. Oh, God, I need to stop unloading all this on a stranger..."

Eliza laughed. "It's all right, Frank, I don't feel like we are strangers, not anymore."

"The fact is I had seen it all coming for years and ignored it. We both made little gestures to try and get the romance back, but she wasn't interested. It was so obvious. After Benny went off to college she turned the guest room into her own private sanctuary. I don't know what Ben thought of that, given he was rarely home, and I was finally a full professor at the community college. I thought life was good."

She couldn't help smiling when he mentioned being an academic, giving herself a mental pat on the back for that one. Maybe he really did teach Shakespeare.

"But seriously, never mind what Benny thought," Eliza interjected. "What did you think? Didn't you have something to say about it?"

Frank closed his eyes for a moment, remembering the night he had tried to discuss it. The shouting on the stairs that ended with both of them slamming doors in separate rooms. Abby stating that since Benny was at school they could end with the pretense.

"It wasn't an easy thing for us to talk about," Frank admitted. "She wanted her own space. I just didn't know she was completely moving out of our room."

Eliza suspected there was more to the story, but she let it go and focused on him again. Everything about him from his intelligent dark eyes to his easy-going posture, not to mention his attire, confirmed his collegiate background. Heck, she'd even categorized him as the professor within the first few minutes.

His willingness to stumble over tough topics was so endearing she found herself opening up to him in response. Things she normally didn't tell anyone, even after she got to know them. The heartbreak of losing a wonderful husband. He'd gone to off to a charity golf tournament and never made it home. A drunk driver had crossed the yellow lines to hit his truck head-on. And how her children were now like mother hens; everything had gotten topsy-turvy, with them being the ones to suddenly look out for her. Like she was somehow fragile.

The rain started up again as they lingered over their coffee. They watched together as the crowd left the front doors of the Marriott and headed towards the parking garage. Most of them were alone, holding their coats around them as they leaped over puddles. Eliza realized then that their coffee cups were empty and she was going to have to let him go home.

"I am so happy we did this, Frank. Got out of there where we could really talk." She waited, letting the silence stretch. Hoping he would ask for her number or for another date.

He nodded and turned to drop his napkin and paper cup into the trash. He then took hers, repeating the process. It occurred to her he might be so out of practice that he wouldn't. She curled her fingers around his hand where it lay on the table. "I would dearly like to see you again."

He relaxed and smiled, his hand turning under hers. "I would too." There was something about this woman, the way she carried herself, the way she smiled and set him at ease that made him want to walk on a beach holding her hand.

Eliza pulled her purse up into her lap, and fished in the front pocket, not wanting to take her other hand out of his grip. Her card was wedged down at the bottom of the bag, of course, but after a moment she retrieved it and held up the small plain card.

She turned it around for him to see. "Elizabeth Hamilton" printed in the center, and then her phone number in the bottom right corner. Nothing else. She'd had them made for just this occasion. She knew they could have pulled out their cell phones and added each other to contacts, but somehow this seemed more intimate.

She tucked the card into the breast pocket of his coat and stood. "Give me a call this week, Frank. We really should get together again."

Chapter 2

Frank felt a little thrill of excitement as he dialed Eliza's number just after nine the next morning. He still adhered to the old social etiquette that dictated calls prior to nine am were rude, so he double checked his emails and text messages, waiting for the time to pass. He still felt a little awkward, calling a woman to ask her out, but he decided it was almost the same as asking the ladies in his department to join him for lunch. Almost.

Eliza happened to be in the car. As soon as her phone started to ring at 9:01 the next morning Eliza realized she should have anticipated he would. She saw his name flash across the screen on her cell as she pulled into the parking lot at work. She was only the tiniest bit late, and as she reached for it the phone slid off the console as she turned and skittered across the floorboards on the passenger side.

"Dammit!" she breathed as she slammed on the brakes, skidding to a halt and fumbling with the cord. Checking to be sure she was out of traffic, she swiped in her code and tried not to sound breathless.

"Hello?" So much for not sounding out of breath. Her voice sounded thin and wispy. A horn blared behind her, followed by a screech of tires as an angry car swerved around her and headed down the aisle. She cleared her throat and tried again. "Hello! Frank, nice to hear from you again."

"I hope I'm not calling too early." She almost laughed at that comment. She'd been up since 6:00. Up and thinking about when she might hear that velvety voice again. Excited by the possibilities.

"No, no, sorry. You just caught me on my way into the office." She hesitated, and then dove in. "I had a really nice time last night. Usually, those events are such a drag. Watching the clock, and all."

"Oh, you're not in the office yet?" She could almost picture him checking his watch. "I can call back in an hour?"

She eased the car into the first open parking spot she saw and shut off the engine. "No worries, Frank. One of the perks of being the boss is that no one mentions it to me when I am late." She had started High End Design in her basement years before, making party invitations and birth announcements for her friends. Growing steadily over the years, it had been enough to support her and her lone assistant over the years.

There was a long silence on the phone. "I was hoping we could get together again later this week. Are you free for dinner on Friday?"

She flipped her calendar open, happy she had never done as her kids pestered her to do and loaded everything up digitally, because if she'd had to start swiping the phone while she had him on the line, she'd end up looking like an idiot.

"Awww shoot, I have a family get together thing Friday evening." It was one of those extended family things where no one would miss her if she didn't appear, but everyone would want to know the details of if she skipped it for a date. Nope, no way to cancel that.

"Well, is there another day? Saturday?"

Eliza scanned the pages and her heart sank. She hadn't ever thought of herself as a busy woman until she wanted to be free and off everyone's radar. She frowned. It was either going to be Sunday or Monday, and she didn't want to wait that long. "I could meet you before my family dinner thing on Friday, say late afternoon? We could be adventurous and do something besides dinner. Cocktails? Something in the open air?"

He laughed. "Meeting for cocktails isn't all that unconventional, Eliza."

She was laughing too. "I know, I know, but I was thinking, if the weather's supposed to be nice this weekend, maybe we could meet in the park, say around 3:30 or so, and have a picnic. I'll bring cheese and crackers, and I am sure you will know just the right wine to bring for Camenbert and Triskets."

"A picnic. That does sound adventurous. And I do have a nice wine in mind. Shall I pick you up? Or meet somewhere?" He sounded hopeful, relieved a little, and happy.

"I have a lunch meeting with a client, but it shouldn't run late. Let's meet at Washington Square, near the memorial. And if it looks like rain, I'll text you. I'll probably text you anyway, just to confirm." She could have sat and chatted all morning, but even the stragglers had made it into the building by now. "I better run. Can't wait for Friday."

She hung up the phone and hurried across the parking lot, feeling just the slightest bit giddy.

* * * *

It was only later, when she had finished with her emails and calls that she checked the weather and started really formulating a plan, guessing what kind of wine he might bring and looking for recipes on the internet. Eliza knew she didn't have a single gene in common with Martha Stewart, so she started a folder for ideas. She could always just delegate to Shelly, her assistant, and not mention exactly what it was for, but for some reason she wanted to be able to say she'd done it all herself. With the help of Mr. Google, of course.

She did more than just Google recipes, in the end. She typed his name into people search and searched through mentions of him on the college website. She checked out his "Rate My Professor" rating, and even found a video clip of him introducing a keynote speaker at a collegiate award ceremony. She made sure her office door was closed when she played it. And then she played it again, smiling to hear that velvety voice. She heard a little knock on her door and quickly added the clip to favorites before closing down her browser.

"Focus!" she chided herself as Shelly, her assistant leaned in and reminded her of three clients that needed attention, as well as a display for a bridal show to finalize. High End Design really could have remained in her basement, if she hadn't downsized her home and ended up with a basement full of boxes. But Eliza had realized early on that mothers and daughters were looking for experiences when they planned a wedding, such as going to cake tastings and trying out champagnes.

That was why they liked to come to her showroom, to feel the samples, the laser cutouts of lace and butterflies, and the raised lettering. Sure, she had brides who wanted to point and order, not even address or stamp the envelopes themselves, but plenty wanted a cozy afternoon, complete with tea. Maybe getting her calendar cleared for Friday would keep her mind off Frank, or at least keep her from reaching for the phone to text him until Thursday.

When Friday morning finally came, Eliza felt a tingle in her stomach she hadn't felt in ages. She dressed with care, selecting a sleek pair of slacks in a dark chestnut color and a creamy cowl-neck sweater. Not exactly in the height of fashion, but the colors looked well against her skin and brought out the warm colors in her eyes. It would serve for work and her lunch meeting with the O'Brien-Smith wedding party as well as her date with Frank later on. That particular wedding wasn't until late fall, however, the young bride was bringing her mother as well as her Maid of Honor to color coordinate and design the perfect invitation.

She chuckled to herself. Thinking about Frank and just saying the word 'date' seemed so odd. Her life had been busy and full since Jim died, there was always something needing her attention: her house, her kids, her work. But something had definitely been missing, too. That little spark of excitement that came from having a romantic interest. She could feel a change in herself already, and was surprised everyone was missing it, the spring in her step, the smile on her face. There had been a sunny smile on Shelly's face this morning, so maybe her assistant was aware of a change, and just not mentioning it.

Eliza knew she was getting ahead of herself, but for the first time in months, no years, she felt young again. Almost like a teenager again. Like some little part of her heart that had lost hope was waking up.

So there she was, in her curve-hugging, slightly stretch pants, perched on the edge of a park bench near the memorial, clutching a small basket covered in a red and white checkered napkin. Her hair was twisted up behind her head, and as always it had decided to go from tidy to disheveled as soon as she stepped into the afternoon sunshine. At least it had held together for her consultation.

The enthusiastic bride, Natasha O'Brien come in with a notepad full of ideas for making her invitation unique, and Eliza had spent the better part of an hour explaining why a pressed flower enclosed in rice paper would be a disastrous idea. She hadn't described it as disastrous, or impossible, even if someone had thought to press seventy-five flowers months ago. She merely mentioned the possibility of loose seeds and flower petals staining the card stock, and steered the group towards some colorful ribbons interwoven into cutouts. As the afternoon dragged on, Eliza glanced at the clock and wrapped up the appointment.

She would still have plenty of time to get to the park, her picnic basket was ready. She had packed a couple of paper cups and plates, as well as some plastic silverware. After all her research, she hadn't been able to decide on one hors d'oeuvre, going instead with a little variety. Pate on bagel chips, and Boursin cheese on tiny sourdough slices.

Eliza had texted Frank just before nine Friday morning to confirm, and she had even gotten to the office extra early. Could it be she suddenly didn't want to look like a slacker? In the end, it didn't matter, since it was just a text, and neither of them was particularly skilled with the phone keyboards. She felt a moment's regret at hearing his voice, before stowing her phone in her purse and admitting to herself she'd been up early, eager to get the day started.

She had tapped the screen and then double checked her spelling. "Weather looks lovely for this afternoon. Looking forward to seeing you."

His response followed a minute later, short and concise, "Perfect day for a picnic. Me too."

Bright sunshine made the day surprisingly warm, and as a result most visitors to the park didn't linger. They hurried down the walkways, passing Eliza without a glance. She wandered away from the statue into the shade of a tall oak with a convenient bench beneath it.

She pulled at her neckline. Wearing a cowl neck sweater suddenly didn't seem like such a good idea, but at least bench she chose was hidden under a tree, with dappled sunlight offering the perfect amount of shade. She had made sure to arrive in the park early, wanting to pick an out of the way spot.

Eliza held the basket in her lap, resisting the urge to look at her phone and check the time. She regretted that the entire world seemed to have given up on watches due to the proliferation of cell phones.

When she finally spotted him strolling down the path she relaxed and took in the easy way he moved. He was dressed almost exactly the way she expected, in a white button-down shirt, creased black trousers, and a sage green sweater vest.

She ducked her head to hide her smile as he approached, wondering how a man could appear so obviously academic and sexy at the same time. He was tall and lean, his hair slightly windblown. He held a blanket draped over one arm and carried a brown paper bag by the handles.

Eliza set her basket by her feet and rose as he drew closer and stopped in front of her. She took a half step towards him, clasping his shoulders and leaning in. Almost a hug, but not quite. And not quite a kiss on the cheek either. Her cheek brushed against his, and she caught a whiff of his unique scent, masculine and somewhat spicy. It was inviting and made her want to nuzzle into the crook of his neck, but she resisted. She drew back and smiled, "Hello."

He smiled back, and it only took a moment for the conversation to flow again. They unfolded the blanket together and set it on top of a low wall. Eliza opened her Tupperware serving dish while he poured them each a glass of white wine.

"I had the feeling you were a white wine girl," he explained and he handed the plastic cup to her. "I guessed you might like it light and fruity, maybe even with bubbles."

* * * *

The day was out of a dream for Frank. He was glad for the familiar task of pouring the wine, otherwise his hands might have been trembling. Thank God for the habitual routine of filling a glass. Everything about this day was astounding, starting with the way he'd nonchalantly strolled into the park, as if meeting a lovely woman there was something he did every day. He'd held onto the handles of the fancy bag from the wine and spirits shop like a lifeline as he crossed the park. She'd stood, wrapped a warm arm around him and stretched up to kiss his cheek. Well, not so much a kiss as laying her cheek against his and whispering a "mwah!" in his ear.

She was everything he remembered. Classy and vibrant, pulling him in like one of those fish with the bio-luminescent dangly things to lure in their prey. He stood patiently while she arranged a place for them, admiring her curvy backside as she bent to straighten the blanket. She seemed so at ease, settling down on the wall and asking about his week. The breeze kept her hair in a constant state of disarray, no matter how many times she tucked stray strands behind her ears.

"It's been a long week," he admitted. "I kept waiting for today."

A smile broke over her face, and she took a sip of her wine before answering. "Me too. I'm sorry it had to be like this, "she shrugged and gestured to the cars going by and the pedestrians crossing on the walkways. "Not exactly private, or a good place for a first date, but we took a chance and the weather cooperated!"

He plucked another cracker from her serving tray. It was Brie on top of a golden cracker, and topped with some kind of sweet jelly or chutney. Hell, he didn't know what it was, but it paired perfectly with the Chardonnay.

"Did you tell your kid about this rendez vous?" Her tone was light, but he had the feeling the question was very serious. She was watching him intently.

"Well, I told him I'd found someone interesting at the dating event, and that we were getting together soon, but honestly, I am so out of touch with dating these days, I wasn't even sure this get together would be considered a date."

Her expression faltered. "It is definitely a date," she assured him, and then she laughed. "Not exactly the best date, but when you're starting over you can make a date out of anything you want. And you're right. I'm not ready to share with my kids that I might be on to something."

He nodded and set his cup down on the edge of the wall. He lay back on his elbows and closed his eyes. He wasn't sure how he felt about it all. Just being near Eliza gave him butterflies in his stomach, made him excited and slightly aroused. He wanted to lean in closer, but didn't dare. Besides, he still felt married, and he was, technically, still married, even if the lawyers were busy exchanging papers.

Eliza drew him in and made him want more, although he wasn't sure exactly what that was yet. More of that allure, that charm.

He heard rather than saw her move closer, turning and curling her legs up under her. One hand cupped his cheek, tilting his face up towards hers. Her eyes were warm, fringed by thick dark lashes and a trace of eyeliner. "Let's keep this feeling that we have between us for now. It's too new. Too young. We can wait until we are sure there's something more there before involving the rest of the world."

He almost laughed at that, considering they were out in the open on a busy afternoon in the park.

But she lay her hand on his thigh, the inside of his thigh as she leaned in. Her lips met his, soft and gently caressing. Her hand slid up to his crotch, lining her fingers up along the ridge of him. He gave a little gasp, and she took advantage, deepening the kiss, her mouth slanting over his, her tongue teasing his lips.

He had been at half-mast since he saw her, and now arousal pooled into his cock, making it twitch in his pants. He hadn't had anyone fondle him in a long time. Not for years, since the time he and Abby had finally decided they were done with each other sexually.

Eliza, with her soft kisses and curvy backside, had captured his interest and made desire pop up and take notice. He liked her bold caresses, and wanted more of those, even here, in the middle of the afternoon, in the middle of the park.

She pulled back, looked in his eyes again, and then dipped her head for a second kiss. Only this time, this time she caressed her thumb over him, dragging the pad back and forth over the head of his shaft.

"Ooooh!" He couldn't seem to form words. His hips pushed forward of their own volition pressing his genitals up into her hand, wanting to feel more. He wasn't used to it, a woman interested in this kind of easy fun.

Her kiss was gentle as she teased him. Back and forth, back and forth. His cock was fully hard under her hand. Soon he was a quivering mess. It had been so long. He didn't think she intended to stroke him off there in the park, but damn, it made his cock twitch even more just thinking she might.

And it was as if she sensed it, that they were about to cross a line that shouldn't be crossed on the first date. Her hand drifted away, and she rested her forehead against his. "That's enough of that for now," she teased. Her tone was playful as she held him close. "Next time," she was chuckling now, "next time maybe we better have a more conventional kind of date. In a restaurant, where we can talk by candlelight and get to know each other better."

She sat up and tipped the last sip of wine into her mouth. "Maybe early next week? You could make us a reservation somewhere?"

He wasn't sure if he should be grateful or confused at the way she alternated between making the decisions and insisting on his role as a gentleman. It was different, but it made things easier. He knew exactly what was expected of him. She was so outspoken and yet so attractive. So confident.

She had found a way to grab his interest, literally, and make sure he had no doubt about the chemistry between them. And then in the next breath made sure he knew there was a plan for their next encounter and she was trusting him to arrange it.

He rolled forward up onto his feet, almost springing off the wall. She was looking at her phone, frowning at the time.

"I'm going to have to get going," she sighed. "Although I am not ready for this afternoon to end."

He took her hand and helped steady her as she uncurled her legs and rose to her feet. She dusted herself off while he packed up her Tupperware and set it back in the basket, corking his wine.

They both lingered, not willing to let the moment end. And when it was time to leave, he let her draw him into her arms and press her face against his chest. He thought she might have even rubbed her face on his sweater. "You even smell good," she said softly.

He tightened his arms around her for a second and then stepped back. "I'll call you Sunday about dinner arrangements for next week." He wanted to kiss her again, but she glanced at the time again and hurried away, stopping to turn and reassure him.

"This is really going to be wonderful, Frank. And don't worry, I'll text you before Sunday."

***

Frank stood there long after she ducked into her Subaru, standing and staring. The sunshine was still there, the breeze just as gentle. The same curl of heat was unfolding inside his gut. He thought about the way she had laid her hand on him and felt his shaft start to stir again. He felt like a geek in high school again, and the pretty girl in the front row had just asked him to the prom. Of course, his prom had been a fiasco. The gymnasium was decorated with balloons and streamers, and he'd worn one of his father's suits. St. Matthew's had been an all boy school, so he wasn't the only one who had scrambled to find a date.

Long after her car disappeared from sight, he smiled and walked away, wondering what her Senior prom had been like, making a mental note to ask her about it next time. His car was where he left it, and he drove home still thinking about her. Still planning.

Arranging dinner was going to be easy. He knew exactly where he wanted to take her for dinner, a little Italian place he knew in Center City. It had gotten a little touristy lately, but he was sure Marco would be able to find a quiet table and maybe even throw a red and white checkered tablecloth over it. After that, adding a vintage looking candlestick would complete the scene. He wanted to really wow her with the ambiance and a corny attempt at recreating the spaghetti scene from Lady and the Tramp.

It was an easy decision to take her there, where he knew the wine list and the menu, and the staff, of course. They might wonder who the lovely woman at his side was, though. Maybe this was going to take a bit more planning. He didn't want anyone asking where Abby was, or thinking he was stepping out on his wife.

The street outside his apartment building was quiet. He lined up his Accord and hit the switch for the automated parallel parking. He never did that, always parked manually, and yet today, everything seemed different. He held his hands poised above the wheel as the computer did its thing, waiting to grab the wheel and steer should the system suddenly fail and go off course.

But trying the auto-parker felt right, trying new things felt right, like he was finally getting back in gear, finally in motion again, after being in limbo for so long. Finally part of the future. He knew that sounded insane. But technology had moved on and while he resisted, he resolved to push forward with it. Eliza motivated him to catch up. To not tread water anymore, while the rest of the world moved on.

He had been stationary. Not wanting to move on from his failed marriage. He still didn't see why it had to fail. They had been college sweet hearts and remained together after graduation. They had both moved to South Jersey and gotten jobs in the school system. Between the two of them, they had scraped together enough for the security deposit on a minuscule apartment. Making ends meet had been tough, but at least then they had been into each other, excited to see each other.

And then somehow one child, 5 or 6 job changes and 3 housing upgrades later things had started to fizzle. Abby had started working late, going out with her co-workers after work and not returning until midnight. He should have known way back then things were so wrong they couldn't be fixed.

Their sexual encounters seemed more like a chore for her, a chore she resented. At first, he had worked harder, bringing her flowers, arranging to leave Ben with his grandmother and taking her for a weekend at the shore.

Looking back now, he wondered why she hadn't asked for a divorce sooner. There hadn't been anything romantic between them in ages. They had been friends, decent parents. Two people who lived in the same house, but not in the same bedroom. Each doing their part to raise the kid.

Frank realized he was still sitting in his car, and switched the engine off. He gathered up his things, and went into the house. He needed to start making a list. Because he hadn't realized how much the spark of romance he felt could ignite his life. Now that he'd felt it again, he couldn't remember when the last time that joy had leaped inside him. Back in college? Sneaking into the girl's dormitory? Ooooh, or reading a really kinky letter in Penthouse, with a take charge kind of woman, who knew what she wanted and went after it.

He sat at his desk, stacked the legal documents and correspondence off to the side and started planning his next date. His cock hardened, wondering if she'd run her hand over him under that red checkered table cloth. Oh, God, he hoped so. He squeezed his thighs together and shifted his weight side to side, so the fabric tightened over his shaft and rubbed back and forth slightly. The arousal coursed through him, returning like an old friend. More like a wave breaking over a damn and chastising him for keeping it at bay too long.

How long had he been moving through life just making do, just taking the ordinary and the day to day? Going to work, teaching his students, going to family holiday gatherings without ever wondering where the joy had gone? He was done with that. He hadn't been the one to call a divorce lawyer. Would never have been. He was old school, and a marriage was meant to last forever. But this sudden freedom... to hell with his dreary feelings of rejection. No more crying over not being wanted. Eliza sure as hell made him feel wanted.

As if on cue, his cell phone buzzed in his right front pocket. He wrestled it out of his pocket and saw her name in his text queue. "Today was perfect. Thank you. Next time will be even better."

He realized was smiling so hard his cheeks were starting to ache.

Chapter 3

It was hard for Eliza to keep him, and their budding romance a secret. Every time she talked to Mother or the kids, the happiness came bubbling up and it was work to thrust it back down and sound normal. Jenny had begun asking how the speed dating went almost immediately and didn't seem to want to be put off by platitudes. "It was exactly what you would expect it to be. A hotel air quotes "ballroom" set up to look like a receiving line at a wedding." Sometimes her daughter reminded her so much of Jim it made her want to cry. "You would have been out of there as soon as you stepped into the room. But I took a few turns, sat at tables with men who are 45 and either claiming to be single because their wife ignores them or still single because they have a mother who picks their socks up off the floor, and no woman in her right mind wants to take over that role."

"But seriously mom, there must have been something about it that seemed positive. Sooner or later someone new might turn up there, or I have this new website that does group activities and even provides background checks."

"Honey, are you hearing yourself? Have we gotten to the place and time where a background check is a prerequisite for a date?" Maybe finding love in the computer age was going to be a very scary thing. For everyone else, not her. She already had stumbled onto someone fabulous.

Her lengthy hesitation must have aroused Jenny's suspicion, or perhaps it was just a different tone she heard in her mother's voice.

"There's something you aren't telling me, isn't there?" Her voice was all too knowing.

Eliza released the breath she'd been holding and gave up. Sometimes her daughter was too intuitive for her own good. "Well, yes... "

"I knew it! I knew it. I was telling Josh you were busy doing something more than working later than usual." Eliza could practically hear her daughter doing a victory dance on the other end of the phone.

"Jenny... Jenny!" Eliza kicked herself for letting the cat out of the bag. "It's not that big a deal, Jen. It was just nice to find someone to talk to, don't go telling your brother or making a big deal out of this yet."

"Oh my God, mom, I won't tell anyone. But admit it, I was right, that in-person middle-aged dating group was the way to go. I knew you'd never sort out the messaging and profile reading from online dating."

"Yes, you were right. The less technology involved, the better for me. And I mean it. Not a word to Josh. Or your grandmother, either." The last thing she needed was to have her mom prying into her new romance. "The last thing I need is her advice or her meddling."

Eliza had been fending off suggestions and dating advice from her mother, as well as the members of her mother's book club and knitting group. All of them were very dear to her, her mother's staunch friends, but Eliza couldn't help feeling as if even after forty years, they didn't really know her. "You should join my gardening club, Eliza, dear," one of her mother's most elegant friends had suggested. "There are always younger men who give presentations." Those kinds of comments made Eliza want to laugh. The young man might be anywhere from twenty to seventy, and he probably worked at the local gardening supply shop.

They had no idea what Eliza needed, the private woman deep inside. The only one she was trusting to find the perfect match was herself. She felt good about how it was going so far. She was eager for their next encounter which happened to be on Tuesday. Eliza managed to squeak out of work early to get home before five. Frank was due to pick her up around 6:30, and she wanted an extra long shower and time to try to coerce her hair into staying put.

Eliza stood in her closet, hoping something would speak to her. She almost wished her daughter Jenny would drop in and pick out the perfect outfit. Pants didn't seem right for a dinner date, so she shoved all the pant hangers back into the depths of the closet and focused on what she had left. There wasn't much. Apparently her current wardrobe consisted of work clothes, work clothes, and more work clothes.

She finally settled on a sharp navy shirt dress, espadrilles and a white sweater. Maybe she looked like she was headed down to cocktails at the yacht club, but classic never went out of style, did it? She made a mental note to ask Jenny for some advice on getting her wardrobe out of the distant past. She definitely needed to add some color and some youthfulness to the project. It surprised her how neutral and practical everything was. Probably because she hadn't been feeling youthful or colorful for a long time.

Oh yes, Jenny would probably have a lot to say, and want to take a trip out to the outlet shops. Maybe it was time to stop dressing like Kate Middleton. She definitely needed her daughter's advice, or to start watching more of the makeover shows on TLC.

A shirt dress didn't scream feminine or sexy, but it had a nice slit at the bottom that would show a little leg at the dinner table. And she could tell from the warmth in Frank's eyes when she opened the door he wasn't worried about fashion trends or soft and fuzzy sweaters. His gaze roamed slowly over her, taking in the belted dress that accentuated her waist and the gap below the last button revealed a glimpse of warm skin as she walked. His nervousness evaporated as he realized how much her 'dress casual' attire reminded him of the female professors at County College. "Just like having lunch with one of the faculty," he reminded himself.

He came in and put his hands into his coat pockets, looking around the foyer while she collected her purse.

"This is quite a nice place you've got here," he said.

Eliza couldn't tell if he was being serious or not. The house was small, with the original 1950s metal cabinets and painted wood trim. The hardwood floors had polished up nicely in the living room and foyer, where they stood. The best feature of the house by far was the enormous picture window overlooking the front yard.

"It's a work in progress, and I know, whoever lived here before I bought it should have hired a professional instead of doing the work himself. You should have seen it when I bought it. Everything was dark, dingy, and probably the best part about it was whatever he hadn't tried to update. There's a bit of original charm under all his efforts at home improvement."

Frank was his usual quiet self. "There's nothing wrong with fixing things one small project at a time." His hair was brushed back, parted on the side, still slightly wavy. She envied him the ease with which it fell into place and stayed there, and made a mental note to run her fingers through it to test it, to determine if it was natural or some kind of pomade that kept his locks in check. He had traded in his suit for a sports coat over spotless pressed trousers. Maybe he didn't even own a pair of jeans, or if he did he only wore them for raking leaves or shoveling snow.

She checked her hair one last time in the mirror beside the door, patting a stray curl into place. "My son, Josh, spends the summers and winter break with me. Sometimes he's home on the weekends, if his girlfriend is in town. Two years ago he went away to college and I didn't see him for weeks, and now, since he met Lauren, he's suddenly a commuter, home all the time and only going off to classes."

Frank walked her to the car door and opened it for her, gently closing the door once he was sure she was settled neatly inside. She watched his profile as he slid behind the wheel and then backed out of her drive. "I am fine with however you want to handle it, Eliza," Frank finally spoke when he was out on the highway and headed downtown. "With your kids, I mean, and the rest of your family. There's no point in rushing around with news until we've had a chance to be sure of it ourselves."

For a split second, she thought he was being standoffish. Was he having second thoughts? Eliza peered at him in the dim light. He didn't look tense or strained.

He turned and smiled at her. "Don't worry, Eliza. I *like* this easy fun attraction. I am a little out of practice, and the culture of the entire country has changed. I'll do my best to catch up." Eliza relaxed back into her seat and balanced her elbow on the armrest, her hand half extended to him. He picked up her proffered hand, and almost giggled when she traced a figure eight on his palm. Such a simple gesture, but one that got his heart pounding. It was so normal, and yet so suggestive.

"And just like that," he continued, "It's like you can sense when I am running on and on, and find a way to make me feel wonderful." His hand was warm and reassuring, and his driving was still relaxed, as he threaded the car through traffic and then off onto a side street.

"You don't have to, Frank." He shot her a quizzing look as they turned into a small parking garage and pushed a button for a ticket. "You don't have to catch up. With the culture where a man doesn't know if opening a door is an insult or a compliment. Or where spending your day with your nose buried in your phone is considered normal."

The evening was finally cooling off as they walked down the ramp of the parking garage and out onto the sidewalk.

"I'm so glad you get me." They strolled down the sidewalk together, his palm resting on the small of her back. He wasn't exactly sure how much she understood him yet, but whatever instinct was urging her to express her interest in him with little touches and caresses only served to make him crave more. She forged the connection effortlessly as if maybe she did know of his secret desires for a strong woman to please, who understood her appeal conveyed her needs.

He almost walked past their destination. "And here we are," he said, turning.

Eliza came to a halt and took it all in, peering through the old-world style windows at the crowded tables. Frank pulled open the door with a grand gesture, and she stepped into a tiny, out of the way restaurant that looked straight out of The Sopranos. It had a dark awning that fanned out over brightly lit windows, and the inside smelled mouth-wateringly good, like fresh-baked bread and spicy Italian sausage.

The maitre d' met them by the door as if he had been expecting them, and greeted Frank warmly before leading them to a small table in the back corner. It was set for two and had a single, waxy candle in the center. Frank spoke easily with the staff, listening to the chef''s recommendations.

Eliza poured over the menu, ruling out anything in red sauce, fearful it would end up splashed on her shirt dress or cardigan. Even still, in an establishment like this, the classics were bound to be exceptional.

"Do you trust me?" Frank queried as the waiter approached their corner table.

Eliza laughed. She found his leg beside hers under the tablecloth and dropped her palm onto his thigh. "As long as whatever you select for me pairs well with prima vera…"

"Oh, it will." The timber of his voice changed as her hand caressed up his inner thigh. " I knew I was right about you being a white wine girl." He scooted his chair closer and leaned over to drop a kiss on her cheek.

It was very apparent that this place was a favorite haunt of his. The waiter was attentive and members of the staff were stopping by to chat and be introduced to her.

In between bites and tiny sips of wine, Eliza encouraged him to talk about himself, "What made you decide to teach at a community college, Frank? The right location?"

He looked chagrined. "No, it wasn't what I had hoped for, initially, I was going to work for a drug company and make the big bucks, but somewhere along the line I became aware of the good that community colleges do, how much they help the kids from the poorest areas get job skills and opportunities they wouldn't likely get anyplace else. They can't afford the four-year schools, not to start."

Eliza thought about the tuition she was currently helping Josh with and nodded. "I pushed Josh to look at the local school just for the sake of finances, so I get what you mean."

"It's not for everybody, but for some of these kids in urban areas, it changes their lives. I see them go on to get good jobs in health services and law enforcement. I don't know. I like making a difference.

Some of the comments Eliza had seen on his 'rate my professor' page flashed through her mind. "Gives good feedback and is clear on grading criteria. Helps students better their performance." Yes, it was all starting to make sense.

"We are very alike in that, Frank, wanting to help people and helping them achieve their dreams. Even if mine is just through a little thing like pretty invitations."

Their eyes met for a moment, and Frank almost leaned in to kiss her. "Don't trivialize what you do, Eliza. You make them happy. You make *me* happy."

She grinned and stuffed the last bite of pasta in her mouth. "Aren't you too cute for words," she laughed. And he did lean down and drop a kiss on her lips.

Luckily she had saved room for gelato, and they lingered over coffee. "The food was outstanding," she told Marco, the manager when she finally met him. "As authentic as I've found since I last visited in Italy." Her complements were heartfelt.

She shook the man's hand enthusiastically and was surprised when the manager leaned in for a private word. "I hope you and my friend Frank will dine with us again soon, Eliza," he said softly. "He deserves some romance and happiness."

Eliza walked out the door feeling like she'd just met Frank's fraternity brothers or his closest friends, and that she'd somehow won their approval. How often does a man have to dine at the same establishment to get that close to the staff?

Her quiet professor walked lightly beside her, his hand resting on the small of her back, not pushing or guiding, just a light touch to connect them, to keep her close. She got about halfway down the block before turning and grinning up at him.

"Thank you, Frank," she said. "For going to all this trouble, for sharing that wonderful place with me, even the references to the show. It made for a really special evening.

He leaned down, placing his lips within her reach but hesitating. "I knew you would get it, Eliza. I figured most in our generation would get the connection. The romantic scene."

"Oh yes, the candlelight, the dark wood, the paintings on the walls" and she laughed, bouncing up on her toes and kissing him. "But really, it looks like most Italian restaurants in the northeast. We must just be of the same mind." A confused expression passed over her face. "Wait, what romantic scene?" she asked.

"From Lady and the Tramp…?"

She burst out laughing, bending over trying to catch her breath laughing. "Oh my God, I thought you were going for Artie's restaurant from the Sopranos." He wrapped both arms around her and pulled her close. Eliza was still chuckling as she stretched up to kiss him more fiercely this time. Her hand settled on his waist, and then slid lower, over the curve of his hip. Her fingers fanned out over his taut buttocks and urged him forward. The intimate contact got her blood flowing, the hard feel of him nestled against her belly.

Frank was becoming used to it, her hands touching him so frequently, cupping and teasing. Her bold caresses made his breath catch and his cock throb. It had been unsettling at first, and yet so exciting.

His arms tightened around her, lifting her, centering the hard bulge of him at the apex of her thighs. It felt so good. So right.

Eliza didn't feel manhandled, she felt cherished. His lips felt warm and smooth, and her free hand snaked up to curl behind his neck. He groaned softly, and she savored the taste of him as his lips parted. It was intoxicating, the lingering taste of chocolate and red wine. She had him right where she wanted him, wrapped all around her. She had the giddy thought of making out with him there on the sidewalk, or in the car. Or better yet, at home, in a bed.

She pulled back and looked into his heavy-lidded eyes. "Oh, Frank!"

He broke the tension and smiled. "Oh, Eliza! Even when you don't get me, you get me." He set her down carefully on her feet and took her hand. "I am so unused to a woman who enjoys this." She thought he might say more, and explain, but instead he took her hand and continued walking.

Eliza's heart plummeted. "Of course I do! Many women do!" She tugged his hand until he looked back at her. "Wait, are you telling me you didn't do this kind of sexy teasing when you were married? Or with other girlfriends?"

He didn't answer until they were in the car and heading back to her place. He had taken so long to respond, she worried he wasn't going to.

"There were no other girlfriends. Just Abby, my college sweetheart. We got married straight out of college. Neither one of us was very experienced, but we did all right. It all seemed pretty straight forward."

Straight forward didn't seem like a very exciting way to describe a sexual relationship, so she pressed him, half joking, "What do you mean, 'straight forward'? Missionary position every Friday night after the kid went to bed? Both of you slipping under the covers naked, with the lights off?"

He glanced sideways at her, his lips twisting up in the hint of a smile. "Not quite that bad, Eliza, but more the usual, me trying to wait for the right time and hoping not to get put off by a headache or a sore tooth."

"No quick blow jobs, giggling and shushing each other so you don't wake the baby?"

Man, she didn't pull any punches, and yet sometimes her intuition was so on target it scared him. He had always suspected other couples enjoyed oral sex, but he had never wanted to rock the boat and ask for it. "No... no blow jobs ever, not playful, or clandestine."

She gave a sad sigh. "Oh, Boy, Frank. Am I going to enjoy showing you everything you've missed." Her mind had been churning over various scenarios for when she'd finally get him alone and private. Suddenly she wanted it sooner rather than later, and she had a lot more planning to do. "Will you let me be the one to introduce you to the fun and games?"

"Fun and Games? God, yes, Eliza. Please!" She smiled silently in the darkness, knowing there was a similar smile on his face. How had they gotten to this point so fast? She had no idea, but it felt right. Those butterflies were back and they were flopping away. Now she just had to find a way to make sure they had some alone time.

She waited until they stood under the yellowish glare of the bulb illuminating her front porch. She'd swung his hand lightly as they strode up to the house, and squeezed it tight as he stepped back.

"Good night, Eliza," he said. He still sounded excited. She was always aware of his response, be it the timbre of his voice, the warmth in his eyes, or the bulge in his pants.

There was no way she was letting him go so quickly or so easily. She had been thinking about this moment for most of the car ride home. Envisioning their goodnight kiss, maybe leaning across the console to kiss him before they got out of the car, or pulling him close as they reached the front door. For a minute she considered inviting him in for a nightcap, and then chided herself. There was no need to rush things. They had all the time in the world. In fact, it felt thrilling and old fashioned to have a little make-out session on the front stoop.

She closed the distance, settling his hand on her hip, twining her arms around behind his neck. She knew he liked it when she took the lead. High time he understood more of what that meant. She stretched up, pressing herself flush against him, meeting his lips softly at first, and then with increasing pressure.

He gave a soft moan and gathered her up closer into his embrace, tightening his grip on her curvy hips. She slanted her lips over his, licking, teasing at the seam, feeling triumphant when he opened his lips a fraction and she was able to tease her tongue in between.

Time slowed to a crawl as she savored him. No need to rush, Eliza just took her time, exploring, getting to know him. Learning what flicks of her tongue made him catch his breath, and which ones made him tremble slightly and grip her harder. She loved every minute of it. He responded so easily, so honestly.

She finally came back to reality, remembering where they were and settled back on her heels. Not quite ready to let him go yet, she curled one hand behind him and cupped one taut ass cheek in her palm, maintaining the intimate contact. It would be so nice to invite him in, to stay for a drink, or for more. But she just couldn't spring this on her son yet. She didn't think Josh was home at the moment, but he might yet turn up this evening.

Eliza leaned close and whispered in his ear, "You like that, don't you? When I grab your ass and put you where I want you?"

He shuddered and nodded. "I aim to please, ma'am," he joked. It wasn't so much her words as the way she said them. The tone, the frankness stirred something unexpected, made him want to see what else this lady might want from him. He held her gently while she kissed him again.

A laugh burst from her lips and she resignedly stepped back from him. "I like your attitude, soldier." She tugged him down and gave him one last peck. "Drive safely."

He was already down the steps and heading around his car, the light of his headlamps giving her a clear view of his blushing cheeks and bulging trousers.

"And Frank," she called out. "No touching that until you get home." She pointed at his distended trousers, illuminated clearly. His step faltered a little as he reached his door. He looked up at her and grinned. "Yes, ma'am!"

Chapter 4

Frank followed up their Lady and the Tramp date with a more conventional one, a Friday night movie. They texted or spoke every day in between, but it was difficult, since he was working relatively little and her days were slam packed with work. Periodically he would stop by the old house to go through dusty boxes in the basement, discovering that most were filled with clothing and toys Benny had long ago outgrown. They had been boxed up and hidden away, forgotten until displaying added storage in the cellar became a selling point.

With the spring semester wrapping up, he organized his office and got roped into carrying boxes and moving furniture as one of his colleagues accepted a promotion to run the department and moved to a corner office. He spent the afternoon toting boxes of textbooks down the hallway.

Always his mind was drifting back to Eliza, especially when he spent the time hitting the gym every morning. He slung his towel around his neck and moved from the treadmill to the elliptical. She was unlike any woman he had ever known, forthright, personable, and yet also attractive in a way he hadn't expected to find. Almost as if she understood him, those secret fantasies he barely remembered, but now found constantly parading through his mind.

His phone would ring, and he'd recall he was still in the middle of divorce paperwork, and he'd try to organize the finances for his lawyer. He had never known how invasive getting divorced could be. He was getting tired of answering, "Who is listed as the beneficiary on the life insurance policy?" and "how much is in the 401(k)?"

By the time the following Friday rolled around Frank felt like it had been ages since he'd last seen her, and his heart was beating just a little bit faster than normal as he pulled into her drive to pick her up. He found himself smiling, or drifting off into a moment of daydreaming, thinking about her. He always felt it, a surge of excitement when he pulled up at her house or opened the door for her. She greeted him in the doorway with a warm kiss. Her wavy hair was pulled back in a clip that allowed most of the curls to cascade past her shoulders. He had never seen it down and wondered what it would be like to run his fingers through it.

"I'm glad you like it," Eliza teased. She fluffed up her tresses and spun around to give him the full view.

Of course, he liked it. All those curls that were usually pinned up behind her head, refusing to stay tucked in place made her look younger, sexier. As if that woman needed to look sexier! He caught her hand and raised it to his lips, placing a gentle kiss on the back of her knuckles. "What makes my lady think I like it?"

The evening air was perfect, cool for early June, and the sky was just dampening from fiery orange to the grayed-out dusk, when the sun has slipped from view, but lingering rays of light still illuminate the clouds. Eliza pulled a navy sweater out of the closet by the door and draped it over her shoulders. "I know this theater, it's always cold. And if you had just seen your face when I opened the door. Or your fingers, looking like they were going to lift up a curl and smell it!"

"I did not!" They headed down the steps and over to his Honda. "I'm not that much of an easy read am I?" She swung his hand and walked nonchalantly, enjoying his befuddlement. "I mean, I do like it. How is it you manage to do this to me?"

"Me thinks the gentleman doth protest too much!" she quipped, shoulders shaking with suppressed mirth. She dropped easily into the passenger seat and waited while he walked around the car. "All right, all right. It was your eyes, and your dick that gave you away," she teased further.

"My dick…. What are you talking about?"

"I was looking at it. It's what I like to do. Check out my man's sexy chinos and see if he's got some kind of magic wand in there for me." She liked flustering him. His voice was so low and smooth, but when he got worked up, it rose in pitch and sounded wispier.

Frank burst out laughing, " All this, and it was you checking out my magic wand!"

"Well, we have yet to see if it can actually *do* magic." That was what he adored about her. She charmed him so easily, and it was like she constantly found ways to tease him or make him sputter.

The drive to the local cinema wasn't far, just a few turns down the back roads. The parking lot was crowded, but then it was a Friday night, and the building had a line out the front door for tickets. They stood in line holding hands, and Frank bought the tickets and popcorn and cokes. The world might have evolved into a place where couples went dutch and gender roles got blurred, but Eliza had confided in him that she was old school, and liked being treated like a lady. And for her man to be a gentleman. That comment still made him smile. Her man.

They carried their drinks into the auditorium and found seats towards the back. They were seeing the latest blockbuster from Marvel Studios, one she evidently had been waiting for ages to see. He hadn't even known there was a Marvel Studios, although he had heard of films like Iron Man and The Avengers.

He would have seen anything she wanted, just to be able to hold her hand and let the world know she was with him, to feel the warmth of her curled under his arm, and hold her while she nuzzled her face into the crook of his shoulder. He smiled, thinking how different she was from him. She had insisted he pick her up early, she wanted to make sure to see all the previews of upcoming attractions. Just the way she said "Attractions…" made him think, "Oh yeah… I feel some attraction…"

He shook his head to clear it, and tilted the sack of popcorn towards her, shaking it a little to entice her to reach in for some. "Only a little bit," she said, and popped a few into her mouth. "I always love to eat this stuff and then I spend the rest of the week flossing to get the kernels out from between my teeth."

That didn't stop her, however. Her hand darted into the bag every time he offered it, and when the lights went down she leaned back and got comfortable, feet on the seat in front. The previews came and went, each one punctuated with a little comment. "That one looks so good!" or "No way are we seeing that!" And he liked the implication. She was talking about the future 'we' as if the two of them would be choosing films together from now on.

The show started, and while he had no idea what was going on, he admired the special effects and tried to work out just who was a superhero, who was an alien, and who was a regular human. Some sixth sense of hers must have kicked in, because she squirmed around in her seat and raised her lips up to his ear. "Do you have any idea who's who?" she whispered.

He shook his head slowly, and her hand landed on his knee. "Just relax then. Hold the popcorn still. Let me see if I can explain the plot." His breath quickened, and her hand inched slowly up along his thigh. He leaned his head back, closing his eyes. Soon her hand rested fully on him, fingers curling down over his balls, palm covering the length of him as blood surged down to his groin.

Her breath was hot against his neck. "See, this guy takes his lady to a movie," her palm pressed down harder over him, feeling the hard ridge of him. "And he has to sit still while she goes into unexplored territory." The bag trembled slightly, and he shifted in his seat, slowly widening his knees.

Her tongue darted out and gave him a little lick on his neck. "This feels good, doesn't it?" Her hand moved over him again, thumb and forefinger tracing the outline of him, base to tip.

"Ummmhmmm" he gasped, the arm around her shoulders gripping tight. He wanted to say more but decided to let her do as she pleased. A brief worry about conventions and manliness crossed his mind, and he felt like he ought to say something or do something, but he tamped the feeling down. The most exciting experiences with Eliza came totally unexpectedly. Like now, her fingers trailed over him, up and down, sometimes forceful, sometimes frustratingly light. His cock pulsed and twitched, wanting desperately for her to unzip his fly and pull him out and yet terrified she might actually do just that.

He liked her warm breath in his ear, the feel of her tongue flicking out, catching him by surprise then swirling around the shell of his ear. He never would have guessed it could be so erotic. But then again, she had his shaft in her hand, her fingers teasing him to a harder plateau.

He tried to sit still and marveled how easily she'd maneuvered him into this. One hand around her, the other holding popcorn, her free to tease him in the shadows. He loved it, and had been waiting for it. Maybe not waiting for it so much as hoping for it, anticipating that she was going to do it or at least praying that she would.

He lifted his hips as she pressed, seeking a little harder touch. She giggled and pulled away. She knew she had him going, had to know she had his cock rock hard, oozing precum , spotting his underwear, if not his khakis.

"Just enjoy it, Frank," her words only added to his passion. "It's a long movie…"

He wanted to throw the paper bag of popcorn onto the floor and tip her face up to kiss her, but somehow he refrained. He kept his face turned up to the screen, once in a while glancing over at her pretty face in the dim lighting. Her wavy hair down around her shoulders was a pleasant change, making her seem more lighthearted. The curls still refused to stay put, framing her ears and face. Her lips glistened like she had just put on lipstick, or maybe fruit flavored lip gloss. He licked his own suddenly dry lips, wishing for a kiss, or something more.

The film seemed endless, and the soundtrack was perfect for an evening of long slow caresses from a sweetheart. One hit wonders from the '70s that took him back to his childhood, to his less than spectacular prom. He re-imagined it all, what it would have been like if he'd known her back then. Ooooh, slow dancing with her to Stairway to Heaven, feeling her hips pressed against his. He would have held her so tight, swaying with his awkward all-boys high school never been to a school dance before non-moves. He probably would have cum in his pants, just like he was about to do here in a crowded theater.

She knew what she was doing, this girl. He wanted more of her touch. She found the sensitive head of his shaft, and stimulated it with rough caresses and little pinches, and then dragged her palm down over him to scrunch up his balls and then massage back up the length of him. He could barely keep his breathing even and tried not to moan. Softer, harder, faster, she was building the need inside him. As if she knew how long it had been, how desperately he wanted to feel this with her.

"I'm, um... Eliza..." he felt she deserved a warning, just in case she didn't want to really see this go too far.

She hesitated but only for a second."Do you want me to stop?" she asked. She gave the head of his cock a cruel pinch and wound him up even closer to explosion. He gasped and was startled that it came out like a little squeak. "I don't think we are ready to stop yet," she cooed in his ear, nipping on his ear lobe and drawing another heavy sigh from him. She found the tab on his zipper and eased it down, letting the fabric part and the solid shaft pop up a little higher, tenting the cotton of his boxers. Her hand slipped inside and wrapped around his pole.

"Oh!" he gasped and straightened in his chair, almost spilling the popcorn. She gripped him tightly, and her thumb curved up and over, stroking the crown. He wanted to spill right there with her breath hot on his neck, her boldness gripping him tightly. He heard her chuckle. "Almost, my sexy. Almost there." She stroked slowly, and his eyes drifted shut, letting her stroke him higher, wishing they were at home in his bed, so they could undress and really get to know each other.

His cock was pulsing, almost at the point of no return. He squeaked again, almost hoping she'd stop and say they needed to rush home. But he knew in his heart she wasn't the kind of woman to start and come this far here and then quit. Or was she? Hell, he still didn't know. As the screen exploded with a battle ending in a fiery crash and the music built to a crescendo, her fingers skillfully built up the need in him, her thumb flicking over his slit, driving him over the edge.

He turned his face to hers at the last second, burying his lips in her hair as he groaned long and low, his cock twitching and unloading seed on his belly and staining his boxers. She kept toying with him until the climax had passed, milking every drop from him.

Long minutes passed as he sat there, eyes closed, unable to move. He breathed in the scent of her hair as strength returned to his limbs and reality returned. The credits were scrolling.

Frank held her close while his breathing returned to normal, and then watched in amazement as she pulled a wad of napkins from her purse and plucked the popcorn bag from his hand. "Give me this while you tidy yourself."

Tidied himself? What a way to put it. He pulled his arm back from around her shoulders and hastily wiped up what he could and zipped his pants. It wasn't easy. He felt so self-conscious, and everything was going straight into the wash the minute he got home.

She took the napkins from him and threw them into the popcorn bag, rolling it up and setting it on the floor. She turned his face to hers and kissed him lightly. "Let's not forget to take that out with us when we leave," she added. Her tone was light, and he dipped his head and found her lips again. It felt so good, kissing her softly in the theater. There was no tension, just warmth and acceptance. Her hand came up to rest against his cheek. "Thank you, honey." Her eyes met his. "I wasn't sure how that might go, but it was... beautiful."

He laughed in relief. "As long as there's no test about the plot of the movie later…"

She chuckled and held him close. "Movie? Was there a movie?"

Chapter 5

Frank tried to act like life was normal, as if everything hadn't gone from maintaining a steady trudge forward through the mess of a divorce to feeling like he was walking on air. Songs on the radio made him suddenly want to pull over and check his phone. They played a constant game of sexy texting, but he refused to think of it as sexting, even though the words and the pictures made his insides squeeze up and his shaft want to sit up and beg. The memory of her hands on him in the darkness of the theater made him suddenly ready to take that step. She had awakened his libido and captured his imagination. Soon he would be free and able to actually start to thinking of them as a couple.

He loved the flirty banter, almost feeling like he was someone else. When he was around her he no longer felt like the unwanted husband, but rather she made him feel sexy, as if he were the one that was the sought after, unattainable dream, with a dash of virgin about to be sacrificed thrown in. He was really getting into the game she was playing.

His phone was overflowing with the text balloons and smiley emojis.

> **Eliza:** Can't stop thinking about the
> movie last night.

You: Me too. Well, I don't remember much of the movie. But you know what I mean.

Eliza: I do. Lol It was supposed to be a good flick. Maybe we should give it another go. See if we can actually watch it this time.

You: It had an excellent soundtrack. I wouldn't mind hearing it again.

Eliza: I have a feeling it would end up exactly the same way. We should get together for dinner somewhere nice, instead. That new Steak House in Center City, maybe?

You: I hear it's popular. I'll check and see if I can get us a reservation.

Eliza: You sound hesitant, think it's that booked?

You: I won't know until I try

Eliza: We could always try a place that's BYOB -- save a little there

He hadn't known what to say to that, so he'd sent back:

You: Lol

Eliza: And head back to your place afterwards for coffee and dessert

He could almost hear her say it, the way she whispered suggestive things in his ear, the way she had in those uncomfortable seats in the Movieplex. Something about her tone seemed suddenly breathless and sexy. Like he was going to be the thing served up for dessert. His cock responded and urged his fingers to type, "Yes, yes!" but he had controlled them and responded with a noncommittal

> **You**: "Oh? What kind of dessert would please my lady?"
>
> **Eliza**: Anything with whipped cream on it. Straight out of the Reddi Whip can.
>
> **You**: I will provide something extraordinary! I'll text you the details
> :)

Frank was so unused to texting and using the little smiley faces that peppered Eliza's text, that he stared down for a moment. He was smiling, and happy... and totally turned on at the thought of having her in his apartment.

So he had set it up, the perfect evening at a romantic French bistro that was both tasty and economical. He was almost certain she had meant the economical thing as a joke. What woman didn't like to be wined and dined? Especially if her escort picked out the perfect bottle to bring along. Eliza must be seeing something in him besides his old-fashioned charm, Frank thought. He suspected that she also saw him as a little bit of a challenge, trying to get him to open up and show his adventurous side.

He had taken extra precautions to have the evening go smoothly, calling ahead to the restaurant to see what they recommended for their prix fixe. Not only to assist in the wine selection, but his instincts told him Eliza was a bit of a gastronome and would want to taste what the French chef had to offer.

The sad thing was, he was so eager for what might come after the meal, he barely tasted it. Oh, his lovely bottle of burgundy wine went well with everything, and he tried to make the evening last, but there was an edge in the air, and he could almost feel his pulse thrumming a little bit harder, repeating, "Tonight, tonight, tonight!"

She had scooted closer to him after the hostess seated them at a small square table. She looked beautiful, in her usual calm and understated way. "Just the two of us on another 'get to know you' date," she whispered. He didn't know who she was trying to convince.

They studied their menus in silence. The waitress approached and studied the two of them as she shuffled papers on her pad. "My name's Melinda, and I'll be your server this evening." Frank smiled up at her while she recited the specials, and then went on to describe them in greater detail.

"Are there any that you recommend?" Frank asked in his smooth, slightly accented tones.

"Any that might be available more quickly than the rest?" Eliza couldn't help laughing at the expression on Frank's face. Oh God, it was like he expected everyone in the place suspected they were running home to get intimate after dinner.

Eliza caught his eye as she clarified for the waitress. "We are trying to make a 9 o'clock movie," she lied, and winked at Frank. "Do you think we can be in and out in less than an hour and fifteen?"

Melanie didn't bat an eye. She scribbled down on her notepad as she decided for them. "Boeuf Bourguingnon, times two, and your sides?"

"Roasted potatoes and mixed vegetables." Eliza enjoyed seeing Frank out of his comfort zone. "Times two." He was almost like a teenager in some ways, and it was such a contradiction. He was so polished, so professional when it came to his classes, his responsibilities at the college, and then every evening out with her it was like he was trying to get used to taking a girl on a date.

Her sexy professor had the respect of his students as well as his peers, a professional air complete with the wardrobe and briefcase to match. Even the video clip she had seen of him at the college included both students and faculty stepping forward to shake his hand.

Melinda the waitress moved on to other customers, and Eliza took hold of Frank's hand where it rested beside her on the table. She shook it a little and looked into his intelligent eyes. "What is on your mind, Frank? As far as everyone here knows, we are an old married couple. No one is wondering at all what we might have planned for after this."

She was right. He knew it. He was wound so tight, and there was no need. Really. He let out a breath he hadn't realized he was holding. "It has been so long, Eliza. I am so out of practice. Excuse me, for over thinking all this." His thumb gently traced over the back of her knuckles.

"I am a little out of my depth," he continued. "Give me a room full of rambunctious teenagers who know nothing about chemistry, and I can take all that in stride." He sounded so earnest. She could just picture him in a white lab coat, and a pair of safety goggles.

"So you set up all the experiments and roam around the room to make sure no one leaves the Bunson burner on or drops a Mentos in their diet coke?

"And I man the fire extinguisher! That's one of the most important jobs. Although most of the students are familiar with how to run an experiment. It's all pretty straight forward, and if they have prepared for class at all, they know how it's supposed to run, as well as what they need to write up in their report.

"Every once in a while I get a student from a school that never required a lab science, but I can usually spot those a mile away."

Eliza sipped her wine and tried to lighten the mood. "Are they the students who wear chef's whites like a lab coat and even add the hat to the ensemble?"

Plates delicately decorated with drizzles of gravy and delicious looking beef Bourguignon appeared. Melinda tucked a plate in front of each of them and topped off their wine glasses. She bowed herself out with minimal fuss, barely interrupting their conversation.

"Honestly, Eliza," he snorted, "It's never what they wear, just the look of terror as they first walk into the lab, and the way they circle around pretending to be a shark, but they are really sniffing around for a lab partner who looks like they know what they are doing."

She bit back laughter, wondering if his comment had anything to do with his search for a romantic partner, but apparently, it wasn't. He was giving his usual straight answer. Once again Eliza wished she had known him back in his college days. "I would choose you as my lab partner, Frank, any day. I would have been worse than the chefs. Lab sciences were never my thing; I got by on compiling the reports, because of my handwriting. Back in the dark ages, before everything was done on a computer."

The scent rising from the plate of beef was impossible to resist. Eliza took a bite and savored it on her tongue. She hadn't tasted anything this authentically French in years. "I bet the chefs aren't required to take a lab science, and those who do are probably up enough on their cooking and flavor skills to know that it's all based on chemistry anyway."

Frank smiled over the table at her. "Smart girl." He took a bite and moaned softly in pleasure at the exquisite taste. He ate slowly, deciding the meal deserved at least a little attention, given that he was passing up on lingering over the blend of Burgundy wine and beef.

Eliza slipped off her shoe and tucked her toes up under the hem of his pants running the smoothness of her stockinged foot along his calf. "Now eat up. I have a show I am trying to make... staring one sexy professor..."

She giggled as this time he deadpanned, "No dessert for you, young lady, if you can't do justice to some French chef who no doubt has his whole self-worth wrapped up in that dish you are consuming right there. He will be heartbroken. We can't have that."

"I have been wondering about it all day, Frank, what did you make for dessert?" she asked. All right, she had been thinking about it since the minute she'd decided to invite herself over to his place.

Enough trying to figure out when she might have her own house to herself. Enough trying to get a straight answer out of Josh about when he might be home. She wanted her privacy back, dammit, and then it had hit her. Frank's place was 100 percent his own. No stray friends dropping in, no kids turning up in the middle of the night.

So she had arranged the perfect plan. It was so easy. It didn't matter what he produced for coffee and dessert. It could be a mint from the tray as they left the Bistro. She didn't care.

"I cheated," he confessed. "I bought a pecan pie and a few cans of whipped cream." He had stood in the bakery section of the grocery store wondering what Eliza would like. He could clearly remember her mentioning chocolate, and the Bistro was French, so somehow cannolis hadn't seemed right, or cake, or brownies. It had been miraculously easy once he had whittled down all the options of 'what went well with whipped cream on top' to pie.

In the end, he had gotten a pecan pie and two cans of whipped cream. The baker behind the counter at the grocery store suggested it would be best if served warm, with a scoop of ice cream, or doused in whipped cream. There were certain parts of his anatomy, and hers, that he would like to see with a dollop on top. His tongue tingled, imagining what licking that fluffy whipped cream off would be like.

She must have been reading his thoughts. He could see the candlelight reflected in her eyes, and see the warmth of a light blush spreading up over her cheeks. "I'm glad you remembered the Reddi-Whip, Frank," she said. "It might be the highlight of dessert!" She took a few more bites and then winked at him, sitting back in her chair and announcing, "I'll have to ask for a box. I couldn't eat another bite!"

Why did everything she said make him want to laugh? He laid his fork down beside his plate and scanned the room for Melanie. "Well good manners dictate that I follow suit," and to his pleasure, the waitress cruised up to the table without much delay. Frank held up two fingers in a peace sign. "Two boxes and the check, please…"

Chapter 6

Settling the bill was quick and simple, and Frank left Melanie a hefty tip. She deserved it for the dinner recommendations and attention that got them in and out in record time. The evening hadn't started out feeling rushed, but after sensing Eliza's eagerness to get home for dessert, well, it was easy to catch that feeling. He made a mental note to bring Eliza back for another, more leisurely meal at the French bistro so they could linger over good French food and good French wine.

He held the door for Eliza on the way out and felt her slip her hand into his, her grip firm, tugging him close while she stretched up to kiss him softly. She must have caught his quick glance around the environs afterwards because she chuckled and gave his hand a squeeze. "I forgot, you still get nervous about public displays."

"I don't, or at least I shouldn't," Frank replied. "I don't know why I do that still, just trying to shake the feeling that we're sneaking around. But my ex, or soon to be ex, uses anything as an excuse to reopen negotiations." He kept her hand in his and hurried in the direction of the car, settling her in the passenger seat before taking the wheel and threading them through the late evening traffic.

Eliza wanted to ask him more about the divorce negotiations that seemed to stress him out so much, since he had mentioned them a few times now. She waited, hoping he would bring up the subject again, but as fate would have it, the ride to Frank's apartment took only a few minutes. The parking space Frank had pulled out of in front of the building was still open when they pulled up, and Frank slid the Honda into place.

Eliza reached back to snag their leftovers off the back seat and then waited while he hurried around to open the door for her. He shut the car door gently behind her and locked it with a beep from the key fob. He knew he was overdoing it a bit, but the grand gestures seemed to make her smile.

Eliza stood on the steps outside the building while Frank unlocked the door, admiring the contour of Frank's buttocks in the bright light that spilled down from overhead. Other than the distinguished form of the gentleman on the stoop, there wasn't much to differentiate this building from any apartment building she had been in lately. There was a pass-through vestibule which lead to a wide staircase of dark polished wood, and to the side, a row of mailboxes jutted from the wall with tenant's names penciled in.

Frank's mailbox was open, jam-packed to overflowing with newspapers and envelopes. He yanked the whole wad of it out and tucked it beneath one arm. His smile was apologetic. He gathered up her hand with his free one, and drew it up to his lips, gently kissing her knuckles.

"It's gotten to be a standard of living around here these days. Legal correspondence." He gestured vaguely to the wad of mail.

His hand gripped hers firmly and reassuringly as she followed him happily up the stairs, a little bit amazed she had wrangled an invitation to his place so easily. She admired the view of him from behind as he lead the way up, finding his slim hips and sexy ass right at eye level. She liked the view, she admitted to herself, and she was getting used to it, even if she was feeling a little jealous of his tight, muscular behind.

She continued to stand behind him as he fished again for his keys, and took great delight in touching that fabulous butt. His jacket rode up as he bent down, and it looked like it would fit the curve of her palm perfectly. It was so close and so irresistible, so why not?

Just one small caress, she thought, hadn't he commented several times how much her sexy caresses turned him on? How it made him feel sexy and desired?

He gave a little 'umph' of surprise when her hand cupped one taut cheek but held still as her hand caressed down over him. Not groping, per se, just getting acquainted with the feel of him.

With a little jingle, Frank opened his door and flicked on a light switch. Now that he had Eliza here in his apartment, he worried about what she'd think of it. The place was small and crowded with mismatched furniture. A heavy, maroon-colored wing chair he had brought home from his office at the college squatted between the closet door and the entrance to the kitchen. The old gray love seat that had been in Benny's room for years was slightly tilted from so many teenagers leaning on the one arm, but it was the focal point in the room facing the flat screen. In front of it, a glass-topped coffee table split the distance to the TV, and behind it was the main walkway between the kitchen and the back hallway.

As Frank took in the sparse furniture and over-sized windows on the far wall behind the couch he hoped she wasn't too disheartened. At least the flat screen TV was new. When he glanced at Eliza, she was turned the other way, examining the most impressive thing in the room, his roll-top desk. Even though it was currently piled high with correspondence from lawyers and accountants, the dark mahogany gleamed. The top was thrown open, revealing an assortment of carved doors and drawers, and even the green corner of a desk blotter. He tossed the new mail on top of the old and closed the covering slats about half way.

"You wouldn't believe the amount of paperwork so far in this divorce," he said angrily. "At first I thought she was being difficult out of spite. But the longer this goes on, the less sense it makes. Assigning things sentimental value, and what not."

Eliza said nothing, just stood in the doorway while he rearranged the over-sized envelopes and closed the lid of his desk. "It seems like every week something new comes up that we have to arrange how to split. She keeps sending me lists of the most outrageous things. Like every savings bond or piece of fine china has to be equally divided."

Eliza took his hand and led him towards the love seat. "It's going to take time, Frank. We both know it, " she reassured him.

For one minute he let the frustration of it all get to him. He waved an arm around the spartan room. "Does this look evenly divided? She can just leave and take everything?"

Eliza sank down onto the gray love seat that looked like it had seen better days. She bounced up and down on it a little, testing the springs. "I don't know... this might be a little tight for us to stretch out and get comfortable on..." she gave him a knowing look and then a saucy wink. "Do you really care about the Lennox teacups?"

"No," he admitted. "But it's not right."

She smiled and the room was suddenly brighter. "I'll test out the furniture, and determine which one will be best for making out on later. But before that, we should probably at least pretend to have coffee and dessert."

The air in the room suddenly seemed hotter, and he pulled at his collar, loosening his tie and slipping the top button free from the clasp. She looked playful, comfortable on the cast-off furniture, and he would be an idiot to let his simmering anger over his legal problems get in the way of enjoying the evening with her.

He headed for the kitchen, making a quick stop to hang up his jacket in the coat closet. "I'll see about that coffee, and heating up that pie," he called over his shoulder.

The tiny kitchen was all original tile and appliances. The only light source was an overhead bulb, and it was way too bright, but at least he could see in the cabinet as he hunted down the old Mr. Coffee machine. Nowhere near as easy or efficient as the brand new Keurig he had used until recently. Somehow that was also a casualty of war, something he had lost custody of in this mess even though it had been a gift to him from the science department at the college to celebrate his 20 years of teaching.

He turned the oven on to 350 and set the pecan pie on the rack without letting it preheat, and then scooped coffee into the filter. He was setting out two coffee mugs, one from a vacation to Maine and another that said, '#1 Teacher'. He could hear Eliza moving around in the living room, probably doing exactly what she'd promised, investigating his furniture for a good place to cuddle. The mental image of her perfect, round ass occupying every seat made him smile.

Somehow the idea of her lightheartedly bouncing on every piece of furniture, just to tease him out of a mood really did ease his tension. She was not going to let his current situation detract from their evening, and he would be insane not to allow this classy lady cheer him up.

Frank set the kitchen timer for 10 minutes and went in search of her. The living room was empty when he got there, and he continued down the short hallway, ascertaining there was light under the bathroom door. He double checked that his bed was made and the bedroom somewhat presentable, and made his way back to the kitchen. He wondered once again what had made her want to see his place, and hoped she wasn't going to write him off because of it. She'd have to know this was all just temporary, wouldn't she? He propped one shoulder against the door jam and waited.

"Oh, I like your bedroom, Frank!" There was a little tell-tale squeak from the bed springs, and he could just picture her in there, bouncing lightly on it, assessing the comfort level of that too. For later.

Wow. Suddenly the prospects for this evening sizzled through his brain, and he felt his dick stirring at the thoughts. He liked the idea of her in there, on his bed. Her ass, on his bed.

The timer sounded with a low buzz that drew him back to the present. The coffee was finished dripping, and he could actually smell the pie. Frank opened the oven door and pulled back as a blast of hot air hit him in the face. He hesitated for a moment and looked around the cook space blankly.

The timer kept on buzzing.

Eliza hurried in, drawn by the delicious aromas of coffee and pecans. She stopped short when she saw the look on his face. It almost broke her heart. "What is it, Frank?"

He stayed bent over, peering into the oven. "I don't seem to have any pot holders." He said it like it was the end of the world, and she realized it was probably just one more thing in a long string of hurts. His life had been organized, secure, and now he was finding one thing after another that was out of sync.

But really, that's what this was about? Pot holders? Eliza glanced around, and then pulled open the cabinet under the sink. She pulled out an old dish towel and nudged him out of the way. She folded the dishtowel a couple times and yanked the pie plate out, setting it down on the stove top. A quick (if forward) look in a drawer revealed some knives and forks.

"You pour the coffee, hun, and I'll take charge of slicing this pie. And doling out the whipped cream," she joked.

He had two mugs of coffee ready, light and sweet, in the amount of time it took her to cut two large portions of pie and overload them with whipped cream. Which, as far as she was concerned, was the recommended way to eat pecan pie.

They made their way back to the living room and settled beside each other on the sofa. Eliza made herself comfortable, sitting on one foot and leaning against the slightly wobbly arm. It had a nice amount of give, and she braced her elbow on it, watching Frank set his mug on the table and sit somewhat stiffly beside her.

"How long have you lived here, Frank?" she inquired, wanting to see him relax a bit. "I like it, it kind of reminds me of a place I rented in my college days."

The sound that he made was a cross between a laugh and a snort. "I have been here over six months, and it looks about the same as it did on day one."

Eliza sipped her coffee and then set the cup down. "And how did it happen, did she move out, or tell you to move out? How is it you're here and your house is sitting empty?"

"I look back, and try to figure out where it all started, I try to chart where things went bad, you know, look at the situation with a scientific approach." He paused to wash down a bite of pie with some coffee. "There were trouble spots, times where she wanted things I couldn't give her, or times I messed up and planned a work trip to D.C. when she was planning a weekend away with her friends, but lately, this past year she has been so... unforgiving."

"What do you mean, unforgiving?" Eliza asked. "There was no pleasing her, or she was pissed about everything?

"She got erratic, almost greedy, and then it was like it never happened. She moved out, moved in with this flashy day trader, and wanted to sell everything, just take off."

Eliza nodded encouragingly. "Sometimes people get wrapped up in their own problems they forget other people have them too."

"But my desk," he gestured towards it with his fork. "She wanted to sell that, even though it is mine, left to me by my uncle. And when I said no and brought it here, she was mad about the empty space in the house, which she wasn't even living in anymore."

Eliza loaded up a perfect bite, small amount a pie and the last of her whipped cream. She held out the fork to him and waited while he slowly leaned in to accept it.

"All couples disagree and let their emotions take over. There was a time after Josh was born when my life was crazy, and I got no sleep. I was struggling to lose the baby weight, and barely even trying. And Jim, in his own out of touch way asked if he should move the treadmill up from the basement and put it in the dining room." She casually scraped up the remnants of Reddi Whip with the side of her fork, and then continued, " because I seemed to forget that we had a treadmill, hidden away down there."

Frank chuckled, 'I bet that didn't go over well."

"No, but after he went out and bought one of those speed-walker strollers I really let him have it, blasting him for his insensitivity, and he ended up taking the kids out for walks in it, leaving me time home alone for a combat nap."

"That was what you really wanted, wasn't it?"

"It was! I hadn't realized how well it turned out in the end. I was just so worked up over that treadmill comment." Eliza sat and smiled as she sipped her coffee. "The pie was delicious, Frank."

She was also silly pleased that he had remembered how she liked her coffee. "It makes me feel good that you remembered how I take my coffee," she admitted, trying to get the evening back on track. As always, the crust was never as appealing as the innards of pecan pie. She had nibbled a little crust with each bite but mostly centered her efforts around the good stuff.

Frank watched her and laughed. "It never ceases to amaze me. You know what you want, and you go for it, with no worries about social convention or what anyone else might think."

Her plate landed on the glass table with a little clink, and she took another long sip of her coffee. "By taking the best part and not worrying about what's dry and crusty?" She was talking about more than pie, and he knew it. She licked a little bit of whipped cream off her lip, and his eyes followed the pink tip of her tongue. He couldn't tell if she was doing it on purpose... but now all he could think about was her soft, full lips, and kissing them.

Chapter 7

Eliza scooted a little closer beside him, feeling him stiffen as she pushed him out of his comfort zone. Such a simple thing, to lean in holding her coffee mug lightly, and hover close enough to remind him of their evening in the movie theater. Her lips were a hair's breadth from his cheek, bringing back the sensation of how her warm breath had felt on his ear, as if she knew how badly he wanted it again.

And he did, she could tell. She caught a glimpse of his tongue as he wet his lips. She didn't even have to look down at the crisp folds of his pants. It seemed his wardrobe consisted of work clothes, work clothes, and more work clothes, just like hers. She made a mental note to come back to that later, and plan a shopping trip for something more casual than casual Friday.

His face was just inches from hers. There was a hint of five o'clock shadow, but her nose was still drawn to the crook of his neck. A light aroma, manly and yet not overpowering. She couldn't resist. She sniffed, making him laugh.

"I have been meaning to ask you, what is that scent you always wear? Is that aftershave? Body wash?"

He laughed again. "Body wash? Sorry, no. Tell me, do you like it?"

She leaned in again and breathed deeply. "Whatever it is, I approve. I am not sure I have ever encountered this scent before. Old Spice?" she joked.

"Eternity for Men," he grinned. Then he turned his head, gathered her up in his arms and kissed her. He pulled her close slowly, feeling her warmth and her curves. His lips lingered over hers, tasting. Her lips parted under his in a small sigh, opening and offering his tongue a sneak inside. She tasted of pecan pie and Maxwell House coffee. He heard her coffee cup land on the glass top coffee table with a clink and she turned in his arms, rising up, straddling him and locking her arms fiercely around his neck.

He rested his hands on her hips, settling her into place. Her most intimate place pressed against the hardened length of him. He lifted his hips slightly, stifling a moan as he felt the sensation of her pussy rubbing along the length of his cock.

It was time. She hoped he was ready for a sexy reality check. If she was going to give herself, she thought, it was going to be on her own terms. Her fingertips caressed over his earlobe as she smoothed his hair back, and then suddenly her hand was tight in his hair, pulling his head back, forcing his eyes up to meet hers. "So that's how you want to play it, Frank?"

She thrust against him again. He resented the fabric between them. His pulse was pounding and his cock felt constricted by his clothing. The rush of sensations had garbled his thoughts. He had never acted this way with a woman in his life. Frank pulled himself together and pinned his gaze on Eliza's face. Her eyes met his fiercely, and he slowly nodded yes.

"I thought I was going to show you the ropes. Explore the fun and games with you," She sounded a little breathless. She felt so good in his arms, so good in his lap. He recognized her experience in the matter, it oozed out of her. This lady was the real deal, normal, rational and erotic, too. The role reversal aroused him, and he would willingly follow anywhere she wanted to lead.

He loosened his grip and relaxed back on the couch. "You're right, Eliza. I didn't mean to rush things." A wry smile played across his lips. "You're the teacher tonight. Consider me the apt pupil."

She chuckled at the thought of him imitating a little schoolboy and knew that was absolutely not what she wanted. Not tonight, or any night.

She dipped her head down and dropped a little kiss on his lips, and then leaned back, pressing herself against him intimately.

He sounded a little breathless. "I don't know how you do it, but you get to me so quickly, Eliza."

"Does that mean you can't control yourself? You feel the urge to reach out and take and there's no finesse?"

Her fingers were making short work of the buttons on his work shirt, spreading the crisp edges and fanning out over the dusting of hair on his chest.

"Your job is to enjoy, and allow me to have fun."

"Oh, Hell," he chuckled. "I think I have been the recipient of your fun before…."

The ancient sofa creaked a little as she rocked back and rose up, pulling him to his feet beside her in one smooth motion. She turned and lead the way down the hall to the door at the end. He had a brief worry as the thought entered his head that he still wasn't officially divorced yet, but she turned as she entered his bedroom and he could see the tight peaks of her nipples under her silk blouse. In another world, where he was a jock or a superhero or even one of the cool kids at school he would have dipped his head and sucked that pointy little nipple into his mouth. But this lady had made it very clear.

There were some kind of rules. No rushing things. They had the whole evening, endless nights in the future to explore each other. He wanted her to show him how she liked it. How she wanted to be undressed, and how she wanted to be made love to.

A shiver went through him. Making love. Something he hadn't done in a long time, and something he had a feeling Eliza Hamilton did very well. The inner student in him respected her as the instructor, and the giving soul inside him hungered to please her, to maybe try some of the things he had only read about in men's magazines or online erotica sites. Oh, God, he hoped she would do some of those things. She sure hadn't held back in the theater.

He tried to keep his breathing even as she finished unbuttoning his shirt and smoothed it back off his shoulders. She took a minute to match the shoulder seams and lay it flat over the back of a chair. He felt ridiculously pleased. She really did know him well.

Next, she hooked her fingers through the waistband of his belt and jerked him a step closer. He came willingly and felt his dick respond every time she took a little bit more control or shook him a little more roughly.

She slid the leather strap out of the buckle and opened his button fly, easing the zipper open. She examined the telltale bulge that tented his boxers out towards her hands.

"These are pretty, Frank. Too bad they aren't boxer briefs. Anyway, you can be sure to have those next time we go out?" He stood staring as her perfectly manicured pink nails plucked at the fabric.

He nodded dumbly and prayed he'd remember. "Boxer briefs."

Eliza took hold of the waistband on each side and shucked him out of his pants like an ear of corn. One smooth motion and suddenly he was stepping out of them. She lay those, too, neatly over the chair back. "Thank you," he mumbled.

She smiled brightly, taking a moment to send her gaze over him. Now that she had him stripped down to his boxers and in good lighting, she liked what she saw, broad shoulders, a trim waist, just the hint of ab muscles, and below those abs… evidence that he was very much enjoying their evening.

"You look so sexy, Frank." He stood rooted in place while her hands went to the deep V of her neckline and unbuttoned a few invisible buttons, letting her top drape open as she shimmied out of her black crepe pants.

Then it was his turn to admire her lush body. Her skin was pale and smooth, and she was a sight in her lacy black bra and panties. They matched her dark hair and black heels perfectly. Eliza took his hand and led him the few steps to the bed.

"You promise to let me have my fun?" He couldn't resist her teasing tone or the quirky brow that arched high on one side. Her dark eyes held him, framed by thick dark lashes and perfect eyebrows. He had never paid so much attention to the details of a woman's face, before, but Eliza charmed him, drew him in.

"You promise?" she asked again, a little more forcefully.

"Ummmhmmm, he moaned softly. " He wasn't sure what he was agreeing to, but with this woman, it was bound to be explosively sexy. He had secret hopes, fantasies he had boxed up and put away, that maybe this sexy lady might reopen.

Eliza turned him and crowded him back towards the bed. She pressed two fingers lightly under his chin, and that butterfly touch was enough to guide him, to move him back, and then draw his face down for a soft kiss. One step back, and then another, until he felt the bed bump up against the back of his knees. He felt a rush of sensations: anticipation and arousal.

A gentle push with her fingertips and he sat down and scooted back on the bed, making room for her to lay down beside him.

She crawled up onto the bed, giving him a perfect view of her heavy breasts down the gaping top of her bra as she drew closer. His throat went dry. He wanted to kiss her, to touch her, and to have her touch him. God, she was good at this teasing thing.

Eliza moved to lay beside him, and he guessed her intention. Laying down flat he pulled her close and curled her up in the crook of his arm, letting her settle in, fitting beautifully. He dropped his nose and smelled her soft, shiny hair. Her fingers traced patterns over his chest, teasing lower, but still not rushing it.

"I love cuddling like this, all warm and snug." Eliza said, "Safe and protected."

Frank nodded. The feeling of her next to him, skin on skin, felt so right. Somehow she made him want to puff up his chest and respond, "I'll protect you!" But he held back, watching her and seeing where she was taking this encounter.

Her fingers found and teased into the opening in his boxers, her nails gently scraping over the sensitive head of his shaft and making him squirm. It was too much, and it wasn't enough. He was disappointed when Eliza dropped a kiss onto his broad chest and reared back.

"I forgot my purse in the other room. Why don't you wriggle out of these plaid boxers while I go get it."

She slid back and bounced off the bed. He watched her sexy ass sway as she disappeared back down the hallway.

She amazed him. She dumbfounded him. He wasn't sure what she needed in her bag. He hoped it was full of condoms or a diaphragm or something of that nature. He did have a brand new box of Trojans in the nightstand drawer. It had seemed a little presumptuous to buy them, but better to be prepared, even if tonight wasn't the night.

The door hit the coiled up doorstop hard as she swept back into the room. The twang of the vibration hovered for a few seconds in the air as she stood there with her red handbag in one hand.

"What is going on in here?" Her tone sounded a little less playful and a little more harsh.

"Welcome back…" he smiled.

"I could swear I suggested you step out of those boxers while I was in the living room. I went all the way there to give you privacy, and I come back and you're still laying there daydreaming."

His hands flew to his shorts and started pulling them down. To hell with modesty.

"Just because I phrase it as a request, doesn't mean it's up for discussion."

He got the undershorts untangled from his foot and tossed them onto the floor. "Yes, Ma'am," he joked, still smiling.

Eliza's eyes glanced at him splayed out there on the bed like a feast for her. Her eyes shone with heat as she kicked out of her pumps and shrugged out of her silk top. She crawled back up onto the bed in slow motion, liking the way his eyes followed her breasts.

"I think I like it when you say, 'Yes, ma'am'."

She took hold of both his stockinged feet and pulled him roughly down towards the foot of the bed, and then lay herself down along his left leg.

"Reach those two hands back up behind your head and take a firm grip of the headboard." Her tone was no nonsense, and he complied immediately. He'd do whatever it took to continue this game.

"Yes, ma'am" She could hear the laughter in his voice. But for all the humor, the tension in the air was very serious.

Her hand slid up the inside of his thigh, crinkling the hair, getting to know the feel of him as she draped herself over his leg. He loved the feel of it, the smooth heat of her skin, and then the slightly rougher edge of her panties. Her weight was slight. She propped herself up on one elbow and leaned over him.

She turned and smiled up at him, and his insides unfurled, knowing she was about to introduce him to a whole new world. Her dark eyes looking up at him over the length of his nude body.

Eliza seemed to want to touch all of him. She nuzzled close to his belly, inhaling the musky smell of his arousal. Her hands roamed the velvet skin of his inner thighs, and then found his heavy ball sack.

She couldn't wait to show him what he'd been missing. Ever since he first mentioned he had never had a blow job, she had been planning this.

Her palm cupped him, lifting his balls, cupping them and giving them a gentle squeeze.

He moaned softly, twisting, turning towards the warmth of her mouth. But her grip tightened threateningly.

"Hands on that headboard, sexy, and just relax your legs. You will enjoy it, I promise."

His cock was bobbing already, and she gently lifted it by the base and steered it towards her lips. Her eyes were up on his face, focusing on him, taking in the look of pleasure and the way his eyes rolled back and a soft moan blew out on a breath when she pressed the crown of his cock to her lips and welcomed it into the warmth and wetness of her mouth.

"Oh, shit" Frank bit out... her mouth, her tongue... just the thought of such intimate attention from her made his hips rise up off the bed. It was silky sweet hot blinding ecstasy, but he quickly recalled her words about not ruining her pleasure, and even though he could have easily exploded right at that moment, he got himself under control and held himself still. He pulled himself somehow back from the edge and let her lips roam over him, licking down the sides of his cock, flicking along the rim under the head.

And those hands, massaging his balls. He spread his legs wider, inviting her to play more, although he wasn't sure how much longer he could keep from cumming.

Eliza had him right where she wanted him. His muscular thighs spread wide, her body contoured against one, and the space between allowing her hands free to roam, touching, stroking. His low moans told her all she needed to know. He was enjoying their interaction as much as she was, or more.

He had fussed a little at the start, not 100 percent willing to commit to letting her be in charge, but once they allowed the passion to rise he had become more receptive to her lead. Most men did, and that thought made her chuckle. As far as she knew, all men responded this way. She was more confident he wouldn't doubt her leadership again.

She gave his throbbing cock a leisurely lick and left her lips surrounding the head. She looked up at him through her dark lashes, met his eyes from across the bed, and once again was amazed she had found someone so perfect. He was in good shape, much better than she herself was. Not sharp muscular definition, but just enough that he probably went to the gym a few times a week. She was going to have to go with him and get herself toned up.

Enough, she pressed him down into the sheets and slurped his heavy cock into her mouth. He gave a ragged groan and thrust up against her. She slapped his opposite thigh sharply and turned to him. "Frank! What did I say about controlling yourself?"

"I know, Eliza. I am doing my best, but you have to know..." He shook his head and turned to wipe the sweat from his brow onto his biceps. "This is all new to me. Forgive the interruption. Please continue..." His smile was contagious.

She laughed again. "Since you asked so nicely, let's see what else I can think of that might be new to you."

"Oh, God..." he sighed.

She sucked the tip of him back between her lips. A soft moan of her own echoing his. He was heavy and thick. Strong and sure of his masculinity. He was content to give her whatever she wanted to take. And man, did she plan to take a lot.

Eliza kept hold of his balls and gently nudged his legs farther apart.

"Here's where you have to trust me, Frank. Can you do that? Trust I know how to make you feel good?"

In response, he spread his legs wider and relaxed his death grip on the headboard. He was eager to see where this led, eager to see how far she'd go. He was still somewhat dazed she was so into the practices and games most other ladies considered 'naughty', but he didn't mind. He figured he had struck gold the day he met her.

She turned away from him for a moment, and he watched her fishing in her purse. Too big and too disorganized, as usual. He watched in fascination as she applied lip balm and then dropped the tube back into her bag. Next she pulled out another tube of balm, or Vaseline or lube.

She applied a dollop to her finger, and then she bent back over his hip. He closed his eyes, scarcely daring to hope she might be about to go into such unknown territory for him.

Her lips returned to his shaft and built up a slow rhythm, bringing him higher and higher. The tension built, and he held onto the headboard, enjoying, and keeping his passion tightly controlled.

He wasn't afraid of what might happen, he knew he would allow her to use his body for her pleasure, and he knew she was a woman who knew how to express her passions is ways most others didn't. He felt her warm hands caressing his inner thighs, his balls, and his taint. He sucked in a breath as her finger found his tight little rosebud and swirled around it, spreading lube and then slipping in.

"Shit, Eliza..." he could scarcely breathe as she slowly worked her forefinger up inside him. He had a moment of nervousness, wondering if he knew this woman well enough for this, and he gave a snort of laughter. He was so far out of his controlled existence. Not going to be possible, he thought, to rationalize being swept up in desire and romance.

"Something funny, sexy man?" Her finger was deep inside him, his inner muscles gripping her tight. His cock was thrumming, wanting to cum hard and heavy in her mouth.

"No, Ma'am. Well, I just had the thought that we seem to have come a long way down the road to new experiences."

She pressed a little farther in and gave her finger a teasing wiggle. "What, never done this before? Never allowed your lover to feel you on the inside?"

He gave a squeaking laugh and conceded. "No! Forgive me, Eliza. It's just that I am a bit rusty…."

This time it was her turn to giggle. She pressed in, feeling the warmth of his skin and smoothness of his inner muscles. She got a serious look on her face and her finger wiggled and probed.

"Nope, not finding anything rusty in here, mister." She had him laughing too, shedding off the worry and tension of such an unusual circumstance. "But let me check again, just to be sure!" She explored deeper and gave her finger a second teasing wiggle. His whole body shook with laughter as he squirmed and thrashed on the bed.

Eliza nipped his cock playfully, "Even if you are rusty, I bet all your plumbing still works just fine!" She placed her mouth back on him and sucked deeply, like she loved the taste of the slippery clear fluid that oozed out of him. She teased the opening it seeped from with her tongue. "How's my rusty lover feeling?"

"Like I could cum at any moment…"

"Good," she chuckled and went back to work. Easing her finger in and out, letting the slow drag of skin on skin combine with the feel of her lips and teeth on his shaft. "Give me a heads up when there's no stopping it…"

He gave a little teasing thrust, feeling his cock bump into the seam of her lips. "Yes, ma'am!" he replied, all enthusiasm. He hadn't been this enthusiastic about anything except Eliza in years.

He closed his eyes and just felt her touch all over him, in him, teasing him, stroking him, and her mouth, oh God, the feel of her mouth on him. She was such a sensual lover. Nothing could have prepared him, that this was what she would choose. It blew his mind. He could feel the orgasm building inside him and let it grow. Let her feed the fire, stoking until he finally ground out, "Point of no return, Eliza…"

She sucked harder, drew him deeper, and froze like she wanted to feel every twitch and every jerk of his cock as he came for her. He arched taut against the bed and groaned hard, air escaping in a long breath broken up by energetic spurts.

When he could finally think straight again, he could feel Eliza's warm body fitted into the curve of his side again. Her head on his shoulder and his arm curled protectively around her. He hadn't even felt her move. It was like his world had shifted. Suddenly she was there in the center of it.

"I think you were really out of it there for a minute, Frank." Her voice was a husky chuckle.

"Not like I have my world blown like that every day, lady."

"Haha... Lady," she muttered. "You didn't even stir when I went to the bathroom to clean up, or when I put your bathrobe on!"

He looked down at her and squinted. "That is my bathrobe! And yes, of course, you may borrow it!"

She laughed outright this time and swatted him playfully, "Somehow I know better than to walk around naked in a strange apartment with no window treatments when the lights are on at night. Have you never wondered if you have neighbors who can see in?

"Well until tonight I am sure whatever they might have seen would have caused them to fall asleep. But after tonight, if they maybe saw us doing what we were just doing, I am sure they are going to shake my hand and pat me on the back when I see them at the bagel shop across the street tomorrow morning."

Eliza scooted closer and got comfortable. "I was thinking both of us needed to hit the mall for some casual clothes, like shorts and T-shirts, but now I think the first order of business is going to be hitting up the department stores for curtains and shades!"

He laughed and squeezed her tight, not worried at all about falling asleep or having to explain her in the morning. It felt wonderful. He hadn't had so much fun or laughed so much while doing it in, well, forever.

*****

Many hours later he came out of a deep sleep as he felt the bed shift. The lightening sky outside his curtain-less windows let him know morning was fast approaching, and he knew he would have to let her get home to her own life.

He rolled in her direction, taking the sheets with him. "Don't go, Eliza," he said sleepily.

She paused, one foot still in mid-air as she lifted a shoe. "I didn't mean to wake you," she paused for dramatic effect, "Rusty."

Once again he was chuckling. " I'm really sorry about the curtains, or lack thereof. It's just not something that I ever really worried about. I was shown the door and there was a list of things I was permitted to take…"

He sounded so sad she couldn't take it. She climbed back into the bed, shoes and all, and let him wrap her up in acres of sheets. She rested her head on his and held him close.

She looked around the room and saw that aside from his neatly arranged clothes, there was very little else of a personal nature.

"Don't worry, sexy. Starting over doesn't have to mean starting at the beginning again. Sometimes it's just a clean slate. A chance to do things differently. We will find a Kohl's or a Macy's having a sale, and get the immediate needs of this apartment taken care of. And next time you cook dinner for me, we'll have oven mitts AND privacy from the neighbors!"

The sheets felt warm and smelled of him. His strong arms closed them all around her and spun her into a cozy cocoon under him. She kicked off her heels and pressed a kiss up under his chin as he stretched for the nightstand. One flick of the switch and the room was bathed in the pale glow from the streetlight outside.

"No need for the neighbors to see any more," he whispered. "Can we have round two, Eliza? Or more dessert?"

A giggle escaped her, and she kissed his jawline again. His skin was rough against her lips, and her heart twisted a little, remembering how she had laughed and teased Jim over his scruffy facial hair in the predawn hours. It felt scratchy, definitely masculine. She sniffed in the faint traces of aftershave and rubbed her fingertips over his cheek.

"I think I like the feel of your scruff, Frank."

"You ok, Eliza? You looked a little far away for a minute there." His own hand joined hers, rubbing around over his chin. "I probably do need a shave. It will only take a minute. I don't want to give you any razor burn."

Wow, razor burn was something she hadn't thought of since her teenage years. Creeping into the house past curfew and knowing her parents would take one look and know she'd been making out.

"It all depends on what you meant by more dessert."

He hesitated a moment, choosing his words carefully. "Well… in a night of very delicious firsts, there was one more thing I would like to try. To get off my bucket list, if you know what I mean." His lips descended down to find hers in the dim light, touching softly.

Eliza went over their conversations in her mind. Wondering what else he might have confided as a secret desire. "You're going to have to give me more of a clue, baby.

The two I had on my list for tonight we managed to complete. Let's see if I can help you narrow it down. Does it involve you, me or both of us having more dessert?"

"Oh it's definitely me that needs more to eat."

"Something from the kitchen?" she teased. "More pie?"

"Oh, I have heard it called pie, but not the kind I have in my fridge.

"Okay!" Now that she had an idea what he wanted, she found herself eager to get started. That little tingle of excitement was back, and the warmth between her thighs was spreading. Eliza climbed out from the nest of sheets and found a pillow. Frank was watching her. Waiting. She shimmied out of his bathrobe and the black lace panties.

She arranged herself on the bed, comfortable with the pillow, and grabbed Frank by the hand, urging him to sink down lower on the bed and settle into place between her thighs. There was a glimmer in his eye and a hungry look on his face. Like a man about to dive into a feast.

"What did you mean, get this off your bucket list?" She murmured. "Wait… is this something else you have never tried?"

His hands slid under the globes of her ass and lifted her slightly. His nose dropped low, inhaling deeply. "There's a first time for everything." His breath was so light, so soft, as he flicked his tongue over her, pressing between her soft folds.

"Ummmhmmm, there is, and I have a feeling you've done lots of reading on this subject."

"Uh huh" his words came out garbled, not wanting to lift from the nest of wet curls. He had read about it, in detail. Wanted to try it many times, and had never been welcomed to try on his wi— Abby in all the long years of marriage.

Her fingers touched his hair softly, drawing his attention back to her. "It's a marathon, not a sprint. You have to go soft and slow. Gentle licks, flicks of your tongue. Oh yes," she sighed. "Feel it with your tongue, the little nub down in there. That's where you focus your attention. Nothing too hard, just pay attention, you will know from the sounds and shivers when you have it right…"

He didn't answer. He didn't have to. He just put her instructions to good use, judging which licks got little gasps of breath, or caused her hips to rise under him. It took time, but he didn't care. The heat and the smell of her filled his senses. She was winding higher and higher, he could feel the tension building in her. And God, he wanted to feel her explode under his lips and tongue.

She was close, they both knew it. He lifted his head and gave her a long sexy look up over her pretty breasts. "Is there anything else I should be doing? Something that would get you higher and over the edge?

His giving nature again made her smile. What a shame he had never been able to hone this talent. She'd never let a man go with this kind of oral aptitude. "It might really do it for me if you had a nice plump ass plug in your backside." She loved the way his breath sucked in with a hiss when she teased him. "Or you could reach one hand up here and tease my nipple." She took the taut peak of her nipple between finger and thumb and rolled it around gently. Within seconds, his fingers replaced hers and his mouth descended on her again. Flicking, moaning... she felt the pleasure build, racing her up the mountain until suddenly she was at the top, and then flying, soaring as her body convulsed and her sexy, rusty lover slowed his tongue down as she coasted back onto solid ground.

He levered himself up beside her and wrapped his arms around her waist, resting in the crook of her arm the way he had held her in his earlier.

Eliza grinned at him and said,"I don't know why you say you're Rusty. I may have to start calling you 'Not Rusty'." She liked the smile of satisfaction that put on his face. "Or maybe I should just call you Mr. Helpful. Or on second thought, maybe my A student!'

"Hahaha, Mr. Helpful is fine, but I was starting to really like Rusty."

Chapter 8

Their quick trip to Bed, Bath and Beyond the next day
turned into a series of trips to the big box stores over the
course of the weekend, with stops back at Frank's apartment
in between to take copious measurements, and then trips back
to the store. Eliza wanted Frank to stop worrying about
whether or not she approved of his house, so she stocked the
kitchen with the bare essentials and added some window
dressings. Some accent curtains at the top of the wide, over-
sized windows would draw the eye up and help balance the
room. They added privacy plus a touch of softness, a bit of
pattern in masculine shades of sage green and gray. Throw
pillows and a matching rug helped blend the haphazard
furniture and make it look like it belonged.

Eliza marveled at how some fabric and pillows could
bring such a change, but if she really asked herself about her
true motives, she was building a love nest. Frank had laughed
when she'd brought the subject up.

"There's no way that shabby apartment is going to be a
love nest, Eliza. And we are too old for that anyway." He was
still chuckling as they made their third foray out to the store.
He hadn't worried about making his new place homey

because it had never before felt like home. It was the place he slept and did his laundry. Eliza had the same effect on his apartment as she had had on him. She had swooped in with her soft smile and warm heart and started making changes. Nothing crazy, just small steps at first. Precision cut shades, and the tools to hang them. Frank stood on one of the rickety kitchen chairs with a brand new electric screwdriver in his hand. His apartment looked different from up here, but maybe it was the fact that he had a fascinating woman keeping one hand on his knees so he didn't fall, and she was practically nuzzling his ass.

Once the biggest issue of privacy was scratched off their list, they had drifted around different home stores, trying out furniture and cuddling right out there in the display areas.

He liked it, ok he more than liked it. The feelings he had, how good he felt when she slipped her hand into his to pull him into the linens section of Lowes and ask about the monogrammed bath towels she'd seen in his bathroom. With time and use, color had been washed out of them and frayed the edges.

"Are they yours, Frank, or more of the stuff she's so kindly allowing you to take?"

"A bit of both, I suppose. She was pretty clear about what I was allowed to take. And then it's like she changed her mind and sent me a list where she assigned all the linens to her side of the column. She even designated them as monogrammed and wedding presents."

Suddenly a pad of paper and a pencil were thrust into his hands. "Add over-sized trash bags to the end of the list, and help me pick out what color towels you want. Our love nest doesn't need to have twenty-five-year-old towels. And certainly not ones from a bad break up."

He agreed, even if he didn't like Eliza's innocent remark about a bad break up. He didn't get choked up anymore looking at the constant mail over the split or her need to stamp her own taste on his place. He hadn't thought redoing his place would be so much fun, pushing a cart along behind a beautiful woman with a sexy, curvy ass. The cost of it wasn't an issue. He'd shop all day if it pleased her, especially if it meant she'd spend another night and blow his mind again.

He didn't have much in the way of time constraints this time of year. The spring semester was over and he only had one online course this summer, so he was pretty much available. His life even felt like summer vacation, complete with a new romance that made him feel sixteen again. Playing house with Eliza all day was fun. It took his mind off the stress he felt over the divorce. When she was around, he barely remembered he was in a legal battle over every gift and knick-knack. He didn't care about their things. He could replace all of those. What mattered was this feeling of rejection he had been carrying around like a lodestone. Everything he'd done for years had been for her, for them, and suddenly she wanted someone younger, better looking? He didn't understand what it was soon to be ex was thinking.

Eliza made him feel like a man again, sexy and wanted. He wanted more than a summer romance with her. In fact, he wanted the court date that would signal the death of his marriage to Abby to come sooner rather than later, so he could get on with his life and start thinking about where the two of them would have Thanksgiving or spend Christmas. He'd bet money Eliza and her family spent the day together sipping wine and cooking. She took her time when things were important. His mind drifted, just for a moment, back to the way she had laid him out and used her lips, tongue, fingers and palms on him the night before. His dick stirred at the thought, wanting more. She sashayed ahead of him as if she knew he was staring at her ass.

"Don't get lost, Frank," she called over her shoulder. He hurried to catch up and turned a corner to follow Eliza down into a deserted aisle behind the key maker stand. She was about halfway down, past the mailboxes and adhesive house numbers, fingering a spool of soft rope. "I think they sell this by the foot. We'll have to get someone to come measure it out for us." She looked at him innocently. "Or is it too soon for us to be buying this kind of thing?"

Frank choked and felt heat pool in his groin. What had been at half-mast became stiff as a post. He shifted uncomfortably, aware his boxers seemed suddenly too tight. She couldn't mean what he was thinking? Or could she?

"For, um, for what?" he asked.

"For tonight… or any other night, when I feel like tying your hands to the headboard, or behind your back. This stuff is soft and thin enough we can use it a million different ways." Her smile was still teasing and infectious.

She wasn't shy, his girl. He couldn't help smiling in return, adoring her playfulness. "I saw a man in the next aisle.

You're the expert, ma'am. You know what we'll need. A few different lengths?"

Frank was already around the corner, hailing the employee at the key stand. The poor man kept it professional the whole way, as the grinning couple looked at each other and winked as they decided what lengths they wanted of what. He finally stuck his scissors into the pocket of his blue apron and wound up the cuts Eliza requested in both soft cotton cord as well as some thinner rope. He ignored the looks passing back and forth between the couple and handed Frank their slip for the register. He left in silence, not positive what they were planning, but the burst of laughter that he heard after he left put a big smile on his face.

Frank was sure the day couldn't get any better. He was enjoying himself, holding his lover's hand in the check out line at the home store. She was tracing circles with her thumb on the back of his hand, reminding him of that first afternoon picnic they'd shared in the park.

"Still got that pad and pencil?" she asked absently.

He fished it from his shirt pocket one-handed. "Right here."

"I want to stop by Kohl's on the way home. There are a few things we need there."

"So you want me to write Kohl's on the list, or tell me what we're getting there?"

Eliza thought about telling him but decided to keep it a surprise. "We could both use jeans and sneakers," she said non-committally.

"Ok!" there it was, that enthusiasm again. That's what she liked about Frank. His ready answers, always eager. She found herself suggesting odd little things just to hear him say, "Sure!" or "You bet!" Like any idea she had was great, and he couldn't wait to do it with her. That's what drew her to him, his eager willingness to be... willing. She had no doubt he'd be as excited about handcuffs and toys as he was about ropes. It was just his personality. He called himself 'Mr. Helpful." At work or with most people, he was just exactly that. She was the one digging down into the repressed sexual desires to see what Mr. Helpful might really be capable of. She'd felt his need to please a woman from almost the first moment, when he'd laid his hands on the back of her shoulders to smooth down her coat.

Eliza also had the feeling he didn't get much back in the way of helpfulness or kind gestures, at least not from his former partner. What a terrible term. Former partner. Eliza couldn't bring herself to say, ex-wife, because she wasn't officially an ex yet, and there was no way Eliza wanted to think of her as his wife. The woman had let go of a treasure, and Eliza planned to hold on to Frank, to make him feel appreciated and wanted. Already he noticed the little things. It was so easy when the things he needed were so simple. She planned to spoil him and give back the way he gave to her.

Eliza handed her Visa card to the checkout clerk, despite Frank's objections. "I'm the one who asked for shades, so the neighbors don't see us, and I'm the one who decided your monogrammed towels need to get chucked in the trash." A gentle tug on his hand brought him down to her level, so she could whisper in his ear, "And I am the one who needs those ropes, to continue your education in fun and games..." The slightest turn of her head, and her lips pressed against his cheek, then dropped another kiss lower, at the corner of his mouth. He needed no further encouragement. His lips met hers in a gentle kiss that lingered until the clerk gave a small cough to pull them back to reality.

"You win, Eliza, but I am paying the bill at Kohl's. And anywhere else we might end up shopping this weekend." He was still smiling as the clerk handed over the bag, and he reached to take it before Eliza could.

"I'm good with that, just there might be one thing I have to separate out and get myself. But for the most part, we're here for you."

The blast of heat when they left the store reminded her of a sauna. Eliza was still wearing the black pants and silky blouse she had worn to dinner the night before, and it amplified the temperature. The afternoon sunshine made it feel like full summer, and the air conditioning in Frank's Honda was just barely putting out anything after the short drive down the highway to the mall.

It was a place that had seen better days. The parking lot was riddled with potholes and a quarter of the stores were empty, but the Kohl's was still flourishing. There were better places Eliza might have taken him clothes shopping, but none that would have the value and style of other items she had in mind. Plus she probably had some coupons folded up in her wallet somewhere.

They headed straight for the men's department at the back of the store, where she loaded his arms up with three pairs of jeans and three polo shirts and set him off into the dressing room. Knowing he'd be busy for a while, Eliza wheeled their empty cart over to the appliance section and found a top of the line Keurig and tossed in a big box of variety cups for good measure. Oven mitts, dish towels, a pretty jar filled with miscellaneous utensils. She tried to remember what he had and didn't have, and decided on a starter set that included spatulas, serving spoons, a pasta fork, and a pizza cutter, all in no-nonsense stainless steel with black accents. It was then she admitted this was a far bigger job that she'd anticipated, and wheeled the cart back to the dressing room.

The idea of working on their love nest over time was a pleasing one. It sort of reminded her that there was no rush. They had all the time in the world. What a wonderful thought. Her feet barely touched the floor as she headed back to check on him.

The far back corner of the store was deserted, there was no one at the sales desk or supervising the dressing rooms. As she approached, Frank ducked out of the changing area and struck a pose. His broad shoulders filled out the polo, and the close fit of the cuff accentuated the smooth curve of his biceps. He was grinning. He turned and showed her the back side, and oh my goodness, Eliza admired the way he filled out the back of those jeans. The denim clung to the curve of his backside, fitting perfectly. He wore the shirt tucked in. Of course, he did, she should have expected that. She was going to have to teach this boy how to relax.

She gave a low wolf whistle while he modeled and resisted the urge to touch. "You're looking hot there, lover" she teased. He spread his feet to shoulder width apart and hooked his fingers behind his head, turning his head to view her over his shoulder. The muscles along his back and arms flexed.

"You like?"

She swatted his taut ass. "You look good like that, like you're about to get frisked!"

"Oooh!" he gasped in surprise, and then thought it over, playing out that scenario in his mind. His smile grew, and his gaze grew more intense.

"You don't seem a bit rusty at all at this, Frank. When you get back to that pad of yours, I think we better plan a trip to party city, so I can see if they have a cop's uniform for me. I am definitely going to be pulling you over later."

The thought of that had him laughing, and yet also trembling a little just wondering how that scene might play out. "On what charges! I wasn't speeding, officer, I know I wasn't!"

"Being too sexy in those jeans, disrupting traffic, and…" She hooked a finger into the waistband and looked inside. "And still wearing boxers, when you were told briefs!"

"You only mentioned that last night! Unfair!" Fortunately, there was a tall display rack between them and the men's jeans department with assorted brands and styles of underwear. Frank studied it for a moment and grabbed a package of Hanes in dark colors of black, maroon and gray off the shelf. He checked the back to be sure he had the right size and dropped them into the cart. "What my lady wants, she gets," he joked. The words that sounded light and commonplace now carried different undertones now, and he liked it.

The cart had more than just clothes in it, he noticed, seeing the little things she had selected for his place, as well as the coffee machine. He didn't know whether to laugh or cry. "You are too good to me, Eliza," he choked out.

"Nothing is too good for you, Rusty."

He pulled her into his arms and kissed her soundly. They fit together so perfectly. He could tuck her head under his chin and feel his cock starting to stir against her belly. She clung to him for a long moment, and slowly slipped out of his arms, looking him up and down. "I hope all those shirts fit like this!" Her hands slid off his shoulders, down over his arms. He liked that appreciative look in her eye. "Go get changed, so we can get out of here and get some dinner on the way home." She swatted his ass playfully as he turned to go.

He jumped and chuckled, double-timing it back into the fitting room.

Eliza worried only briefly that she'd been gone from her house for over 24 hours as they sped back down the highway, the back seat of the Honda piled high with shopping bags. The air conditioning had decided to cooperate, and she pulled out her phone and checked for texts. Nothing but a text reminder for a dental appointment. Josh either hadn't come home for the weekend or hadn't noticed his mom was MIA. She tapped in a short hello and slid the phone back into her purse. She wasn't ready for this weekend to be over yet. It was just getting started.

Traffic jammed up as they got closer to the city, where mall shoppers and tourists had to merge down onto increasingly fewer and fewer lanes. Frank leaned on the horn and worked the small car through the merge. "Why aren't these people at the shore? God, it feels like August instead of June." The flow of cars stopped and started until finally the expressway cleared and they were back up to speed.

"It's not a big deal, Frank," Eliza sounded relaxed, almost sleepy. "We can't possibly finish everything in one day." He gave a brief nod of agreement. "Besides. We have all the time in the world. That's the beauty of it. We can take our time. I mean I get it, this is very exciting, but we don't have to do it all in one day."

That sounded wonderful. All the time in the world. Tonight was more of the beginning. Even his cock liked that idea, and he let his mind consider it, tonight, and after that all the other nights to come. He relaxed a little and shook off some of the urgency that had been riding him.

"At least we are ahead of the Saturday night traffic." Every time a new highway merged in they slowed to a crawl, and then sped back up again on the far side. "Did everyone decide to leave for home at the exact same time we did?"

Eliza fiddled with the air vents and aimed them directly at her face. The cool air was welcome, and she arranged the airflow on the driver's side right onto Frank. "As long as it's cool in here, I don't mind. In fact, the longer it takes, the less likely we'll have to unload this car in the heat."

"Oh! Was there another store you wanted to hit on the way home? I mean, I'm not sure we spent enough yet today..." He caught her eye and winked. "I haven't hit my daily limit yet!"

She wasn't going to let that one slide. Teasing begot teasing. "Well, I seem to recall we might have some items to get at the Adult Outlet...."

His eyes darted to the side of the road, almost like they were searching for an immediate exit. He flipped on his blinker, headed for the right-hand lane. "You're going to have to look up directions, or is there maybe something similar at one of the bigger malls?"

Obviously, he hadn't put two and two together yet, to discern what kind of establishment she was proposing. "I'm pretty sure they don't have an adult toy superstore at the mall there, dear. Maybe something like Spencer's Gifts, but not the hard core stuff we're after.

"Hard Core?" He barely got the words out, and then stopped himself from repeating them again louder. But damn, those words got to him, and he suspected she knew that and had used them on purpose.

It was hard for her not to laugh. Eliza loved it when he was aroused and sputtering in shock at the same time. She hoped he never lost that charming gullibility.

"Yeah, what kind of things did you think they'd sell at any store with 'Adult' in the title? And don't worry. I don't want us to go through all the new adventures in the first weekend. I plan to take my time with you, Rusty. Break you in slowly, as it were."

His eyes were on the road, his hands on the wheel, gripping and ungripping. Things always got serious when she called him Rusty. It made him sit up straighter and his knees spread a little wider, and his pants feel a whole lot tighter.

"So where is this Adult Outlet? And when might we be headed there?" Oh she did love that smooth baritone voice, lightly accented and only slightly raspy. Eliza had no doubt he'd be ready to go anytime she asked. Taking him there was going to be so much fun. She couldn't wait to turn him loose and let him explore. But first, they had work to do. A love nest to outfit. At some point, they both needed to find a way to spring this relationship news onto Josh, Jenny, and his son, Ben. Somehow telling the inner family would make it all feel more permanent.

"We can go on Wednesday, after my trip to the dentist. I'm taking the afternoon off, and if you don't have office hours or classroom set up, we could meet at Starbucks and go from there."

"Sounds like a plan. But you still haven't mentioned what you think we might be buying. Any hints?"

Eliza just laughed and gave his knee a good squeeze. "Maybe after we hang some curtains and order some dinner we can check out their web site and make a wish list."

"Ok!"

Chapter 9

Eliza looked forward to the dentist's office only because her mind kept coming around to what she planned to do afterward. She just had to sit still for 45 minutes for a cleaning, chatting with Kelly, her long-time hygienist, about the wedding invitation business and comparing notes on their kids while the cheerful redhead took x-rays. A steady stream of conversation flowed even though Eliza could barely respond with her mouth full of dental tools.

All of the employees Ultimate Dental Care were knowledgeable and kind and had earned Eliza's trust over many years. She lay back in the chair and relaxed, willing the time to pass quickly. It was hard not to smile as she thought back to the email she'd found in her inbox that morning.

Evidently, Frank had been doing some research on the local toy shops and worked up a spreadsheet on the size, variety and Yelp ratings from the top stores in the area. He's begun with her old stand by, The Adult Emporium, and gone on to give alternate stores such as Spencer's Gifts, Passion Works and Adult World some kind of quantifiable score to determine which they might want to eventually visit. A few options might require more than a day trip, and he'd included suggestions for dining and accommodations in neighboring counties. The scientist in him was showing, and she liked it.

It seemed she had opened up a new world for him. They hadn't even talked about anything special they intended to shop for. She just wanted to walk around the place holding his hand and let him see all the possibilities.

Because that's what their time together had become. An open book of possibilities. All they had to do was get together and find ways to get closer, to please each other more. His scientific mind would probably rate and categorize items in order of preference and degree of excitement they engendered.

Eliza didn't doubt Frank would be excited and a little anxious about it. She knew from experience that a faint feeling of unease, mostly from stepping into the unknown, combined with sexual arousal could create a wild, intense feeling of excitement. She herself had been in stores like these many times with Jim. Her late husband had been a fan of any kind of triple X shopping and had been an expert at finding kinky uses for everyday items. He had always been solid presence beside her, laughing and getting ideas just looking at the vast displays of bondage gear. Jim had bee a fan of anything made of leather and buckles, whether it was cuffs on his wrists or the wrap-up closures on her strappy sandals. In his easy-going way, Jim had conveyed his openness to try anything and everything.

Eliza felt the familiar sting of tears at the bittersweet memories. It was strange how similar things were turning out again this time. She knew Frank's hand would be there on the small of her back as they strolled around the display area. His hand would be warm in hers as they selected merchandise. Anything they found would be fun, whether it was lingerie for her or cuffs for him…

"Are you all right, Liza?" Kelly had stopped her assault on the plaque, and Eliza cracked one eye open and peered up, meeting the hygienist's eyes on the far side of her face shield.

"Un huh" Eliza blinked the tears away, rinsed and spit. "Just a sad memory got me there for a moment. You weren't causing me any pain." She opened her mouth again and kept her mind focused while Kelly finished up and spun the polish onto her teeth.

Before she knew it she was stepping out into the sunshine, running her tongue over her exceptionally smooth teeth and practically skipping to her car. She checked her phone and sent Frank a quick text. "On my way. See you soon!"

She let the engine run long enough to pump out cool air, and played with her hair in the rearview mirror, tucking away stray curls. She added a touch of lipstick and brushed on mascara. Then she laughed at herself as she donned her sunglasses and opened the window, letting in the breeze that undid all her handiwork. She turned up the radio and headed for Starbucks, where she found Frank waiting beside his car as she pulled in, looking fine in his sky blue polo and jeans. She leaned over and gave him a quick hard kiss as he climbed in.

As soon as his seat belt clicked she swerved across the lot and into the drive-through. "Ever had a mocha

Frappachino?" She had a feeling he hadn't, and the slow shake of his head confirmed it. She buzzed the window down and leaned out. "Two Mocha Frappachinos, with extra whipped cream!" The expression on his face was priceless.

She could almost see him replaying their experiments with whipped cream in his tiny apartment. Oh yeah, he was remembering her lips on him, her tongue flicking, and her control.

"Do I need to tease you about getting turned on at the mention of whipped cream?" Luckily she had rolled up the window and pulled away from the speaker. She reached around behind him, fishing for her handbag in the footwell.

"You always know, Eliza. I don't know how you do it. Am I that obvious?" He dragged her purse up from out of the back seat and handed her her wallet. "You get this, and I'll buy anything else we purchase later on...."

"Hahaha, I can imagine we might be finding a few things to add to our stash. But it's a deal." She happily paid and settled the two drinks into the console. "So my store first? Or did my scientist determine after careful experimentation that another locale might be more productive?"

Frank blushed slightly and took a long draw from his coffee. He swallowed slowly, savoring it. "That is amazing. I don't know how I never tried one of those before! And your store would be a fine place to start. It did compare very well to the others, and it has the closest proximity to our current location."

"Aye aye, Spock, plotting a course to closest adult supply store. Warp factor 6." She headed back into town, shoulders shaking with mirth as he sputtered.

"I'm not that bad! You think I sound like Mister Spock?"

Eliza grabbed his knee and squeezed. "Are you kidding? Spock was the unemotional, un-fun, un-excitable one! You don't qualify on any of those. You are very excitable!" His hand covered hers, feeling warm and secure.

The drive was quick to the Adult Emporium. The building itself was wedged back off the main thoroughfare hidden behind a fast food restaurant, and aside from the tall sign out front, it looked nondescript. A boxy, faded yellow facade with no windows overlooked the parking lot where only two other cars waited. Eliza pulled up in front of the door and sat there for a minute before getting out.

She tugged his hand until his eyes met hers. "I know this place is safe, and I have been here many times before, but I wouldn't venture in there alone. So please stay beside me."

He nodded in understanding and sat up a little straighter. "Don't worry, my lady. I know how to be a good escort. You don't have to worry there might be creeps in there that would bother you." He drew her hand up to his lips and kissed the knuckles softly.

She smiled at his antics. "Well honestly, it is more that I don't want any of the women in there thinking they could make a move on my guy."

He gave a shout of laughter, so stunned she might worry about such an unlikely thing. And so pleased at the way she called him her guy. "I doubt very much there are any single women in there looking to make off with your date."

Eliza pulled her hand out of his grip and exited the car, waiting while he circled around to stand beside her again. "But what's the point of taking my sexy man into a place like this if I can't show him off? I want the creeps and the woman behind the counter to know you're with me!"

Frank hadn't expected her to put it that way, but it felt good. He reached the door first and drew it open with a flourish. "I believe I understand my assignment, and never fear, I am honored the be shown off as your chosen escort."

He followed her into the establishment which turned out to be brightly lit, as well as surprisingly empty. He felt relieved and a little disappointed at the same time. As usual, he was torn between wanting people to see them and dealing with his own awkward still-married feelings. God, he couldn't wait to be free, plus he couldn't see how think Abby would even mind at this point.

Early in their marriage she had worried and fretted when he wasn't home on time or if a faculty meeting ran late. The change had come when Benny was in middle school, and Abby's life had been taken over by carpools to soccer and karate class. Suddenly she was the one who was out late, and Frank was the worrier when the hour grew late.

A gentle tug on his hand drew him back to the present, pulling him down to hear her whisper, "It is the middle of the afternoon on a weekday." She led the way towards the back of the store, giving a little wave to the rough looking woman behind the counter.

The back half of the shop was a treasure trove. Racks of men's magazines, erotica, and everything in between in book, magazine and newspaper format. Eliza continued like she knew where she was going and stopped in front of a long wall of cuffs. Handcuffs, leather cuffs, fur-lined cuffs. She picked up a simple pair that looked about the right size. They were black leather with silver grommets and a large steel D ring.

"These aren't expensive at all, and would be easy to attach to your headboard, say for instance with all that rope we bought last weekend."

He took them as she handed them over, and he studied them, comparing them to the rest dangling from the wall. His voice had that familiar rough quality it got when his cock started to swell. "They would do nicely."

Eliza wasn't going to let him off the hook so easily. "You want them, don't you, Rusty?"

"Oh, God, yes."

"Just to be clear, what do you want them for?"

He moved closer behind her and pressed up against the sexy curve of her ass, letting her feel the excitement thrumming through him. His cock twitched as it pressed against her. "I want you to cuff my wrists to the bed, or behind my back, or anywhere you please…" He leaned down and buried his nose in her fragrant hair, dropping small kisses on top of her head. "I also remember you mentioning a nice plug for my ass?" His voice was low and breathy. He almost sounded like a different person.

"Oh, yes! I have a feeling you will love it." She caught his hand and pulled him across the store. An enormous pegboard covered half the back wall, displaying what the sign above declared, 'insertables.' The selections were organized by different materials, different sizes, and some were made exclusively for female anatomy, and some for male.

Interspersed with the plugs were dildos, some with vibration… and Frank's breath caught. This was so unexpected, and yet it was so obvious that places like this existed. That people came and shopped in establishments like this. Not just creepers slinking into the back, God, they probably hadn't been doing that for years. They could sit at home and watch porn in privacy on their computers.

All manner of regular people came in here, including couples, and not just lonely men skulking to watch movies in the back. This place was all brightly-lit shopping area. The merchandise ranged from XXX to playful items like massage oil, lingerie, and games.

Frank's eyes went to Eliza again and he marveled that he had found her. It now seemed so easy and so natural to come here. He would gladly buy whatever she wanted and try to refrain from running home to play with it. He cleared his throat and asked, "What kind do you think we should start with?"

She pulled a small white device off the shelf. "Something like this. Silicone, easy to clean, comfortable to wear…" He looked at it, almost disappointed.

"But it's so small…"

"You did ask where we should start. I didn't mean to imply that's all." She headed down to an end-cap display and pulled off a larger container. He read over her shoulder, 'Anal

Training Kit"". His cock jumped. It liked the sound of that. Really liked the sound of that. "Hmm, three plugs in ascending sizes... plus a tube of good lube. I think this would be good." She sounded so serious. "These look like they'd get you accustomed to the feel of it gradually." She looked up at him and quirked a brow. "You want to try these, Rusty?"

"Just thinking about it makes my cock hard as a rock... and if it gets you hot, that's even more important. So far, any time the conversation turns intimate or sexy, you get my complete attention, upstairs *and* downstairs."

Eliza tried not to grin and ended up nibbling on her lower lip instead, feeling his giving side slip him farther into her grasp. "What are we going to do with these, Rusty?" she pressed with an iron thread in her voice.

He swallowed hard and hesitated. "You're going to lube it up and sink it deep in my ass while I lick your pussy."

She rose up swiftly on tiptoe and kissed him quickly. "I have such a sexy lover. Not really all that rusty." Her hand closed reassuringly around his. "I can't wait! But let's keep looking. Maybe find a thing or two to put on our wish list. Or into our shopping basket."

"Did they have shopping baskets by the door? Or by the check out maybe?" It was always possible Eliza was messing with him... teasing him the way she always did. He looked over the displays towards the register.

Frank found the cuffs and training kit thrust into his arms, and her hand sent him off towards the register with a loud smack. "See if the cashier will let you stack them there on the counter while we finish shopping," she called after him. Loud enough for everyone in the store to hear. The woman at the counter cleared off a space and grinned at him as he set the packages down. She had her short dark hair buzz cut on one side and wore a tight black shirt that emphasized the size of her breasts. Part of a butterfly tattoo was visible on one breast in the vee of her neckline.

"And ask her where the floggers are," Eliza called out in his general direction. "The good ones, from leather and rawhide. Not the cheap plastic ones."

The sensation was indescribable. The way everything that happened made him feel more hers, and more like he was definitely in lust with her, borderline in love. The only problem was he had never believed anything could happen as fast as it had. In a sense, his emotions were still processing. Being with Eliza felt good, despite how recently he had met her. Periodically he felt like he needed to stop and catch his breath, but when she was absent for a few days he spent his time wanting to call her and wishing she would drop by his apartment. He wasn't even a free man yet, technically.

But he loved it. The way she made it clear he was her man, and the way she took charge of the shopping, his apartment, and the sexy stuff. A few weeks with her had been life-changing. The thrill of it made his heart pound and his cock fill. He still didn't know how she'd done it, wrapped him around her finger so easily. How she sent him off to ask about floggers and he wasn't blushing in shame, he was thinking, "Hell yes, where have you hidden the good floggers?"

He hadn't mentioned all of his fantasies to Eliza, but it seemed like she knew them. Or predicted them based on his responses. The thought of her cuffing him and binding him and then taking a paddle to his ass. Oh, God. His pants had to be straining to contain his protruding cock. It was cradled comfortably by the boxer briefs, which he had been sure to wear. Maybe she really did have a reason for insisting on them. Half the time he wasn't sure if she knew something he didn't, or if she was just insisting on things to establish control.

"Quit daydreaming, Frank!"

He glanced over his shoulder and then back to the cashier, who gave him a knowing look and pointed to the far side of the shop. "You'll find what you're looking for over there, hun."

At first glance, it didn't look like they had all that many items in the whip display, but he discovered it was a series of peg boards that slid back and forth. He saw the first set did look like cheap plastic. So he shoved the board aside and examined the items hanging on the next one. He knew Eliza was standing behind him as he studied the options.

"Lift them up, and see how the strands feel in your fingers. Feel the weight of it. If it's too heavy or the strands are too long, it will just be awkward. Remember, the room is small and full of furniture. It's not like we're doing calisthenics."

Frank lifted one and gave a nod of understanding. "Some of these are so big they should just be a display item on a wall." He picked up a smaller one, gauging its weight.

"Give it a swish. We want one we can really use, don't we?" She lifted one and flicked her wrist a few times." The sound sent chills through him and a quiver of anticipation.

"You would use that one me?" His smooth voice had lost some of the velvety quality. He sounded rougher, a little lower on the register.

"Trust me, Rusty…." She gave his ass a playful swat with the flogger. He barely felt it through his jeans. "It's a toy. And toys are supposed to be fun, aren't they?"

He nodded. She wanted it. And because she did… he did. He had sneaked Penthouse magazine into his dorm room years ago and read the forums, never quite believing that there really were women who liked to tie up their boyfriends or take a man over their knee. It was so arousing that she enjoyed these things.

"It will be fun for me, at least," she continued. "We will have to see how you hold up to it. Maybe we'll have to give you a safe word. Let's find another big bottle of water-based lube and then head to the checkout."

He rearranged the display and followed Eliza back to the checkout desk. He admired the way her ass filled out her cropped linen pants. She was soft and rounded, so feminine in her looks and manner. And then once she got to the bedroom, look out! It wasn't that she was aggressive or hard as nails. He couldn't put a finger on it. Sometimes it was a look in her eye or a no-nonsense tone in her voice that got his motor running. She just knew; she had the right experience, and he thanked God that for whatever reason she had picked him that night.

There were two young coeds at the register when they got there. Frank felt a little self-conscious at first. The more he looked at them, the more he thought "cheerleaders" and "Sorority girls." They bounced up on their toes, and their ponytails swung.

The unfazed cashier ignored their giggles and bagged up their magazines, lube and thigh-high stockings. It occurred to Frank that they were the right age to turn up in his classroom, but then he remembered how far they were from his campus. They were miles from anywhere he'd encounter someone who might know him.

Besides, the two girls were probably also trying to go unnoticed themselves.

"Earth to Rusty!" Eliza called for a second time. He saw their purchases were rung up and bagged, and the two women were looking expectantly at him. He stepped up beside her and handed his card to the cashier.

Eliza chuckled and took him by the hand. "You have to excuse him. It's his first trip to a shop like this, and he's a little overstimulated."

Frank almost choked… what a way to put it. Overstimulated. But he said nothing and signed the slip.

Eliza put a hand beside her mouth and whispered, "He's really eager to get home and try everything out!" She waggled her eyebrows for emphasis. Both ladies laughed, and he relaxed and joined in. He did some eyebrow waggling of his own.

"You bet your sweet ass I am!"

The cashier laughed and nodded to the tall, handsome man. "If I was heading home with that beautiful lady, I'd be in a hurry to get home too!" she whispered conspiratorially.

Chapter Ten

The car was strangely quiet on the ride back to Starbucks. Their departure from the counter had been smooth and almost carefree, but then right as they exited Frank had stopped to stare at a display of what looked to him like dog collars. "Are these good for bondage to, to complete the set?" he had asked in his usual mild-mannered way. "Shouldn't we be getting one of these, too?" He had said it with the usual amount of longing and eagerness in his voice.

Eliza had considered for a moment and then taken a stern tone. "You aren't ready for that yet, Rusty."

His crestfallen expression made her hurry to explain further.

"A collar is probably the most meaningful piece of equipment you can buy." She reached out and reverently fingered some of the collars. The variety of styles and sizes impressed her. There were dainty little chain collars, thick heavy leather posture collars... even some that had spikes like a guard dog. "Someday soon I am sure we will get you one, but it's not something we can just buy and take home as part of our bondage gear. It will be for the evening when you are truly ready to make yourself be mine."

"I want that now," he informed her, his smooth as silk voice washing over her and making her long for the day when he would be really free to make such a commitment.

"I think we both want it now, but it's serious. There's almost nothing out there that can symbolize the dominant/submissive relationship better. Some people might use a collar carelessly, but for me, once you put it on, it means something." Her hand drifted further down to a black posture collar fitted with D rings all around and a locking mechanism. The post that fit through the slot of the buckle had a tiny round ring for a lock. Someone had also carefully attached a bone shaped owner's tag with a small round holder. She reverently lifted the tag up to show him. "Bowzer" it read, followed by "Miss Maria Farnsworth" and a telephone number.

Frank's fingers traced the lettering on the tag.

"We could take a technical approach," Eliza began, "set stages for bringing you to full understanding." She thought for a moment and then counted them off. "Stage One, when you're a newbie. Everything is fresh and exciting and you can't wait to try, but at the same time you are wondering if you're nuts."

He smiled, thinking briefly about how had been doing just that and nodded for her to continue.

"Stage Two is the exploratory phase. We experiment, try some test runs and see what excites you, we determine what you might or might not be ready for yet, and where it overlaps with my interests."

Frank had almost laughed when she mentioned her interests, but she was on a roll and he was curious to see where she was going next.

"Stage three, when you are under consideration. That's when we decide if we are playing at this or taking it seriously. Really, all three I have mentioned fall under the umbrella of under consideration, but they all result in a decision about the deepest aspect of the relationship, and if both parties want it, that's when you're ready to come back and buy that."

He peered over her shoulder again, down at the owner tags one last time. "Don't worry. I understand the meaning, Eliza... umm, Miss Eliza. But I hope that as soon as I am free, and you think I am ready, we can come back here."

And so the first few minutes of the ride back through town were silent, and Eliza started thinking. The two of them were driving two cars back to Frank's place and the fact was that no one would be at her house to worry when she didn't return until late. Or morning even.

"You said it was almost the most significant thing a man could do for his lady," Frank said out of the blue. "What did you mean almost? Is there something more?"

She parked beside his car and twisted around in her seat to explain. "I have heard of very rare instances where a couple has a small ceremony in front of like-minded people, and there's an agreement that's signed. I am not sure if it's a legal document, but there have always been stories of sub contracts, and signing over authority to the domme."

"You keep saying domme. As in dominant?"

"Yes, in just about any kind of relationship you can think of, there are some where one person is dominant. You're just used to seeing it where it's the male who calls the shots."

Frank mulled that over for a moment. He wanted to talk more about it, but maybe sitting in the car in the heat wasn't the right place. He gathered up their bag of purchases and exited the vehicle. He leaned back down and looked across the car.

"You're the expert in these things, Eliza. You make it easy to follow your lead." He grinned and waved. "I'll see you back at my place in a few."

"I have an errand or two to run on the way. I'd like it if you showered and shaved, and did NOT open any of those packages until I arrive. You may wear a towel around your waist while you wait."

His eyebrows shot up, but he grinned. "Yes, Miss Eliza."

She laughed as he closed the door and then she hit the button to lower the window on his side. "I just remembered. There is one other thing a sexy male sub can do to prove his devotion to his lady. I'll give you the details later on."

He nodded and waved as she pulled out.

Eliza threaded her way through traffic to the local hardware store, kicking herself for not remembering to purchase small locks when they were at Lowes. Of course, that was before she'd mentioned the sex shop and realized there was another area of his education to concentrate on.

Thankfully, the hardware store was quiet and she was able to get in and out quickly. They would not really be necessary to affix the cuffs onto Frank's wrists, but sometimes just knowing a lock was there added to the thrill. It added a little something to ensure he couldn't undo the buckle with his teeth. It would give him an extra level of arousal and deepen his sense of giving. Not that Frank needed either of those, but she was enjoying giving him the full treatment.

She walked out of the store, locks in hand, and phoned in an order to their neighborhood restaurant that offered pick up at the curb. After pushing buttons and finally getting to the ordering menu, she kept it simple and got two Caesar salads with grilled chicken to go. Somehow she had a feeling once they were in for the night and breaking in new toys, they weren't going to want to call out or head out for food. Some cozy together time afterward would be perfect, intimate and romantic.

Eliza checked the clock. Her little shopping spree hadn't really taken very long, so she dawdled as she made her way to pick up dinner. Of course, she was in a rush to get home, eager to walk into the room and see if he had taken one more step to surrendering and giving. It was so easy to read his eagerness for the same thing.

She picked up dinner, giving the waiter a handsome tip, and then headed to Frank's. She wanted him to have just enough time to get freshened up and start to feel a little vulnerable before she went knocking on his door. She had given her little suggestions casually, and yet she was counting on the fact that he'd take them as directions.

There was nothing worse than feeling like every instruction had to be barked out like a drill sergeant.

Well, there was nothing wrong with putting a little no nonsense bite into a suggestion just to be clear, but she knew he'd respond well and if he didn't, well, that was what they'd bought the flogger for.

His neighborhood was surprisingly empty for a Wednesday afternoon, and she got a lucky parking spot down the block from his building. There was a buzzer by the door with his apartment number on it. All the other residents had their names listed, even if it was only hand-written in, but Frank's was blank. Eliza pressed it and wondered about that, as well as why he wasn't buzzing her inside.

"Just a second, Eliza," he called from the top of the stairs. He came running down the steps, barefoot and wearing his terrycloth bathrobe. He swung the door open and stood back while she passed inside. She gave him a cool look.

He cinched the belt tighter about his waist as he led the way back upstairs. "The buzzer doesn't seem to be working from my apartment," he explained. "I hope you don't mind that I improvised."

In his usual Frank way, he stood to the side and propped the door open allowing her to enter first. The tantalizing aroma of his aftershave was in the air as the distance between them closed, and Eliza breathed it in deeply. It would be so easy to gather him up in her arms and tuck her head up under his chin. To just get comfortable in his arms and inhale.

Instead, she refrained and made a gesture with her fingers about his outfit. "What's with the robe?" She asked. "That's not what I suggested you wear."

He plucked the food delivery bag out of her hands and bustled into the kitchen, tucking it safely away in his fridge. "I don't know how long my com system has been out of service. I rarely have anyone ring that bell there. I knew you couldn't hear when I tried the speaker button, and the door wouldn't unlock. I had to run down and let you in."

"I could swear I made it clear I wanted you naked, or wearing a towel when I arrived." The bag of recently purchased toys was sitting on the couch. It looked unopened at least, so he had followed most of her instructions.

He quickly shrugged out of the bathrobe and laid it over the back of the couch. He was bare underneath except the short white towel tied around his hips. "I had gotten ready for you, Eliza. I only put the robe on to run out into the hall."

"Even so, Rusty. I still think you know what happens to a boy toy who won't follow directions." There was a certain emphasis on the name 'Rusty'. She moved purposefully behind the couch and closed the curtains with a jerk. A quick look into the Adult Emporium bag revealed their assortment of goodies. Eliza dumped them out onto the couch and picked up the leather flogger. She used it like a teacher uses a pointer and gestured to the sofa.

"Back here, behind the couch, Rusty. Feet spread. Bend over the back of it, palms down flat on the cushions."

It was like he was moving in slow motion. Here he was at that juncture. Wanting to try it all and yet wondering if he was crazy for wanting to. He stepped into place, set his feet, and gave Eliza a long lusty look as he bent forward, a look that said, "come and get me".

Frank had spent the time awaiting her arrival mulling over her words. Her long list had seemed so technical. Taking a scientific approach should have appealed to him when he was wondering if he was getting into more than he could handle. However part of his brain insisted this sexiness with Eliza should be spontaneous.

He had stood in his bedroom, wearing only the towel and thought for a moment about doing an internet search for "steps to submissiveness" to see if such a thing even existed. He half-suspected she had made it all up on the spot, just for him. She probably had; it would be so like her. And drawing that conclusion eased his mind and made the technicality of it... just perfect. He was going to try everything she had to offer, with gusto.

There was no sound in the room for a long moment except the harsh sound of their breathing as she moved into position behind him. Eliza knew instinctively he was ready but wanted the anticipation to build. His tight little buttocks was intriguing. The tiny white towel barely left anything to the imagination. It didn't resemble anything she had seen in his linen closet. She half-suspected he must have stolen it from his gym.

Her hand cupped over one ass cheek, caressing, sliding over the rough nap of the towel, then slid lower, to the crease where ass met thigh. "Oh!" his usual velvety tones sounded high and excited. She delved further, caressing back even more. Slipping between his thighs and rubbing over his balls.

Eliza leaned down, resting her weight on him, pressing him down more fully onto the backrest of the sofa. "This is your last chance to back out, Frank. For the record, your safe word is 'Time Out'. Just nod if you are clear on that and how to use it."

Her words were barely out of her mouth and he was nodding. Emphatically nodding. The palm she had been caressing over his heavy balls curved, cradling his sack, and then took in a light grip. Her warm breath caressed his earlobe as she leaned close to whisper, "I am hoping you enjoy this as much as I do. There is no pressure. It is my job to make you long for more."

This time he nodded more slowly and moaned softly. "You are good at your job," he chuckled.

"And you probably don't need this, my sexy." She took hold of the towel and gave a sharp tug. It came away easily, and she liked what she saw. The muscles of his tight buttocks were toned and firm. Pale white, and utterly kissable.

Eliza bent down and surprised him, pressing her lips to the faint tan line in the small of his back. Her right hand caressed up and down over the smooth surface, and then teased up and down the cleft between his cheeks. "Shall we begin?"

Frank moaned softly. "Yes, please... although I am not certain what I did merits a..."

Whack! The long fibers of the flogger came down suddenly across his backside, changing whatever he'd been about to say into an "oomph!"

Eliza swung it again, harder. "Ten here, and ten more in the bedroom, after I have you secured. And those two first swats were just for giving me lip about what you do and don't need!"

He took a slow breath, almost shuddering, and nodded. "Yes, ma'am." He braced himself, squirming as the whip landed twice more, hard enough to pinken the white skin. She was learning from his reactions, and gradually increasing the force. Another blow landed hard, right at the top of his thigh.

"You aren't counting out loud. How many was that?" The edge was back in her voice. His hips thrust slightly forward, pressing his shaft up against the couch as he thought about it and then answered.

"That was five, Miss Eliza." He sounded confident and eager.

"Five total, yes, but the first two were for giving me sass. That was number three. We are going to have to start all over again." He groaned again and spread his feet a little wider. He kept his head down and watched her subtly over his shoulder.

The repeat blows fell in quick succession, making him jump and squirm and grind his cock into the fabric. Eliza caught him watching and took a handful of hair, turning his head roughly to focus down at his hands on the seat cushion.

Once she had him back in position, she tucked the flogger beneath her arm and examined him. Her palm ran over the warm skin of his ass while he caught his breath. His backside was heating up nicely, and everything about him proved how right she had been that he'd love it. His hips swiveled, stimulating his sensitive cock. He was tense but still moaning and sighing. What a natural he was. He hadn't been kidding when he'd mentioned how he had always longed to try some of the lighter BDSM stuff. She could well believe he had been fantasizing about it most of his adult life.

It was like he woke out of a daze and remembered he was supposed to be counting. "One. Two Three, Miss Eliza."

Her eyes closed as she felt his skin. There were just a few places where the beginnings of a welt might be forming. Perfect. She wanted him to feel it when he ran his hand over it later, so she put a little more force behind the next two blows.

There was barely any skin discoloration, and while he jumped and gasped, there was no bruising. He had the perfect ass for flogging, spanking, paddling. She couldn't help smiling as she administered the rest and he bit out, "Eight. Nine, Ten!"

He held his position on the couch as he watched Eliza fold up the strands of the whip in her hand and slide the device into the Adult Emporium bag. Then she circled around the couch and gathered the rest of their purchases off the cushions. "You're doing so well, Frank." He looked up and smiled at her, feeling a little self-conscious that he was naked and spread while she was still dressed.

She lifted his chin and bent down to kiss him softly.

"Now get your ass into the bedroom." She followed along behind him, smiling as he quickly jerked the shades down. Eliza pulled the wrist shackles out of the bag and tossed them onto the bed. "You slip into those while I slip out of my work clothes." It made her want to laugh, how easy the sex was with Frank. How there was no pressure, just a desire to share it all with him. Her heart felt good. It was starting to feel whole again.

By the time she had wiggled out of her cropped white jeans and embroidered peasant top, Frank had secured the cuffs on. Eliza stood in front of him in white panties and a white cotton bra, gesturing for him to hold out each wrist. She slipped the tiny locks through the metal circles on the end of each prong, snapping them closed. He gave a long sigh as the locks clicked.

"I love it, Eliza..." Frank examined the way the locks functioned and then lay back on the bed, lifting his arms up to the headboard. He smiled at the woman who had opened his world so completely and made him forget about the pain of his divorce. He grinned at her as she crawled up and twined a length of rope around the base of the bed frame and then threaded it through the strong rings on the cuffs.

"Yes ma'am, I am ready for more."

Frank felt his heart pounding as Eliza straddled his chest and secured his wrists over is head. He could smell the sweet musky scent of her arousal, and he remembered flicking his tongue over her labia and clit. He wondered whether she would roll those panties off her legs and come back and straddle him some more.

Instead she scooted back and knelt between his outstretched legs. Her soft hands found the hard length of his cock and caressed it, delving down to encircle his balls and give them a gentle squeeze.

"Pull your knees up, and keep your feet wide, sexy. Don't move please."

Frank nodded and positioned himself the way she asked, watching in wonder and anticipation as she found the bag of toys and pulled out one of the smaller plugs. She showed it to him, and then coated it with shiny gel. She squirted one last dollop of the goo onto her fingers and dabbed it around his rosebud. It felt cool and slippery at first, but she teased her fingers around, slipping inside, and finally declared he was ready.

"Just relax and take a deep breath, my sexy man. I have a feeling you have been thinking about this for a while now, and it's going to feel as good as you remembered."

"Oh, God, yes ma'am..." He was ready.

He felt her fingers gently part his cheeks and press the tapered tip of the plug against his dusky rosebud. Her touch was light, but she worked the length of the silicone plug steadily into his ass, easing it forward and back, until it finally slid into place. He clamped down hard with his inner muscles and shifted his hips slightly, getting used to the feel.

"It's nicely tapered, and has a curved base and a long neck. It should be comfortable and not pop out." And then when his inner muscles clenched at her words she laughed and gave him a small slap on his hindquarters. "Now roll over onto your stomach while I wash my hands. I need to finish whipping that ass of yours before I fuck you.

Chapter 11

There was enough slack in the bindings for Frank to comfortably turn over, and he lay there on the bed marveling at the circumstances he found himself in. He could hear footsteps and then water running coming from down the hall. It was like he could still feel Eliza's touch all over his body, and he was ready for more. The sensation was incredible, he was feeling all in. Whatever she wanted. He found everything she did arousing, from the way she took charge to the way she made him feel like offering up his ass for a whipping or a plugging was the most natural thing in the world.

His ass still felt warm from where she'd spanked him before, and the plug inside him was keeping his cock rock hard and oozing. He flexed his glutes and thrust his dick slightly in the tangle of sheets beneath him.

This no-nonsense side of Eliza flipped his switch from aroused to high voltage in an instant. He adored this side of her. It set him off-kilter, made him feel slightly vulnerable, and yet he never felt in danger, like he suddenly needed to ask for a safe word. She talked about building anticipation and oh my God, was he anticipating. He moaned and pressed his hips down into the sheets again.

"I see you started without me," she accused, and he felt rather than saw her climb up onto the bed beside him. "Let's do this right, so we can move on to the good stuff. Lift your hips slightly... yes, that's good... and clench those ass cheeks together. I want you to feel that plug way down deep inside. Are you ready, Rusty?"

Frank remembered the first time she'd called him Rusty, lying here on this bed with her fingers penetrating deep. He looked back at her and took a tight grip on the ropes that went from his wrists to the headboard. "Yes, please!"

He tried to keep his ass raised and his muscles tight, but each swat left a little bloom of heat on his buttocks. He kept count in his head, as well as aloud. It took very few for him to be squirming and twisting under her whip. The muscles in his back and shoulders flexed as he pulled. He felt hot drips of sweat slipping over his skin. How had it come to this? He wondered. He loved every minute of it. He wanted more.

"More..." he whispered when she finally stopped. "It feels delicious... please."

Eliza laughed and mentioned again how she'd known he would be a natural. She pulled back her arm and gave him three more hard swats with the flogger, each one harder than the last. They stung, and took Frank's breath away.

Then he felt her fingers on the plug, pushing it deeper, as if it had been about to slip out. He clenched down on it and followed her guidance to roll over onto his back. His dick bobbed as he did so, long and fully hard. The crown was slick and coated with shiny, oozing precum, anticipating whatever might come next.

Frank watched Eliza as she stood by the bed and stripped off her bra and panties. Her dark hair was loose around her shoulders, and he thought she looked magnificent with the whip in her hand. She nodded to the drawer in the nightstand. "Condoms in there?" She asked.

"A whole box of them," he joked. Only when she opened the drawer, there really was a whole box of them, Trojans, Bareskin.

She pulled them out and gave him a teasing look. "A box of 10? How did you decide? Did you stand in the CVS and think 'I need more than two but not as many as 15?'"

"No…" he moaned as she flicked open the box and pulled one out. "I asked the pharmacist which one was the best…."

Suddenly Eliza was laughing as she bit open the foil packet and unrolled the latex over his shaft. "Of course you did. My sexy scientist." Eliza was smiling broadly when she threw her leg over his hips and positioned herself above him. His cock rose up, seeking the soft folds of her sex, trying to stretch up for contact.

Her palms were braced on his chest, her heavy breasts the first thing he saw when he looked up at her.

"I think I am going to like fucking you, Professor Rusty. How's that ass plug feeling?"

He gave a little laugh and looked away. "It feels good, Eliza."

"Say the whole thing, Rusty." She had a serious note in her voice, so he thought back to their shopping trip.

"The ass plug feels amazing. I want to feel it when I fuck you. I want to feel it when I cum."

In response, Eliza pushed her hips forward and lowered herself slowly. Frank gave a moan of frustration as his cock was trapped between them. Between the soft folds of her sex and his belly. He could feel her warmth, her wetness as the head of his shaft came so close to penetrating,

He heard her soft chuckle as she repositioned and teased again, letting him feel the drag of skin on skin. She let him feel the heat, feel the pressure, but not the wild thrill of actually joining. She kept it up, letting the velvety length of him press so close to her depths, gliding over her most intimate place, and then stimulate higher, over and over her clit. A ragged sigh escaped her, and the area between them grew damper... wetter.

"How do you like this?" she teased. "I love the feel of this, almost like your tongue circling over me."

His hips pressed up, slightly harder as he rasped, "I seem to remember something about licking your pussy like this... that it would help push you over the edge..."

"Oh, it would, but I'm not in the mood to untie you yet." She braced her hands on his ribs and moved over him, keeping the tip of his shaft pressed close against the sensitive nub of her clitoris. Her body quivered as she moved over him, hips barely moving, keeping up the pressure, building the pleasure. His cock was coated in her juices, sliding easily.

Eliza looked down through her lashes at him, flushed and tense. Concentrating on the micro movements as she sought her own pleasure from him. As much as he wanted to find his way home inside and pump himself inside of her, he wanted her to do this, to take her pleasure from him. He wanted it to go on and on.

His lady knew so many things he had never thought of. He could never have dreamed a woman would want to feel him sliding between her slick folds this way. That she'd ride him without actually riding him. Now that he'd felt her shudder and cum under his tongue he wanted to feel her come apart here over him. The thought of it made his cock jerk and rise up, and he held his breath, fighting back the orgasm that was suddenly there about to erupt from him.

"Oh, I felt that, you naughty boy!"

He closed his eyes and tried to slow his breathing, but every time he raised his hips to thrust against her the plug moved so deliciously in his ass, pushing him towards a release like he had never felt before.

A small swish was the only warning he got, before the thin leather strands of the flogger connected with his chest, biting into the hardened nipple. His eyes flew open and watched as she struck the other one. "Not yet, Rusty! Don't you dare cum yet. I am not through riding you yet."

A shudder went through him, and he nodded. "I want you to take what you need from me, Eliza…"

Whack! Another swat on his chest, and the sting got his mind off his heavy balls. "Thank you, Miss Eliza" Frank kept pace with her, wanting to reach for her, and every time getting jerked back to reality by the cuffs and bonds. He yanked hard on them, but they didn't budge.

"So sexy to see you realize there's no escape…"

He yanked on the bonds again, expressing the desire and frustration that mingled into a growing passion. "Oh, God, I don't want to! I just want to hold you, feel you under my hands..."

She laughed, and lifted slightly, positioning him at her entrance. Her eyes fixed on his as she slowly lowered herself down on him. Her hands felt good on his chest, her arms braced to keep her weight up, allowing her to take him one slow inch at a time. She looked down at him and when he was in all the way to the hilt she leaned back and began to move, riding him slowly. The need was still on him to hold her, to put his hands on her hips and show her how he wanted her to move, but he liked this twist she put on things. Her words were so sexy... her kinks, kept him teetering on the precipice. He was at her mercy, and she was the one setting the pace.

"Ready, my sexy?" She gripped him with her inner muscles and started to move. "Let me ride that marvelous cock of yours, Rusty. You like the feel of me on you, don't you?"

"God, Eliza. Yes, of course."

"Hmmm just like you loved my fingers fucking you the other day... and the way you love the silicone plug fucking you now. Such a perfect little boy toy..."

Frank twisted in the ropes and moaned again. "Your words... may push me over the edge..."

Eliza paused her movements and flicked his nipple. "That's when you ask me if I'll permit you to cum... do it, thrust harder, fill me, and say, 'Mistress, may I cum?'"

His breath hissed out, and he pressed himself into her. "Mistress," the words tumbled from his lips before he could even think about what they might mean. How they might change his sexuality. "May I please cum?"

Her body gripped him like a glove, and he thrust as fast as he dared, waiting for her permission. He was so close, holding back every time he was buried deep inside her. The silence stretched as she rode him, her head thrown back and her hair cascading in a wild tangle down her back. Her hands went to cup her breasts and finger the nipples lightly.

"I want to watch you cum, to feel your cock jerk and twitch inside me as you unload. Grip down tight on that plug, and let me feel it..."

The headboard creaked as his body tightened, his wrists pulling hard on the ropes. His hips rose off the bed as the pleasure overtook him. He huffed and groaned with the force of it, feeling it from the tips of his toes to the top of his head. Eliza remained unmoving, watching him, reveling in the intensity of his orgasm. His eyes drifted closed as he struggled for breath, and he felt her move to lie pressed up close against his side.

It was long moments later that the locks came unclasped with a twist of the key, and he pulled her close against his chest and held her tightly. "The things that you do to me, lady," he joked. "I love them all...."

Her breath was light on his chest, and she nuzzled closer, sighing. "This quiet time for cuddling after the intensity of sex, it makes me want to wrap you in my arms and keep you there.

His arms closed around her. "I feel the same way... it seems crazy to look up and see it's still light out. It's still the middle of the day!"

Eliza grabbed his phone off the bedside table and handed it to him. "Set the alarm for half an hour, and then we'll shower and see about eating those take-out salads."

Frank managed to wrap both arms around the woman snuggled against his chest and get both hands onto his phone and set the alarm. He was surprised to see it was only 4:45... it felt like it should have been midnight. He nuzzled his nose into her hair and felt her breathing even out. He drew in a deep breath, wanting to memorize the smell of her fragrant curls, and let his body relax in slumber.

Frank felt he had just closed his eyes when the alarm beeped. He sleepily tapped the snooze button, but he knew he needed to get up. He couldn't believe he'd napped for half an hour, or that he'd done it without removing the plug she had slipped into him earlier. He quietly disengaged himself from her grasp and tiptoed to the bathroom.

He cleaned everything up and wrapped a towel around his hips. Then, after a second thought, he took the towel off and turned around to inspect his ass in the mirror. He could just barely see it in the mirror over the sink if he stood on the edge of the tub. It looked the same, but he could feel faint welts when he ran his hands over it. He couldn't help smiling as he hurried to the kitchen and set out placemats, wine glasses and silverware on the rickety table for two. He served up their salads and poured them each a glass of wine, pleased that it was all ready when she turned up wearing his bathrobe.

She padded into the room, barefoot, and eyed him in his tight gym towel. She stretched up to place a soft kiss on his cheek. Her smile was warm, and she had a well-satisfied look in her eyes.

"I'm glad to see you look as exhausted as I feel," he grinned. He pulled out the small wooden chair and scooted it in for her after she sat. He hadn't thought much of the breakfast table in the back corner of the kitchen when he'd moved in, but the idea of little dinners for two was intriguing. Not that he could ever have foreseen doing it dressed in a towel, or his dinner guest rocking his terrycloth bathrobe. Her dark hair spilled down over her shoulders and no manner of tightening the belt on the robe could prevent her cleavage from peeking out of the gap.

He liked to see her all tussled like this, knowing she'd gotten that way in bed with him. There was little conversation as they both sat and tucked into their Caesar salads. Sleep still hadn't fully left either of them, so they lazily ate and sipped Merlot. It was hard to ruin a simple salad, and it always went well with wine.

And when he would have risen to take the dishes to the sink, she picked up his hand and tugged him into the living room. She climbed onto the love seat and patted the space next to her, waiting while he settled comfortably before moving into his embrace. They sat curled around each other and watched the early news, and then The Big Bang Theory. Frank would never have spent the early evening laying on his couch, but today he wouldn't trade the experience for anything. Eliza was languid and happy, her body fitting perfectly against his.

He knew of the show she put on, but he had never watched it before. Somehow she had found yet another thing that would add light and laughter to his life that he hadn't known he was missing. She had laughed and laughed when he'd asked, "Is this show new?" He'd found the premise a little ridiculous, but found his science background served him well. Plus he identified with the awkward characters, felt like his social life had resembled theirs as a kid. Only now, and he grinned as the thought occurred to him, only now it was completely different. He was her boy toy. She had dropped those words on him like a bomb. He chuckled and replayed the words in his mind. His social life had certainly shifted. His lover was akin to Wonder Woman.

He gathered Eliza close and kissed her slowly and sweetly, trying to thank her for the way she'd swooped in and changed his life. She twisted around and pressed her lips more fully against his. Her palm crept up to cup his cheek and keep him close as her lips lingered over his. "I know," she murmured. "I have to go after this show, and I don't want to."

"You could stay the night...."

She pushed herself to her feet and headed to the bedroom for her clothes. "I can't... but we could get together this weekend." She paused a moment and looked back, her expression suddenly serious. "And if you haven't got any plans for the Fourth of July, I have a family get together at my aunt's house. It might be a bit intimidating, meeting everyone at once, but I am sure they will like you."

Frank swallowed hard. Meeting the family. Already. And then joy swelled inside him. Already!

She was about to speak again, but he cut her off, pulling her into his arms and giving a squeeze. "I'd love to!"

She squeezed him back, laughing and pressing her cheek up against his. She was happy and vibrant, and some of that was rubbing off on him, because he felt a surge of joy. Her excitement was infectious, and he was swept up in her charm. He readily followed when she took his hand and pulled him back to the bedroom to get dressed.

Eliza laughed and pulled off the towel, waggling her eyebrows as he fished for boxers in his top drawer and self consciously pulled them on. "Only you would be shy after what we just did," she chuckled. Out of habit, Frank cinched up his belt and tucked his white button-down dress shirt into the waistband of his khakis. A pair of black socks and loafers completed his look, and he was ready to walk her down to her car by the time she had straightened her hair in the bathroom mirror.

"I can manage to find my way to my car alone, Frank, really, I can."

He just smiled and followed her down the stairs. "It's what a gentleman does," he said simply, and she nodded, leading the way down the street. People were out sitting on their stoops enjoying the twilight. Others were hurrying home from work, arms laden with grocery bags. They called out "Heya" or "How's it going?" as he and Eliza walked by.

Had they ever done that before, when he was walking alone down the street? He couldn't remember if they had, but Eliza waved and called back to them, stopping even to take a turn at four square with some kids. She held his hand and drew him into the game. His cheap rental apartment suddenly felt like it was in a neighborhood, and he liked it.

He reached her car at the end of the block and enfolded her in his arms. Her head fit perfectly beneath his chin, and she sighed and held him close. "This is good, Frank," she whispered. "Very good. Always leave 'em wanting more..." He opened the door for her and slowly closed it once she was in and fishing for her keys in her over-sized purse. She rolled down the window and leaned her head out. "I'll text you when I get home."

Frank stepped back and watched as she worked the car out of the parking spot. "I have never had a day like today," he said as she swung out into the road. "Never..."

"You're a natural! I knew we'd click!"

"Seriously, though," he began. "How did you know? When did you know?"

Eliza checked her mirrors to be sure she wasn't blocking traffic. "I am not exactly sure when, but it was all adding up, the mix of good manners, small touches that revealed you were taking my comfort and desires into consideration. And oh, yes, let's not forget that kiss in the park."

His mind flashed back, remembering how it was a whole lot more than a kiss.

He stood with his hands shoved into his pockets, watching her drive down the street, and as he turned to walk home he saw Benny trot across the street and clap him on the shoulder. "It's good to see you, Dad, I hope this isn't a bad time to drop by."

His son was taller than he was and had the same wavy dark hair. He was much more outgoing though, and more athletic. He wore work-out shorts and a baggy tank top, like he was on his way home from the gym.

In a short moment of panic, Frank wondered if they'd left any new toys out and about, but Eliza had insisted on tucking them all back into the Emporium bag and making a special home for it on his closet shelf.

"No, tonight's perfect." The last light had dwindled and the street lights popped on. On impulse, he added, "You just missed meeting Eliza, a lovely lady I met at the Silver and Gold Meet and Greet."

"That's great, Dad, and how come you haven't mentioned her before? No... don't answer that. I'm just glad you're getting your feet wet. Seems to me she's the first woman you've had over here in the five months since you moved in."

Frank had to smile when the thought about how he'd gotten a lot more than his feet wet. He followed Benny into his apartment and realized his kid was gazing around in wonder. "Wow. I mean wow. I like what you've done with the place. This is all new. Like you're finally deciding to live here."

He flopped down on the love seat and clicked on the TV. Frank could only smile, remembering all the days Benny had done that when the sofa was in his room. "Coffee? Or maybe some pecan pie?" It was probably still good, he'd wrapped it up in cellophane. The Keurig gurgled out two cups of coffee quickly, while Frank tossed the containers from Applebees into the trash and stuck the glasses and flatware into the dishwasher. He cut two pieces of pie and added a hearty dollop of whipped cream to each.

He found Benny still in front of the TV. Trust the kid to come to visit and spend the time on his couch clicking through stations.

If Ben was impressed by the pie he didn't say anything. He polished it off quickly, and then turned to his father. "The reason I'm here, is mom called me. She asked me to talk to you. She's changing her mind about selling the house, and she wanted me to see how you felt about it."

Not selling the house would be a bad idea. Initially, the idea of letting go of the home they'd been in for years had hurt, but neither one of them could afford it solo. "We have been working on on this for months, Ben. I had no idea it took months, no, years, to divide up the assets and end a marriage. Your mom moved out over a year ago, and then changed her mind and kicked me out. I am not sure what it is she wants, just that it isn't me."

Benny sat in silence, and Frank didn't want to put him in the middle where he had to arbitrate. Except it was Abby who had sent him and been the one to involve their son.

"Has her new boyfriend decided he wants to live on the Main Line?" Frank tried and failed to keep the bitterness out of his voice.

"Kendrick? I'm not sure she's even still seeing him. All I know is she's scheduled another meeting with the mediator for July 11th. She wants you to be there. I really wish I knew what this was about. She just sprang it on me the other day."

"I'll come, but if she wants that house she's going to have to refinance it and get my name off the mortgage and the deed. I'm trying to move on here."

Ben held up his hand in protest. "Save it for the mediator, Dad. I'm just the messenger."

Chapter 12

After Ben left, Frank climbed into bed with his cell phone. Eliza had texted a simple, "Made it home safe" an hour earlier, but it still wasn't all that late. It just felt that way because they'd had such an eventful afternoon.

He tapped her name on his phone and typed in, "Do you think it's possible my ex knows about us?"

It didn't take long to get an answer. "No. Why? What makes you think that? And it's not any of her business anyway."

Frank settled down more under the sheets. He could still smell faint traces of her in his bed, and thinking about it made his cock stir. "She sent Benny over to talk to me about the house. She wants to keep it. Like she's trying to get more money out of me now, when it's all so close to being settled."

"Lol. I'd pay more just to have it settled and have you officially single."

Trust Eliza to cut right to the chase and say something to bring it all into perspective. He felt like a little kid reading with a flashlight under the covers as he typed back, "But even then I won't be single. I'm seeing somebody."

There was barely a pause. "Lol. Are you now? Oh, hey. I heard a good one. How come chemists have the answer to every problem?"

Frank groaned inwardly, knowing the answer to one of the world's worst chemistry jokes, but he played along, how did Eliza put it? Silly pleased she'd bothered to find a science joke. " How come?" he replied.

"Because they have all the solutions!" He could almost hear her laughing. Then she added, "Good night Frank. Thank you for today. I don't know how we got here so fast, but I wouldn't have it any other way now."

Time seemed to drag by for Eliza as the upcoming week turned out very differently than expected. The weather turned hot and unbearably humid, and Eliza struggled to keep up with her demanding clients.

Her business catered to demanding brides, and June was the season for it. Custom stationery and invitations had suited her art background and turned into a business that flourished, mostly due to Eliza's patience and ability to couch suggestions in a manner that made the purchaser believe it was their idea all along.

But brides, and it seemed anyone getting married these days, seemed to believe they were entitled to be cranky and demanding, flighty even. Nothing demanded more of her attention than a stressed out bride trying to make her celebration unique. They wanted their own colors, their own calligraphy, their own wording. And Eliza made a good living off their discriminating tastes. Usually, the fussier and more exacting the better.

Just not now, Eliza thought. Not now, when all she wanted to do was leave early for the weekend and spend it at the love nest with Frank. With all her distractions, her clientele might have suffered if not for Shelly. The younger woman was a superstar, going through client folders and making slight alterations to the packaging displays.

Setting up for a consultation was usually Eliza's forte, selecting a few colors and designs for the bride to choose from, especially if the wedding had a particular theme or was on a tight budget.

Eliza's calendar usually got less busy as the summer wore on, but whether it was due to changes in the Gulf Stream or global warming, the sunny summer days seemed to be lasting well into October. It seemed early fall weddings were becoming all the rage. Eliza would be busy at work for the foreseeable future.

She was a little bit jealous at all the free time Frank had. Sure, it wouldn't last, and he would be working more once the summer semester started. She had a feeling he would be busy in the fall just when her workload usually dropped off, entering a bit of a lull between the summer wedding season and the holiday party rush.

As usual, June was an abnormally busy month for High End Design, and to top it off Jenny was texting, wanting to know more about the mystery man from the Meet and Greet. "Don't make me bribe my way into their sign up list, Mom," she had joked. "To see what his name might be!"

Eliza gave up trying to put her off and suggested dinner on Friday, with maybe a little shopping thrown in afterward. "I could use a little help finding something casual and yet cool to wear to Aunt Lucinda's barbecue. I look in my closet and all I see is work clothes."

Jenny usually jumped at the chance for some shopping. Eliza had a feeling she would toss out half her mom's wardrobe, as well as shred her current supply of catalogs if she could. "All right, mom. You can tell me about him on Friday. And don't think for a minute I can't hack into the Merriott Hotel's guest list for their single's night. Don't you make me do it!"

Eliza knew the hotel staff would probably read the sign-in sheet over the phone for Jenny if she just called up and asked. Jenny had a sunny disposition that was hard to resist. She'd know all about Frank before Eliza had a chance to explain. She really wanted her daughter to like Frank. In a few months, there would be absolutely no reason for her to object.

There were times when Eliza envied her daughter, with her open smile and take charge attitude. Life seemed so easy for her, dressing stylishly without stress, balancing her work and social life effortlessly. Jenny had been the one to suggest trying online dating as a way for Eliza to get back in the game, and for months Eliza had resisted until Jenny had teased her into it.

"You have been alone for years, mom! You can at least take a look at what's out there before you decide you're not ready."

So Jenny had made time and scooted her chair up beside her mom at the computer to explain the inner workings of online dating sites. She made it look easy, snapping a few photos and putting in the minimal information. Before she knew it Eliza had an active account and Jenny declared her ready to peruse some profiles.

"You will have to add more about yourself later, Mom, but for now, we can start swiping." The notion of swiping was familiar, part of the lingo from all the major sites, and Eliza was excited to see for herself.

The first picture appeared on the screen, a man standing on the back deck of a boat. He held a fishing pole in one hand and a string of large fish dangled from the other. His face was obscured by a fishing hat and dark glasses, and all she could see of his profile was his first name, Howard, and his hometown.

"So what do you think, mom? Yes, or no?"

Eliza grabbed the mouse and clicked the x in the top corner of the window. Howard disappeared, replaced by Bill, posing all in leather on his motorcycle. Eliza closed that box too.

"Wait, mom, no! You have to swipe them, yes or, no, or the program won't ever be able to match you with anyone."

"How can I judge anything from one picture and a hometown? It's too much. Are they going to get some kind of notice that I like them?" Eliza couldn't keep the anxiety out of her voice. "It feels like I am making some kind of commitment, to like some man I saw for ten seconds on the internet."

"But that's how it's done," Jenny said. "It's not so much that you are signaling that you like them, just that you find them acceptable."

"Doesn't everybody lie, on the internet?"

Jenny laughed. "They all expect at some point to meet in person, Mom, so I doubt they are posting pictures of someone else. And there is a way to read more of their profiles, we just have to search differently." She clicked a few times and demonstrated how to search and read, and then went back to the system's choices for her mom. "See? It's not so hard."

"I will check it out, and view some more pictures, but for now, can we just close it, and come back later?"

That was when Jenny had closed it all down, and found the old-fashioned meet and greet at the downtown hotel. She had been right, too, Eliza thought. She was looking forward to sharing her news about meeting someone to her daughter. Jenny really had found her the most comfortable way to meet men.

Wading through a week full of work was making Eliza feel as if the upcoming weekend hidden away with Frank was being overtaken by family and chores. She decided that maybe it would be better to plan something different, something casual, so when Jenny asked she wouldn't immediately know her mom had moved on to spending the night over at her new boyfriend's house. Perfect. This way, when Jenny asked what her plans were for this man, she could honestly say, "He's taking me to the museum tomorrow."

Eliza decided to call Frank just so she could hear the warm tones of his voice, and after exchanging pleasantries she asked him to arrange a visit to the art museum for Saturday afternoon. "We could meet for lunch first, or have something in their cafe, if they have one."

"Well, which art museum were you thinking, Eliza?" Frank sounded pleased with the idea. He was comfortable with art, and an afternoon spent wandering the long, yet thankfully air-conditioned halls sounded blissful.

"There's more than one? Whichever one's the best, or has the best cafe."

He chuckled. "Finally, something I can introduce you to, Eliza. We can do the Academy of Fine Arts. Let's say around 1 o'clock? I can text you the address."

"Don't get too cocky, mister. There will still be plenty of time left after the museum to get you home and out of your clothes." Eliza sounded fierce as she said it, but her insides were feeling steamy at the thought of getting her man alone.

"Oh, yes, Eliza. Yes, please! But maybe we better take the train into the city and meet at the station. Easier than trying to deal with parking."

The walk was only two blocks from the train to the museum, but heat still radiated off the pavement and Eliza felt baked as they entered the building. She brushed her hair back and stowed her sunglasses in her purse. It had to be ten degrees hotter in the city than at home. Cropped jeans had seemed appropriate given the nice day, but Frank had to be sweltering even though he looked put together as well as unbothered by the heat. Maybe he was just plain in better shape. The walk hadn't tired him.

The Academy was not at all what she expected. Even the exterior had a playful air to it, not carrying the weight of an edifice encapsulating an art gallery. The interior colors were warm and inviting, and the variety of the displays made Eliza forget the long hike and instead hurry around every corner to discover whatever was next.

There was nothing stodgy, instead she found color and art made from materials she would never have anticipated. It was welcoming, and drew the viewers closer, almost asking themselves, "What is that made of?"

The crowd grew as the day wore on, and Frank was comfortable beside her, talking about exhibits he had seen before that seemed fresh again as he watched her. Each gallery presented a jumble of various art forms, and crowds of people of all ages meandered through. Frank walked beside her and waited as she took it all in.

Eliza took her time in the gallery, examining the paintings, but finding herself drawn more and more to the mosaics. Her creative side respected the sheer amount of work and talent it must take to create such breathtaking designs, and she made a mental note to incorporate some of the colors and motifs into her invitations.

She snapped a few pictures with her phone, thinking some of her brides might be inspired by the art. It was stunning. Someone had devoted hours meticulously shaping tiles and matching colors.

"I had no idea this was here," she finally said. It was beautiful and totally unexpected. "I love it. Thank you for bringing me here, Frank."

They had reached the end of one corridor and were partially hidden by a colorful sculpture that looked as if it had been woven out of reeds. The strands had each been dyed vibrant shades of blues and oranges.

"Look at this! From one angle it looks like a giant pitcher, and from another it resembles a tree." Eliza stood back and considered the sculpture. "What do you think, Frank?"

"I think the artist wants you to feel that way," he said. "To make you stand back and ask yourself if it is art imitating life, or nature expressing art."

She glanced behind before taking hold of his hands. His presence beside her had been reminiscent of her old married days with Jim. He hadn't crowded though, merely accompanied, not even holding her hand or laying his palm on the small of her back. Come to think of it, he had been a little apart.

"Are you worried we might run into people you know here, Frank?"

His eyes flickered up and scanned the empty hall before relaxing. "Well, it might be a possibility, so I thought playing it safe might be prudent." He gave a sad little smile and pulled Eliza, unresisting, into his arms and dropped his nose into her dark curls. "A few weeks more, milady. However, this close to home, and work, I just prefer not to make waves."

Clasped close to his chest, the subtle aroma of his aftershave teased her nostrils. She sucked in a deep breath and leaned back, smacking a quick kiss on his surprised lips. "Got it. No public displays within city limits." He laughed and so she kissed him again. "So," she teased. "Where's the cafe in this joint? Do you suppose they do afternoon tea here?"

Following signs back towards the entrance, back on the ground floor, they found the cheerful cafe. It was full of afternoon sunshine and less crowded than she'd expected. Three-quarters of the room was floor to ceiling tinted glass, offering a view of the busy street outside, while also giving the uncomfortable feeling that the patrons inside the cafe were also on display to the public at large.

Within minutes they had each collected a cup of tea and a pastry from the friendly staff and retreated to one of the many polished wooden tables with high stools. Most of the lunch crowd had long since moved back out to the galleries. Eliza waited while a busboy wiped down the table beside them and then turned to Frank.

"How old were you when you first started to recognize you had fantasies that were different from everybody else?"

For once Frank wasn't caught off guard by her direct question. He chewed his scone and thought before answering. It wasn't the kind of thing he ever thought he'd share with anyone, but with Eliza, as usual, "Never ever" became "Well, as it happens…"

He gave a wry smile and stopped trying to keep his secrets hidden from her. "As it happens, when I was young, like early teens, I used to have this crazy fantasy of being in the jungle and ending up captured by Amazons. They always brought me back to their village and had their way with me…"

Eliza leaned in conspiratorially. "Had their way with you? You mean they fucked you?" She liked the light flush in his cheeks.

"Well, it wasn't always the same, Eliza. Sometimes they'd strip me in the center of the village and the matriarch would declare I was hers, and take me off to her shelter. When we got there she always made it clear what kind of fucking we'd be doing. And it never involved my dick getting anywhere near her pussy. She always had a couple of her most trusted women get me down on the furs and make me assume the position."

Eliza laughed at his candidness and his youthful recognition of his submissive tendencies. "So the alternative was being lost in the depths of the Amazon, so you really had no choice but to comply."

Now it was his turn to laugh. "Oh, I might have only thought about protesting for a moment. The fact is, I wanted them to control me, tease me, penetrate me."

"And your friends were mooning over Playboy centerfolds," Eliza interjected. "And dreaming of running away to find Christie Brinkley or Farrah Faucett."

"Maybe a few of them. I just knew I couldn't tell them what was on my mind. And really, it didn't seem realistic to expect to find a woman like that anywhere but in the Amazon." Now that he had confessed he felt more exposed. He gathered up their napkins and plates, making a long distance throw into the trash receptacle. He stared at the tabletop while Eliza gathered up her purse and stood.

"You never know, Frank. A woman like that could be right beside you. Are you ready to head home, my little captive?"

A long sigh escaped him, and he pinched the bridge of his nose, almost like his eyes hurt. "Are you going to make fun of me all the way home? I don't need that kind of stress." Maybe confessing something so intimate had been a bad idea. There was a reason he had never shared anything so deeply personal, not wanting to open himself up for ridicule. But somehow he suspected she already knew what kind of answer he would give before he gave it.

They kept the pace slow on the return to the station, as the heat had increased as the afternoon waned. The height of the buildings cast shade on the street, and Eliza would have laced her fingers through his or held onto his arm if he hadn't felt so distant. She had meant to dig into the origins of his sexual submissiveness as a means to tighten their bond and bring him closer, and instead she had stressed him out and caused him to pull back.

"I always knew I liked to be dominant long before I had a word for it," she confessed. "I just knew I liked to be in control." Frank was still walking stiffly at her side, but she knew he was listening. "Don't get me wrong, both sides of the dominant/submissive sexual relationship can be incredibly hot. I get aroused quickly imagining either kind, but when it comes to which I'd like to actually act out in real life, I prefer control. It matches some of my earliest fantasies, just like yours."

A harsh laugh escaped Frank's lips. "You mean you dreamed of being an Amazon with a fresh young captive you found wandering in the forest?"

"Noooo!" Now she was outright laughing. "I was always the tutor who demanded complete control to help my student prepare for an essential exam or the spoiled daughter of the factory owner who blackmailed the young male employee into doing what I wanted. God, I hadn't really thought about any of this for ages. It's really quite extraordinary, to look back and see just how early I was already finding my way to a position of dominance. But it was really only after I had gotten some experience that I really understood it all. Probably by the time I was out of college."

They descended down into the coolness of the station and boarded the train still comparing notes on sexual history, but the tension had fled, and their conversation was more like two accomplices. They sat in the first pair of seats they found together and settled in for the ride home.

"Have you got time to get dinner when we get home?" Frank inquired. "Or we could pick up some take out? Not that I'm plotting to get you back to my place, but Eliza, I'm not ready for our time together to end." Great, now he really was sounding like a Freshman offering to show a co-ed his etchings. He knew she probably had things to do, since she'd been very specific about wanting to get together in the afternoon.

He watched as she pulled out her phone and checked for messages and emails before smiling at him. "No messages. Not even my turn in Words with Friends."

"Oooh!" In seconds Frank had his phone in his hands and was peering over her shoulder. "I play that too. Let me see if I can start a match with you. I usually just play the computer, so I doubt I am much of a challenge."

Eliza smiled as his name appeared on her screen, and she decided their day together didn't need to end early. "I don't see any reason to head home alone and cook something for myself after a day spent in the heat," she said. "I might be free to grab something, on one condition. I miiiight have time to get dinner someplace close by," she teased, "IF you promise to tell me more about your Amazon adventures." Eliza loved watching the different reactions cross over his features. Surprise, dismay, and finally arousal. "You mentioned that clan of Amazon warriors didn't always hand you off to the chieftain. Maybe sometimes you got handed off to the chieftain's daughter… wait, daughters?"

Frank got a reprieve from her gentle teasing when they split up briefly to drive separately to the steak restaurant down the street from the station. Frank tried to compose himself, yet the images of his youthful fantasies came back strong in his mind and he shifted in his seat, once again admiring how easily Eliza kept yanking on his balls with a figurative string.

They paired up down the block and entered the establishment side by side. There was an early Saturday night crowd, and they opted for seats at the bar.

After helping her up onto the bar stool, Frank tried to steer the conversation back to her evening plans. "I was under the impression you had some family reason for wanting to hit the museum this afternoon, some dinner to rush off to?"

"Oh that," she waved off its importance. "I had dinner with Jenny last night, and just wanted to be able to mention we had some intellectual pursuits on our agenda.

"As opposed to sexual pursuits?"

"Hahaha oh, my God, yes. I don't know, I wasn't really thinking. We have done plenty of the typical dating things: dinner and movies. Maybe it's just that when I started talking about you it was hard not to giggle and smile and mention how sexy and perfect it is."

"But she knows about us, about me? That we're serious. I don't even know how to put it anymore. Going Steady?"

Just then the bartender stepped in front of them to get their orders, and as soon as he turned away Eliza explained. "It's called being exclusive. Right now, even though you might have a technical commitment to Abby, you are exclusive to me. You are still in the early stages of proving to me it's worthwhile to be exclusive with you."

Frank frowned into his wineglass. "That hardly seems fair. Not that I mind proving myself."

She leaned over and whispered softly in his ear, "And yet the submissive accepts it. Gives up power and the idea of fairness and trusts their dominant. Giving up power isn't always easy. And it's ok, sweetie. I know you're a little uneasy about the dynamic. I would be too, if I was in your position. You have to trust that you have everything I want, and follow my lead. The things you do for me, and let me do to you, those are very special.

"I like what you do to me, Eliza," Frank admitted. "Pleasing you makes me feel good inside."

"Exactly. I think we are a good fit. I respect you and your desires. They are not something to be exploited." His eyes were warm, looking back at her. "Well, maybe once in a while... to get what I want,' she chuckled.

Eliza left the steakhouse confident in their renewed intimacy. Their highly personal talk at dinner erased the last of her reservations. She had never had any doubts about Frank or his sincerity, but he was still learning, and so excited about taking it all in. He was experiencing a relationship and feelings he hadn't ever spoken of aloud before, so she was glad she had pressed.

Originally her plan had been to head home for an early evening and some last minute emails, but she found herself following him back to his place, taking the stairs quickly and smiling broadly at him as they passed straight through the living area and down the darkened hall, shedding clothing as they went.

Frank didn't know who he was anymore, dropping his socks on the floor and peeling off his shirt, giving it a haphazard toss onto the chair. Eliza caught him up in her playful magic again, and he went with her as she tussled him onto the mattress, reaching up to wrap his fists around the headboard bars. He gladly gripped the wooden slats tightly while she fumbled in the drawer for a condom. His cock was rigid in her hands as she covered him, and he reveled in it, easily accepting she was going to be on top. That was fine with him, for now, and for forever.

Eliza stripped off her bra and panties and straddled herself across his hips. He was more than ready, and she wasted no time, giving in to the impulse to ride, reaching to position his shaft at her silky entrance. She eased onto him, lifting herself up periodically before easing down, coating him and ensuring their joining was slick with lubrication before she rode him long and hard. The intensity showed in his gaze as he watched her, lifting his hips in rhythm with her, meeting her thrust for thrust until she reached her fingers down between them and stroked herself over the edge. The feel of her muscles tightening around his shaft was heaven and sent him flying off into ecstasy right behind her.

His death grip on the bars loosened as she slowly sank down to lie beside him, and pulled him close against her side. He didn't mind it. He liked the feel of her heart beating wildly under his ear as she cradled his head against her chest. She dropped a soft kiss on his hair as she struggled to catch her breath.

"This is the time I like best," she finally said. "The quiet time after, after we have been through whatever we have been through together, where we hold each other close and feel each other's heartbeats return to normal. The time where it's just us."

"Mmmmhmmm," he replied. He tried to remember if he and Abby had ever done this, just floated back down to earth together. And damned if he couldn't bring to mind a single time. He didn't even mind that Eliza was the one was cuddling him up against her. It felt right.

"I don't know if it's the quiet, or the pounding heartbeats, but it brings an intimacy. I love it." She sounded beyond contented.

"I love it too." Frank murmured. There was a long silence afterward that almost got awkward.

"It's ok," Eliza finally stated. "I know you're on the borderline of love with me. Or if we had been together longer it would be easier to say it. For now, just know that I feel it too, and only worry about the speed of it." It was so like her, to just state the obvious like that and have it seem normal.

"I don't want there to be any doubts about us. I want a relationship based on love and respect. I am not looking for a doormat or mindless obedience. Any time you feel it's not what you want, just let me know. I want for us both to want things the way they are.

He nodded sleepily against her shoulder. "I do, too."

But Eliza wasn't done. "It's about love and loyalty, and it's not meant to be shared with anyone except us. I am not sure I can describe it, the strength of the bond. Once, years ago I attended a Munch and I met this lovely young man."

"Wait," Frank broke in. "What's a Munch?"

"It's a gathering of people who all share the same interest in kink. Sort of a BDSM meet and greet. A chance to learn and meet like-minded people. Many are just looking for a hookup or a sexual interlude."

"Sounds intriguing," Frank lifted his head and waggled his eyebrows at her. "Just what did you learn, milady?" he joked, but then got back to being serious. "What kind of people turn up at these things? And how do they find out about it? Are they sponsored by the Adult Emporium or something?"

Eliza laughed. "Sometimes, although I am not aware of any from the Emporium. There are web sites, though. I'll take you on a little tour later." She snuggled him closer before continuing. "But to continue. This gentleman I spoke to had been in an FLR, and before you ask, that's a Female Lead Relationship. One hundred percent, the woman is in control. Anyway, what struck me about Stan was how loyal he was, how devoted. He stayed with his lover through a long battle with cancer that she eventually lost, and he was still heartbroken years later."

Eliza's hand had come up to absently stroke fingers through Frank's wavy hair. She sounded wistful. "I believe you have that kind of potential, Rusty, for that kind of fidelity, I really do."

In response, he curled his arm around her waist and pulled her closer. "I'm honored," he murmured.

Chapter 13

There was a large package leaning against his door when Frank leaped up the steps on his way home from a workout two days later. He wasn't a fan of the big health clubs, so discovering a hole in the wall sports gym in this neighborhood had cemented his apartment choice. Close proximity had been the main factor in joining Atlas gym, as it was within walking distance and overlooked by all the millennials and housewives because of its boxing roots. Even though the place was mostly empty when Frank went in the early morning hours, he liked the concrete and steel feel of the place, even if it stank slightly of sweat.

There were no treadmills facing TV screens blaring Judge Judy or The Price is Right, just a few cardio machines, a weights center, and the corner with the punching bags and practice ring. Every once in a while the staff asked Frank to climb into the ring and hold practice pads, but usually, he stuck to his own routine: cardio first, then weights, and finally finishing with the speed bag.

The package outside his door was a bit of a mystery since he hadn't ordered anything, but he checked the label, and it was correctly addressed to him. He set it down beside the desk, worried it was yet another of his estranged wife's efforts to divide up their belongings. It would not surprise him if she was returning something she decided she didn't want and then going to reopen negotiations.

Frank left the package unopened and showered and shaved, but finally curiosity got the better of him. What if it wasn't from a lawyer?

He set it on the tiny kitchen table and used a steak knife to slice open the box. His first thought was that of course, it was another crazy scheme of Abby's. However, it looked like an old-time suitcase, hard-sided and dark beige in color. He lifted it out by the leather handle and checked out the brass clasps that popped open at the press of a button. The inside was lined in the same beige-colored silk. The fabric was worn in places, but otherwise looked well cared for, and reminded him of the valise his father used to take on short business trips when Frank was in grade school. His parents had long since moved to a condo in Boca Raton, and he had never owned anything remotely like this since.

As he closed the case and reset the clasps, he noticed an envelope tucked under the leather strap. The parchment color had blended in with the valise. It felt heavy in his hand, like quality card stock, and he suddenly thought of Eliza. Heat pooled in his cock as he thumbed the fancy envelope open. It was almost square in size, like an invitation.

The lettering was elegant and tall, and the message took his breath away. The date at the top was yesterday's, and it was most definitely an invitation. He scanned through the words and then sank down into the kitchen chair to read it again slowly.

Dear Candidate,

Due to your success as an initiate in the world of domination and submission, you have been selected to spend a weekend at "The Villa". Your sponsor, Miss Eliza, requests that you present yourself at her residence no later than 6 pm on Friday. Bring both casual and formal clothing (although you might not be permitted to wear either of them) and all accessories currently stowed in the Emporium bag hanging on a hook in the back of your closet.

You will find your 'ticket' inside the interior pocket. This does not involve leaving the country or even the state, However, as a candidate, you must arrive fully prepared to serve. Present yourself in the best light possible, and the removal of pubic hair is encouraged. There may be a surprise inspection at any time, and demerits have consequences.

Remember, your behavior is a reflection on Miss Eliza. She feels you are ready. Your weekend at the Villa will be life-changing and will build intimacy and trust between you and your dominant. We wish you good fortune.

Sincerely,

The Villa Management

P.s. Confirm your reservation by texting Miss Eliza immediately the words "Attendance Confirmed".

Frank slowly tucked the invitation back into the envelope. The gold clasps slid open easily under his thumbs and he turned the suitcase towards the light, running his fingertips over the timeworn silk. He peered into the silk pocket inside the lid and spotted another envelope there, presumably his ticket. He extracted it carefully to examine it, noting the resemblance to a plane ticket on manila card stock. The words "Admit One" were written in bold at the top, followed by his name and address. The only other thing on it was a bar code on the bottom left. He flipped it over and examined the back, smiling to see Eliza's phone number printed along the bottom edge.

He wasn't exactly sure what all this was about, but his cock sure wanted to go. His pants felt increasingly tight, encasing his hard-on in light pressure that slipped back and forth as he shifted his weight.

What day was it? Only Tuesday? Friday seemed a long way away. He barely had a moment's anxiety about attending. He was up for any trip with Eliza. It could be anything, and he would love it, her constant teasing and the way she could say something suggestive and have it resonate in his mind for hours or days.

He was confident this was one of her role-play scenarios. It had to be, didn't it? The mystery of it all was so arousing. His cock throbbed again.

Within seconds his phone was in his hand, and he was typing out "Attendance Confirmed." He had a dozen questions he wanted to ask, but he waited to see what her reply might be first. His screen lit up almost immediately.

"Thank you. Your reservation is complete. Come prepared, and do not be late." She sounded so official, and Frank was sure at some point in the past she had mentioned role play, although it was a sexy traffic stop she'd mentioned. Frank wasn't sure just what this was yet, but he was happy to go along with it. He took a deep breath and typed out his most pressing question.

"Do you really want me to shave my pubic region?" It seemed like it would be a lot of work for not much of a difference. In men's magazines, yeah he saw it all the time, with the ladies. Maybe it'd give Eliza the same kind of rush it gave him.

She sounded a little impatient. " I believe the invitation merely said it was encouraged. Personally, I'll find it very disappointing if you don't. Compliance is not mandatory if you are nervous or afraid to try."

"I'm not nervous or afraid!" God, she knew exactly what buttons to press, to make him jump at the bait and deny the obvious.

"Then stop asking silly questions," she answered. "And by the way, I know your cock is hard right now, and you are probably finding some way to stimulate it." His legs stopped shifting back and forth, stilling the fabric caressing his shaft. How does she know these things? he wondered, but she wasn't done, "That stops right now. No masturbation of any kind between now and our trip to the Villa."

That stilled him right in his chair and he stared at the screen, wondering what to say to that. He felt like a schoolboy who'd been caught with a hand in the cookie jar. But really, there was only one thing to say.

"Yes, ma'am."

The week ahead was going to be a long one, but oh, the anticipation was there. Having four days meant Frank had time to Google and practice shaving his bikini line, as well as carefully pick out which outfits to wear, no wait, which outfits to bring. He still did have a little doubt about what he might be permitted to wear. The thought of kneeling at Eliza's feet naked, God, made his dick swell and jerk in his pants.

He purchased a small duffle to pack the sex toys in and buried it down at the bottom of the valise next to his dress shoes. On impulse, he tossed in the white gym towel that barely concealed anything when he slung it around his hips as well as the Eternity for Men aftershave.

Somehow he got through work, forcing himself to do his course prep work and set up his online class. He struggled to concentrate and get it done ahead of schedule, so by Thursday morning he was done and ready for a long weekend. His lesson plan was ready for the following week, even should he return home late on Sunday.

Eliza was always on his mind. He wondered if she was as excited about this as he was, if she was carefully going through her wardrobe finding the right things to pack. He realized suddenly he wanted to have something special for her. Not something overtly sexy, like lingerie or leather. He wanted something for fun, just to please her.

Late Thursday afternoon he got in the car and headed west, back to the Adult Emporium. The parking lot was nearly empty, and he was happy to see the same shop girl manning the register. He nodded and gave her a little salute as he entered, and headed for the erotica section. There had to be a femdom section, right?

There was one, a small corner of the erotica display that spanned two shelves, as it turned out, and he stood there reading the back cover blurbs, feeling the temperature in the room rising and doing his best to refrain from putting his hand in his pocket for a little friction. It was such a conundrum. Just by forbidding it, Eliza had made it all he could think about. He had never thought of himself as a highly-sexed guy. He had always been ready and eager when Abby approached him, or when he happened to read Penthouse Letters, but Eliza somehow flicked a switch, where he went from simmer to full boil.

Frank selected the three novels that reminded him most of Eliza. He passed over the "Best Women's Erotica" books and concentrated on those that looked realistic and classy. He didn't want to hand Eliza anything with whips or models in corsets on the cover but instead selected books displaying colorful masks and kinky boots.

Finally satisfied with his choices, Frank stopped to chat with half-shaved brunette at the check out line. "Read any of these?" he asked casually.

The buxom cashier pouted and shook her head. "Not really my kink, luv." Frank recalled she had made a casual comment last time about going home with a beautiful lady, and realization dawned. "Oh," he whispered. "But if it was two ladies....?"

She laughed and nodded at her handsome customer. "I'd have a copy of each at home."

As he pulled out his card to pay Frank spotted a basket of mood rings beside the register on the impulse rack, and got one of those, too. Not that he ever had any doubt about her moods. She was crystal clear, but a man needed all the help he could get.

"You want me to wrap these?" the cashier joked.

"Does that cost extra?" Frank started to say and then decided she must be making fun at his expense. But it was worth a try. He leaned down and winked at her, "Miss Eliza would sure love it if they were."

There was a grin on his face as he stepped out of the store a few minutes later, all three volumes wrapped up in pretty paper and the mood ring threaded through the ribbon, dangling from the center of the bow. At last, he finally felt prepared, and more than ready for this weekend, even if he felt a little itchy downstairs.

Frank rolled out of bed early on Friday and wished he hadn't finished all of his course design. Excitement for the weekend ahead bubbled up inside him, making him restless, and he needed a distraction, a way to vent some of his pent up energy. Deciding to maximize his morning work out, he phoned Benny, suggesting they meet up.

Benny sounded pleased to hear from his father. "Sure, Dad, I have time this morning. Give me 30 minutes to finish my coffee and get changed. I'll see you soon."

Frank went through some of his legal mail to kill time before he left, and eventually dropped some older correspondence in the circular file before changing into his workout attire and giving the neatly packed suitcase in his closet a final once over. He had it stowed it out of sight, just in case Ben stopped over after their workout. Atlas was only a few blocks away, after all. He waited for Ben outside on the sidewalk in the cool morning air, and Atlas was deserted when Frank strode in with his son at his side, both tall and dark, their loose tanks emphasizing their broad shoulders.

The building was open and airy on the inside, whitewashed cement-block walls and a high-gloss gray on the cement floor.

"Cardio first?" Frank suggested, picking up a white towel at the desk and heading toward the back. "To get us warmed up?"

The Frank settled into the routine of his workout, stepping up onto the elliptical machine and starting it up slowly. Benny took the machine beside him and the small talk dwindled as they picked up the pace. It wasn't often that Frank had company working out. He wasn't used to talking as he ran, so he gave up trying.

Even though he and Ben were both members here, their schedules hardly ever meshed. Rather Frank hit the gym in the morning before class, and Benny liked to spar in the late afternoon when the more serious athletes turned up. It still surprised Frank that his kid was into boxing.

Frank had been happy to introduce Benny to Atlas, his hidden gem of a gym. It was exactly Ben's style, clean and simple, and the men and occasional woman who frequented the place came to work out, not socialize. Ben had joined on the spot, much to Frank's pleasure. He shouldn't have been surprised when his son had made friends with the staff and gone from being a sparring partner to an aspiring fighter.

The routine of the workout felt good and calmed his insides. Benny's familiar presence on the elliptical beside him reminded him of all the times he had dragged his son to the YMCA as a teenager to get him out on the basketball court or into the swimming pool. Anything to get him off his phone or computer.

Those had been good times, taking basketball seminars over the winter and spending weekends at the crowded pool at the Y. He missed those days when he and Abby had bought lunch at the snack bar and lounged by the pool while Benny swam with his friends. Remembering them now made Frank's stomach twist again that it all seemed to be ending.

He stepped off the equipment and blotted his face on his towel before spraying the machine and wiping it down. He smiled at Benny as the kid did the same.

"Got time for some free weights?" Frank asked. "And then maybe the heavy bag?"

The suggestion of pounding the heavy leather bag caused a smile to break over Ben's face. "Sure, dad, lead the way!"

Frank went through his usual routine. It was fairly simple, but Ben didn't complain, taking turns running through arm curls, squats, and spotting each other on the bench press. Benny kept up a flow of conversation, talking about a new girl at work, so much so that Frank thought maybe his son had a little crush on the girl.

"So what's her name, this new girl who can't seem to do anything right?" he teased. "Is she cute?"

"Jesus, Dad. It's not like that. Her name is Morgan, but she's young, and she doesn't know anything." The younger man was smiling, even though he sounded a little irritated.

"Maybe in time, Morgan might be of interest? If she's cute?" Frank added. "And if she has someone older and wiser, to help her out, to get her past her nervousness." What a crazy thought, to be suggesting his kid was older and wiser than anyone while in his mid-twenties.

Maybe it was a rule of life, that when you found yourself in a happy couple you suddenly wanted everyone else to couple up as well. He desperately wanted to open up to Ben about Eliza, but he knew it was too soon. They needed to talk about Abby first.

Once they had rolled some athletic tape around their knuckles and settled in at the heavy bag, Frank wrapped his arms around it, holding it in place while Benny threw some punches.

"I've been thinking about the house and your mom," Frank stated.

Ben gave a grunt and continued pummeling the leather. Frank leaned his weight onto it more to keep it in place.

"I'm going to check with HR at work, and see if I can pull some cash out of my retirement account to help your mom buy the house, if she really wants to keep it that bad. I think it would be better for everyone if we sold it, but we can maybe work it out this way. I'll get my name off the mortgage, and do what I can to get her financing."

"Are you sure, dad?"

"Absolutely." Frank grinned. "But what I can't have is her changing her mind. I'm not going to pay a penalty withdrawing that cash if she's going to change her mind again."

"I know, Dad. I understand." Benny stopped punching and held onto the over-sized leather bag while he caught his breath. "You take a turn."

Frank stepped back and threw a few punches, getting used to the feel of it.

"That's good, weight forward," Ben encouraged. "Yes, like that!"

Frank grew more confident, hitting harder.

"I know mom's life has gotten hectic since she walked out," Ben continued. "I mean Kendrick was a bit of an ass, but it's only since they broke up that she has gotten a little... erratic."

"Hey, she picked him," Frank gave up hitting the bag and flexed his fingers, finding they were sore. "But don't worry, I've made up my mind to help her with this. Anything to get the paperwork signed and settled." His hands really ached. He had probably been dumb to pound that leather bag so hard.

Benny nodded and checked the time. "Thanks, Dad. But I need to head out if I'm going to shower before work. Let's do this again next week."

Frank clapped the kid on the shoulder and walked him out of the gym. "Sounds good, I'll text you Monday."

Just a few hours later Frank cruised down Eliza's street at a quarter of six, and turned into her driveway. As he did so, his cell beeped, and instructions flashed across his screen.

"Pull around to the back. Park next to the garage, candidate." As if he wasn't on edge enough, his excitement rose another notch. He parked in the empty spot, grabbed his suitcase and hustled around to the front door. Five minutes early was still cutting it close.

He rang the bell, and the door opened immediately. It stayed open long enough for him to step inside and then closed swiftly behind him. Her sparsely furnished foyer appeared transformed and was now brightly lit and had the look of an office to it. There was a long table at one end, and a row of chairs against the side wall. Eliza herself was there, looking very official in a dark blue uniform, complete with an official-looking cap and badge.

She stepped in front of him and led out her hand, palm up. "Tickets, please."

"Oh, yes, one second," Frank mumbled, fishing the envelope out of his breast pocket. He smiled as he placed it in her hand, wanting to grin. She looked damn sexy in a cop outfit.

"Where are you traveling this evening, Mr. Sutherland?"

He cleared his throat and decided to get into his role. Thoughts of her frisking him or heaven forbid, strip searching him made him remember he hadn't cum in almost a week. "I'm headed to 'the Villa,' Officer."

"I see. And the proper title for me is Agent." She pointed to the name sewn on the breast pocket of her uniform: "Agent Suarez". She looked him up and down, taking in the sports coat and trousers before examining the ticket more closely. "Are you traveling alone this evening?"

Frank nodded. "Yes, Agent. Just me."

"Is that your carry on bag? You packed the contents yourself?"

Another nod. "I brought everything that was requested and yes, I packed the bag myself." In a surreal way, he felt like he was in the difficult check-in line at an airline in the years after 9/11.

The lovely Agent Suarez gestured to the table at the front of the room. "Place your baggage up there, sir. Anything you'd like to declare?"

Frank felt a thread of nervousness hit the pit of his stomach. There were some pretty personal items in that bag. Hell if he knew if it was the kind of thing she'd want him to declare. The note had implied it was a domestic trip, so he decided not to mention the Emporium items.

He smiled as he lay the old valise on the table and stepped back. "No, Ma'am. Nothing to declare."

"We'll see about that!" Eliza bit out, snapping the clasps open and lifting the lid. Everything in the bag was meticulously folded and placed. Barely disturbing anything, she looked around the sides of the suitcase, and then pushed some shirts out of the way to withdraw the mini duffle.

She gave him a knowing look and asked, "What's in here, Mr. Sutherland?"

Frank found himself actually feeling a little nervous at this point, and decided to confess. "That's everything from the Emporium bag that was in my closet."

Silence followed that pronouncement, and Eliza swirled her hand at him, gesturing for him to continue. "So this bag contains....?"

His cheeks felt warm, and he was almost squirming. "It's the sex toys, ok?"

Eliza made space in the valise and replaced the small container. "Sex toys, very interesting. Do you travel with sex toys often?"

"Oh, hell no," he laughed, watching "Agent Suarez" continue rifling through his bag. She reached down into the wide pocket on the inside of the lid, and nodded, satisfied. "Looks like this bag will pass the search. Wait, what's this?" She found a small strip of beige silk protruding from the lining. One quick tug and a hidden pocket opened. A tiny Ziplock baggie full of small clear gemstones fell out.

"Ah ha!" she crowed.

Frank stared in horror. "Those aren't mine! I didn't put them in there, I swear. They must have been in the bag before I got it."

Eliza pulled a small flashlight from her back pocket and switched it on, shining a beam of light down into the concealed space. "I think there's another packet in here," she muttered. Her fingers gripped and tugged, and another tiny baggie emerged, this one filled with white powder. She held it aloft and shook it in his face. "Just what is this, mister? Do you know how bad this looks?"

Frank was mesmerized by her. Her eyes flashed and her lips were set in a hard line. He had been hard since he stepped out of his car, but now his cock started throbbing. Somehow she was always one step ahead of him, this woman.

"Please, Agent. You have to believe me, I don't know anything about those packets. They aren't mine, I swear."

Eliza smirked. "That's what they all say," she mimicked his desperate voice, "It's not mine, I don't know anything about it!" She was all business as she turned to squarely face him, arms crossed over her chest. "You are going to have to remove those socks, shoes and that sports coat, sir."

Complying immediately, Frank nodded and sat down in one of the waiting room chairs, kicking off his loafers and then rolling his paisley socks down. He folded the pair up neatly and tucked the roll into one shoe. He shrugged out of his jacket and draped it across the back of his seat. He definitely felt at a disadvantage when he stood before her again.

"Very good," she quipped. Her fingers closed around his elbow and turned him to face the wall. "Hands up against the wall over your head. Feet back, and spread them shoulder-width apart." Her hands held onto parts of him and moved him into the desired position.

Frank swallowed hard. It was so hot, standing there, feeling her hands pat him down. His lovely TSA agent took her time, stroking his hair and neck before patting their way over his broad shoulders. Frank had been imagining a scene like this for days, but the reality of it made his blood pound.

Her hands found their way down his arms, and then over his sides, reaching around to pat him down in front. Those hands stilled for a second when they encountered his flagpole of a cock tenting his trousers, and then they gripped tightly, squeezing and teasing. "What have you got in here, my little drug mule?"

Frank shivered, suddenly getting an uneasy feeling about where this might be heading. "I'm not a drug mule, officer, I swear it!" It was delicious, the way she maneuvered him into situations like this one, where he was practically shaking with anticipation.

She stepped back and then gestured again. "It's Agent! Now remove the shirt and trousers, please. It appears you might still be concealing something.

"It's my dick," Frank burst out. "You can put your hands into my pockets, and feel what it's doing."

Agent Suarez had a shocked look on her face. "Are you trying to manipulate me into groping you?" She took hold of his belt buckle and started unfastening it herself. She yanked it out of the belt loops as he stood there gaping. "This is a very serious matter, sir. I have to report all instances of attempted bribery."

Frank's hands flew to the buttons on his shirt, and he hastily pulled it off. His pants followed. "Please, ma'am. I didn't mean that. I will comply with whatever needs to be done." He turned around, his white boxer briefs standing out against the golden tan of his skin as he placed his feet apart and resumed the position. He leaned heavily against the sheet rock, and gave a gasp of surprise when Suarez tapped the inside of his ankle with her toes, urging him to spread wider.

This time Eliza ran her palms over his warm skin, gripping the firmness of his muscles and then peeking into the waistband of his boxers. There was a pause as she fumbled around for the flashlight, which she shone down into his underwear.

"I can't see much. And you know I am going to have to do a thorough search. Complete and thorough."

"Is there any other option? An x-ray or something?"

"The other option," the feisty transit agent replied, "Is to spend the night in a cell and have a transit official review your case in the morning."

Frank leaned his forehead against the wall and thought about the sexy woman who had him wrapped around her finger so tightly. He wouldn't have it any other way. "Let's get it over with. I am innocent, and a thorough search will prove it."

Chapter 14

The wait seemed endless, and Eliza aka Agent Suarez muttered. "Well, all right then." Frank heard a soft clink, and she stretched up behind him and snapped a cold metal cuff around his wrist, muscling it down to the small of his back. He kept grinning, lowering the other hand so she could close the other cuff. One final click and they were in place.

She took a firm grip of his elbow and steered him over to the table and plucked his valise off it to make room. He wasn't going to make it too easy for her.

"Really, Agent, is this necessary? I have been completely cooperative."

Her touch was expert and perfectly placed, one hand on his elbow and the other between his shoulder blades, tipping him forward. He eased slowly into place and gasped when she nudged his feet together rather than apart. It wasn't hard to guess why.

Delicate fingers hooked into the waistband of his tighty-whities and shimmied them down over his hips. Within moments he was totally nude, and he tried to rise up and entreat her again.

"Please, I am not a drug mule. It is just that your touch got me so aroused..."

Her hand pressed the center of his back again. "The more you resist the search, Mr. Sutherland, the more guilty you look. Now widen your stance, and we can get through this."

Frank lay his head down on the table and spread his feet.

"Wider." She insisted, and when he was slow to comply her hand cracked against his ass cheek.

She knew just how to take advantage of every vulnerability. Once his feet were wide enough and his balls dangled in the breeze, she reached in and caught them in a steady grip. She examined them closely, her grip easing. "Fortunately, all the pubic hair in the region has been removed, this experience may cause some slight discomfort, however, the exposed skin simplifies the search. It will be completed more quickly and easily."

"Yes, ma'am," came Frank's muffled reply.

Her hand clasped gently around his balls. "There's an easy way and a hard way, Sir. And now that you're in position, don't think I won't use these boys to keep you in line."

"Whatever you have to do, Suarez."

She squeezed slightly and pulled back, repositioning him. He closed his eyes, hoping for the feel of her hand or the flogger. Instead of a whip crack, he heard a light snap as she pulled on latex gloves. Then her fingers parted his cheeks and dribbled some lubricant down his crack.

"Oooh, that's cold!"

That earned him another slap, but then Eliza swirled a finger around his pucker, warming the cold gel up, and making sure everything was slippery.

Frank stifled a moan and pressed his hips back, encouraging his sexy security agent to begin the body cavity search.

"Take a deep breath, Mr. Drug Mule, we start with the most likely cavity."

Frank tried to relax, but the excitement was building. Her fingers teasing their way into him, probing so intimately. It was all he could do to maintain his position while she teased in and out, eventually adding a second finger. He felt outmaneuvered, exposed and, oh, so aroused. She wiggled her fingers deeper, commenting, "I don't seem to feel anything, do try to ease up with the clenching, It makes it difficult to complete the inspection."

Frank was grateful for the sturdy dining table under his chest holding him up and keeping him steady. The muscles in his arms bunched and flexed, and one minute he was holding his breath, the next he was gasping and moaning.

At first, Eliza kept one hand on the small of his back, with just enough pressure to keep him in place, but as she teased and probed he went up on his toes, and his fabulous cock was right there in her view and within her reach. It was easy to take it in her grip and tease it with slow, sexy strokes.

"Oh, God, Eliza," he breathed, thrusting his hips in rhythm, wanting more, harder, faster.

She had positioned herself off to the side, as she continued her search. Her slim fingers were very thorough, probing and scissoring inside him. The length of his cock quivered in her left hand, which teased up and down his engorged shaft. Her palm half curled around it, felt the heat of it thrusting forward, wanting her touch. She obliged for a few strokes, all business, enough to keep him on edge, but not enough to push him to orgasm.

After several minutes, she had to admit defeat and withdraw. Playing his part as a suspected smuggler, Frank groaned in objection when 'Agent Suarez' pulled away from his side and peeled off the blue latex gloves. She lifted her clipboard and added a few final notations, before fishing the key from her front pocket. In moments Frank was upright and rubbing his wrists as he smiled down at her. It was hard to resist smiling back up at him, so instead she handed him a towel and pointed over to his clothing piled on the chairs.

"You are free to get dressed, Mr. Sutherland, and then please reclaim your carry on and take a seat in the waiting area." With a curt nod, she disappeared down the side hall, turning into the bedroom at the back of the house. She leaned back against the door after it closed and allowed herself to smile. So far this trip to "The Villa" was going exactly as planned. And her rusty lover was thrilled by it. God! Every quiver and gasp had just made her want to play with him more. He didn't have to say he loved it, it radiated off him.

Quickly she stripped out of the TSA uniform and brushed out her hair, transforming herself back into Eliza, Director of Print Advertising. She pulled on a summery black wrap dress and stepped into a pair of low heels. The face in the mirror smiled back at her, and she couldn't believe that was herself she was looking at. Yes, the unruly hair was the same, the fine lines forming around her eyes, only they weren't frown lines any longer. She didn't feel like an aging widow anymore.

Eliza touched up her make up and twisted her hair up behind her head, securing it with a clip. She was all set to go, but she wanted to give Frank enough time to clean up and get dressed. Plus, it would do him a little good to sit there and wait for a few minutes, to have his mind start to wonder what might be next for their weekend. The Villa wasn't really a BDSM resort. As far as she knew there weren't any in the area, at least not on a permanent basis, merely hotels sponsoring an event for a weekend.

No, the Villa was a going to be their little getaway to amplify Frank's submissive feelings and set the mood for erotic dominance.

Only the feelings were becoming much more genuine, more serious than simple erotic pleasure. Sure, their banter was light-hearted and their rapport was easy-going and fun, but there was a serious thread under it. Whatever she was setting up now was going to lay the foundation for their future. She was willing to work at keeping him sated and satisfied, and she had a feeling Mr. Helpful was eager for the exact same thing. They would spend two nights booked in a local hotel featuring fantasy suites, and immerse themselves in the dynamic.

Deciding he had waited long enough, Eliza dabbed on another coat of lipstick and grabbed her bag by the door. Her little overnight carry on had wheels and hummed down the hallway behind her. Frank looked up and smiled as she entered.

She didn't stop, just rolled on over to him and kissed him where he sat. "A plus for you so far, my sexy student." He stood and framed her face with his hands, kissing her softly. He seemed relaxed.

"Am I through security, then?" His lips sought hers again, caressing gently.

Happiness bubbled up inside Eliza, and her words came out almost like a laugh. "You are! Now we can finally hit the road, and we might actually make it to the Villa at a reasonable hour." She dragged her little bag forward and set it at his feet. "Why don't you take these out to my car, the trunk should be unlocked. I'll grab us each a water bottle for the drive."

Eliza watched as he maneuvered the two bags out the door, and hurried to find her purse and catch up. She was eager to surprise him with their destination, a little-known area hotel. Somehow she had no doubts this would be another first for him, a place meant for lovers, with giant champagne glass bubble baths or private pools.

The place she'd discovered wasn't too far away, and just reading about the amenities made her mind work overtime. Fantasy rooms on themes that ranged from jungle rooms and science fiction suites to Venetian villas. The majority of the guests would be couples, some using the hotel for its convenience to the mountains and antiquing, and some traveling up from the city as they were for the sex appeal.

Eliza took a moment to straighten out the dining room table and scoot it back into place, and then set the chairs back into place around it. She'd never look at this table the same way again. From now on she'd always have the mental image of Rusty splayed out over it.

She took one last lingering look at it, flipped off the lights and headed out the door. Frank was ready by the driver's side door, opening it for her in his typical gentlemanly way.

Chapter 15

"Any hints about where we're going?" Frank asked.

Eliza gave his hand a reassuring squeeze and concentrated on the road. Even though it was well past rush hour, the route was crowded with cars heading to the mountains for the weekend. She found it strange, for summer weekends the expectation was that everyone packed up and went to the shore. At least that had been Eliza's expectation, so she had elected to go in the opposite direction.

"I would never have thought there would be this much traffic this late!"

Going through the towns that spotted the major route were the worst, and Eliza finally pushed the button for radio. "See if you can find something you like on there.

"Sure!" God, Frank thought to himself. He was back to sounding like Mr. Helpful.

Frank scanned through all the stations she had programmed in and sighed. "You have Rock, Talk Radio, Alternative, Country, and Classic. Mind if I look for something different?"

At first, she thought he was joking. Who couldn't find something to like given the sort of customary choices? But she had asked him to put on whatever he liked. She was curious to know what sort of music he favored anyway. "Feel free. I'm not sure what stations we might get this far north."

"You don't have satellite radio, do you?"

She shook her head "Sadly, no."

He cranked the knob around and finally tuned in to a jazz station.

It was surprising and yet adorable that he liked jazz, Kenny G smooth jazz. Somehow it suited the evening, speeding north for a romantic getaway. As if on cue, the Subaru outpaced the other drivers on the road and continued farther off the beaten path.

Eliza wanted to imprint the moment on her memory, holding hands with Frank as the dusk fell, cruising along to a station she had never heard of, but suddenly wanted to program into her radio. She felt euphoric, like the time she and a few girlfriends had bolted off the college campus and spent a weekend at the shore, hands out the window swooping the air as they raced down the parkway. Her heart had that lighter than air feeling, only better.

Sitting beside her, Frank didn't need to ask if she liked it. Her face glowed. Or maybe that was residual from the security inspection from earlier. He lifted the back of her hand to his lips and dusted kisses along her knuckles. He smiled as he did so. All was right with the world. His heart and his mind and even his cock agreed that putting Eliza on a pedestal and keeping her happy was a priority. He liked her take-charge attitude, even if he wasn't he wasn't ready to label it domination and submission. Whatever they had might seem like a game on the surface, but he wanted to explore further, to be the one responsible for keeping that healthy glow on Eliza's face every weekend for the rest of her life.

Frank wholeheartedly believed she deserved it, to be loved cherished. She had freed up something inside him, he couldn't wait to see what the rest of the weekend would bring.

It was late in the evening when Eliza made the final turn onto the long driveway. "What is this place?" Frank wondered aloud. It was looking very remote.

"Just wait for it," she nodded to the lights up ahead. "It may be hidden, but it's a full-fledged resort. You may even have heard of it. They specialize in fantasy suites."

Eliza pulled into the drop off circle and parked. "See? You get our bags while I check us in." She took two steps towards the sliding door and then hurried back, holding out the keys to him. "Maybe you had better park too."

She walked away from the car without waiting for him and hurried inside. Frank found it awkward, feeling like a valet, but as always, being helpful was something he aspired to. He found her finishing up at the desk, pocketing two keys and looking at the restaurant that was closing up for the night.

"Are we too late to get dinner?" she inquired. "It was a long drive."

The desk attendant looked apologetic. "The main dining area closes at 9, but the bar has burgers and bar food until 11, and room service is available until midnight.

The lobby itself was almost deserted, and after the clerk retreated into the office, low conversation and the faint strains of oldies music drifted from the darkened doorway of the bar. Eliza caught hold of his shirt collar and dragged him down for a long hot kiss. He gave no resistance, standing there, holding a suitcase in each hand. He didn't let go of them, but rather let her lips explore his softly.

"Let's not forget why we are here..." she whispered. "Let's stow this luggage and see about getting a nice juicy burger." Frank trailed after her to the room, glancing around at the romantic touches. Floral arrangements set on Louis XIV tables and over-sized gilded mirrors. In the elevator lobby, recessed lighting almost gave a glow of candlelight. The vestibule of their suite was similar. Someone had placed a welcome basket on the sideboard, and a bottle of wine was chilling in an ice bucket.

He parked the luggage beside the door and glanced around, wanting to see if there really was a champagne glass bubble bath, but Eliza caught his hand and pulled him back towards the hallway.

"Dinner," she reminded him.

"Right." He would rather have spent a few minutes checking out their villa. Ever since he'd heard the words 'fantasy suite' his mind had gone into overdrive. The brief glimpse had let him catch sight of an enormous round bed and a separate lounge with a fireplace. The room bore the high round arches and pale plastered walls of a Roman villa, complete with cool ceramic tiles beneath their feet.

A shudder ran through him at the thought of kneeling on those floors, his imagined role would create indelible memories. His mouth went dry and heat pooled in is groin imagining himself naked or dressed only in his white towel kneeling on that stone floor.

Just as suddenly as they'd flicked on, the lights flicked off and he was tugged by the hand back out into the hallway. Eliza was laughing at his curiosity and pulling Frank by the hand back down to the bar.

"Plenty of time to experience the Roman house slave treatment later..." she teased.

Frank stumbled along after her, shaking his head to clear the hum of desire. He followed her into the dim light of the bar and found just what he needed, a quiet booth in a dark corner. Normally retreating someplace out of sight would have guaranteed hours spent waiting for a waiter to remember he had customers. But for a romantic getaway resort? They'd have to be more attentive.

Eliza edged into the seat opposite Frank and soon had a refreshing a spritzer in her hand and a bowl of peanuts to nibble on. She gazed around. The bar was almost empty, just one or two couples lingering, dancing by the jukebox in the corner. She pulled Frank closer and spoke low, "A jukebox? Maybe we have gone back in time a little."

"Your Subaru is really a De Lorean underneath all that paint."

"Yes, I wanted you all to myself, so I not only drove you to the middle of nowhere but also back to 1995."

"1995 was a good year! Benny was born, and I started in the Chemistry department at the college.

"Somehow when you put it like that, it sounds sexy."

He looked her right in the eyes, across the table in the quiet corner booth. "It's you, Eliza. You make me feel sexy. I was always a stick in the mud before this. I did nothing out of the ordinary, nothing kinky, nothing excessive…"

The waiter appeared and interrupted only long enough to deliver their burgers and fries. The tantalizing smell caused her stomach to growl, and Eliza didn't wait to dig in. She shook a dollop of ketchup onto her burger and then laughed as Frank did the same. "Stop copying me!" she teased.

He stopped mid shake and looked up in surprise. "I'm not copying you! I always eat cheeseburgers this way. Half the people in the country eat their cheeseburgers this way. And, oh my God, you're messing with me again!" He squashed the lid back on his burger and attacked it with gusto. "I swear, you do it on purpose, and I fall for it every time."

He looked across at the lovely lady opposite him. Her features were soft in the dim light, but she was laughing hard, at his expense, trying to chew and swallow. She took a long sip of her drink.

"You are so cute when you sputter, Frank. It's a crying shame no one has teased you like this until now. You've gone through 48 years of your life without it."

"The last thing I would have needed in high school or college was a pretty girl like you teasing me and making fun at my expense." The over-sized burger was a handful, proving to be both juicy and delicious. Frank carefully wiped his chin and reset his napkin in his lap.

"Exactly like that, Frank! That's exactly what you needed as a young man. Maybe then you wouldn't have been a virgin on your wedding night. Any girl who teases you verbally… is thinking inside about teasing you sexually. And you wouldn't be so stiff, sitting there, daintily wiping a spot of grease off your chin."

"Daintily wiping, are you kidding me? My mother was the one who insisted," he was sputtering again, and he knew it. "And you are doing it again! Am I that easy? Wait… does that mean you wish you could be teasing me sexually, right now?"

In response her toes caressed along his thigh under the table, slowly working their way up towards his crotch. She found him semi-hard, and wiggled her toes against his package, feeling the fabric shift as she flexed. "Oh, yes, Frank. I am glad you finally understand my meaning. Finish up your meal, sexy. You will need your strength."

He liked her touch, her outspokenness. And it was a simple thing to perch closer to the edge of his seat and offer himself up to those tantalizing toes. The way she smiled when he did it gave him another glimpse into her mind. Maybe someday he would feel like he could keep up with her erotic games, but for the moment, he got hard just wondering what she might be thinking, how she might next surprise and jostle him.

"So tell me about this house you're selling. The one she who must not be named suddenly wants to keep." Reality returned, and he found it was easy to enjoy her playful touch while he explained.

"I still don't understand it, I mean, the house is amazing, just not something that can be maintained on a teacher's salary. We bought it about fifteen years ago, and have been redoing one room at a time. Not every year, more like not in the first five years when Ben was small, but in the last ten." It was evident Frank had pride in his home.

"So why not sell it then? Was your mortgage underwater or something? That you can't clear any money, or have to split debt?"

"No, we did refinance once, but only to get a better rate. We should clear enough that each of us could put a down payment on something reasonable. But it's like one minute she's obsessed with our past and the next she wants everything to stay the same. Only without me in the picture, I guess."

Eliza tossed her napkin onto her plate and pushed it away, leaning forward and stretching across the table to pick up his hand. "Do you know anything about her lawyer? Maybe that is where this is coming from? Suddenly thinking he can get more for his client at the last minute?"

"Hadn't thought of that. Or maybe they are bucking for a price reduction. I don't know. I just want this over. I have moved on, and she can't get pissed that someone wants me after she kicked me out." High time he stood up for himself and went after what he really wanted. His confidence was back.

Dinner didn't drag on. Even the waiter was able to sense their underlying eagerness to get back to the romance of their fantasy suite. He cleared their plates and made a cursory inquiry about dessert, before bringing their bill.

Eliza plucked out of his hand as he was about to set it in the center of the table. "I'll get this, Frank, and you should go see if there's a romantic slow song on the jukebox there, so maybe we can squeeze in one dance before adjourning to our room." She was fishing in her purse, but not for a credit card.

Frank rose and meandered to the brightly lit Wurlitzer, realizing he hadn't put a coin in one of these machines in years. The display glowed with neon lights, and the shape and form of it was comfortingly familiar. He read over the song choices, recognizing most of the oldies, Elvis, Moody Blues, and Whitney Houston. For some reason, he wanted to find something a little more current. He flipped the page and scanned through songs and artists he had never heard of before. He looked over his shoulder and saw Eliza speaking to their waiter and signing off on the bill, charging it to their room.

He hurriedly scanned, hoping something would jump out at him, a song he'd heard his students mention, or something he'd know was a romantic hit. After a few mental kicks, he settled on the last one on the page. He'd never heard of the song or the artist, but the title seemed perfect, "I Could Not Ask for More." He dug a couple quarters from his pocket and plunked them into the machine, hastily hitting J10.

She was on her way to him when he turned, and he met her on the dance floor, drawing her into his arms and giving her a little spin. She flowed into his embrace as the song started. The tune had a slow, heavy drum beat and an easy rhythm. "Oh, Frank," she laughed. "How did you know this was one of my favorites?"

He snuggled her close against his chest and dropped his head low to rest his cheek on her hair. "I didn't, it just seemed appropriate, the title I mean." The song had a country twang to it, but also a little bit of a pop sound, the song of a happy lover realizing he had found a special woman. "I must say," Frank moved easily to the beat and decided he'd made an excellent choice. "I must say, I have a suspicion every song in that machine is probably a perfect, romantic couples song."

In response, both her hands dropped down to cup his ass cheeks, fingers splayed as she pulled him closer. "I have to imagine that dozens of couples dance after dinner when they come all the way out here. We are not all that different from most," Eliza murmured.

"Mmmm," He sighed, cradling her gently as their bodies swayed, reminding him again that this weekend seemed like some sort of initiation.

"I like it this way," she murmured, "That no one knows what we are going to do when we get back to the room. Well, maybe the assumption is that every couple is going to make love while they're here. But for us, it's different. If we come out here later your ass might be bright red from a whipping under your pants, or your balls might be tied up with string, so you feel my touch on you whenever you move or whenever you reach into a pocket and stimulate that naughty cock of yours."

"Ooooh," he swallowed hard, letting her breathy words wash over him, wondering for a moment how she'd managed to see so clearly that his body would respond when she talked dirty like that.

Her face nuzzled against his chest, and he wasn't sure if she was talking to herself or to him. "I love that no one knows all the nasty things I am going to do with you. Where I am going to wiggle my fingers, and how your cock is going to throb when I guide your tongue between my legs."

"Oh, God, Eliza. Yes please!" He stepped back as the song ended but held onto her hand. "Another song? Or back to the room?"

It was an easy choice, heading back through the lobby to the elevators. The place seemed almost deserted, which suited Eliza fine. The decor was modern and the inn seemed well kept. Each fantasy suite had a different theme and finding the Roman Villa available had meshed perfectly with her plans. Their room came complete with the usual hotel bar, but she'd arranged ahead of time to have a bottle of white wine chilling and some chocolate covered strawberries delivered. She pulled Frank to a halt outside the door as she slid the key card into the lock.

"Remember, sexy. Once we walk in this door you are mine, bound to serve the entire weekend. Is this your wish?"

Frank lifted her knuckles to his lips and bowed slightly. "Oh, it is most definitely my wish." He followed her into the chamber and got his first good look at the place. The over-sized bed he had seen before as well as the sitting area with the fireplace, which would be lovely in winter, but useless in June. Thick marble columns separated the sleeping area from the living space, and far to the left was a bar set up in front of a sliding glass door to the balcony.

Eliza gave his hand one last squeeze and pointed to the luggage in the entryway. "See to my baggage as well as your own. There should be luggage racks in the closet. Get out of those clothes and get into uniform. I will be in shortly to arrange my own clothing." She slapped his ass as he gathered up the suitcases and headed for the sleeping area.

"I'm sorry, Miss Eliza, I am not clear on my uniform. There was no mention of it in the invitation. I did bring my white towel, if that would suffice." There was a smile on his face, and a spring in his step as he moved away. His voice was still smooth as velvet moving over her skin. She couldn't wait to see him in that towel again, or maybe in the tiny Roman toga she'd bought for him at Party City. "White towel it is, Rusty," she called after him.

She drifted to the bar and poured herself a glass of Chardonnay before giving in to her curiosity about what her sex toy was up to in the bedroom. Clothes were hung up in the closet, toiletries arranged on the counter in the en suite, and Frank was setting the Adult emporium toy bag on the bedside table next to the nylon pouch containing her own meager toys, mainly lube and a small vibrator.

Eliza smiled to see him barefoot and wearing nothing but the tiny white towel.

"I think you're getting used to that outfit. It suits you."

Frank smiled even as he looked self consciously down at himself. "I am kind of curious about the toga you mentioned. It might cover a little more, and be less precarious."

"I happen to like precarious. I might get lucky and see something magical." She ignored his snort and zipped open the side pocket on her case. "Here, you can try this on. Oh! And I got footwear." She tossed him a scrap of white fabric and a pair of yellow flip flops, trying not to laugh at the dumbfounded expression on his face. "Go ahead, try them on. I promise I won't peek," she teased.

After a couple of hard shakes, Frank pulled the costume over his head. It was short, very short, barely long enough to cover his ass cheeks in the back or provide modesty in the front, but he could tell Eliza admired it. He stepped into the sandals and settled the knotted fabric on his shoulder. "How do I look?" he queried.

Eliza let out a low wolf whistle and gestured for him to do a slow turn. "I like the way it shows off your best assets, but honestly, it would look so much better if you were kneeling."

He dropped instantly, draping the material over his thighs and smoothing it into place. He rested his hands in his lap and looked up. "I hope this meets your approval, ma'am."

Eliza sat down on the edge of the bed and kicked off her shoes. She curled and flexed her toes, extending her foot out towards him. "Much better, and at a good height now to do a little work seeing to my comfort. My arches are killing me. Surely a pampered house slave would eagerly see to his Domina's every need." His cock hardened at the words house slave and domina. He liked the image. Exactly as he had pictured himself doing earlier, he liked to be kneeling, wanted to make her feel good, so he turned towards her and took her foot in his hand, running his hand over the arch. "Oh, yes, that feels so good."

His hands moved tentatively at first, but then with growing confidence, caressing, smoothing the tension away. Every time he found a particularly tense muscle he worked it with knuckles and thumbs until she sighed in pleasure. Those sighs reminded him of the times he had nuzzled between her thighs. His eyes flicked up to hers, hoping she might recognize the same sounds.

Instead, she leaned back on her elbows and extended the other foot. Her eyelids drifted shut as he kneaded the sore spot under the ball of her foot. "Don't worry, Rusty. You will have all weekend to please me with that tongue of yours. But first, finish with my toes."

Chapter 16

The world had gotten very small, shrinking down to the space around the two of them. Isolated in the cocoon in the cool Italian-style hotel room with only the hum of the air conditioner in the quiet of the remote romantic getaway, Frank felt as if no one else existed. It wasn't that Frank seriously wanted his world to be reduced to just two people, it just felt right to have her be at the center of his. These moments when she took charge and commanded his mind and his tongue and his cock felt so right. All she had to do was pat the bed beside her and say, "Time to hop up here, Rusty, on all fours please," and his dick would throb and his heart nearly beat out of his chest.

He climbed up eagerly, feeling the warmth of her hands as she stroked his balls and his thighs. Eliza always knew just how she wanted him, ass up, head down, knees spread. She peeled off her wrap dress and climbed up onto the bed beside him. Her skilled hands teased and dribbled lubricant down his crack and gently massaged it in, working her fingers in slowly. He thought back to the first time she'd done that; when she'd laughed and probed and pushed her fingers deep into his hole. That was the first time she'd called him Rusty.

Whatever rustiness had been on his brain was long since greased and polished away. His sex drive worked like a well-oiled machine, ready for whatever came next. His mind drifted for a moment, overtaken by the image of an auto shop and Eliza dressed in the formless gray coveralls of a mechanic. She would point to him and then to a pair of cuffs dangling from the auto lift. "Just enough time left in the day to get that rusty hatchback up on the lift for a lube job," she'd proclaim.

"Pay attention, slacker!" Eliza slapped his ass sharply. "Take a deep breath, sexy, and relax."

Eliza knelt behind him on the bed, resting hands on his hips, making him wonder for a brief second what it would feel like to have her don a strap on and actually fuck him. The image stayed with him as she pressed one of the latex plugs into him. It felt bigger than the last time, but he was ready, well lubed and relaxed.

With a practiced touch, she eased it in, wringing soft moans and gasps from him. Sometimes pulling back before working it in farther, until it was seated all the way in him, and her hips were pressing up against his hindquarters.

"What do you think of that, Rusty?"

"I love it," he sighed. "I wish it was on a harness and you were going to fuck me with it."

In response, Eliza spread her knees, the subtle pressure causing his legs to spread wider on the bed. Her arms curled around him and she took hold of his rigid cock where it dangled below him. It was lovely, the way his hips moved, thrusting his cock deeper into her fist. "Glad to know you feel that way! We can add that as a goal for your training. Give you something to work up to.

"Oh, yes, please!" he moaned softly. Suddenly her hand was in his hair, pulling back roughly so he could see her behind him, leaning over him.

"That's 'Yes, Mistress', or 'Yes, Domina' slut."

"Yes, Domina," he ground out, grateful when she relaxed her grip. He kept his head down, waiting obediently as she repositioned herself, lifting the white fabric of his toga and slapping his ass hard. It barely hurt, but it made his cock start throbbing again.

She spanked him again, and again, wincing and shaking her hand. "All I am doing is hurting my palm," she declared. "I think the flogger would be better, don't you?"

"Oh, yes, Domina!" He couldn't keep the excitement out of his voice, and soon she had it in her hand, swishing through the air to shake out the strands.

She started without warning, not caring if he counted, just enjoying every gasp and moan. After a few swats, she paused and found his cock and heavy balls hanging low under him, and giving them a slow caress and a quick yank. Then it was back to business, warming up his sexy backside. Before long his butt cheeks were turning a rosy shade of pink. Eliza stopped to run her hands over his skin, feeling the warmth. There were also a few stripes across it, little welts she could feel as she skimmed her palm over him.

"Look how much your cock likes a rough spanking, Rusty." She didn't have to touch it to know, it was fully engorged and shiny with precum on the head.

"I know," he moaned.

She gave him another heavy swat. "Who do you serve, slave boy?" He hesitated before answering, so she smacked him again.

"Ow! Miss Eliza, I serve Miss Eliza!" She lay into him again with the flogger one more time for reinforcement.

"Sounds like you had to think about that for a minute there."

"No, no," he groaned. "Only to decide between Miss Eliza or Mistress Eliza."

She swatted him playfully. "I see. You don't like addressing me as Mistress?" She took him by the hand and pulled him to the edge of the bed, urging him off of it and onto the floor. He knelt there, looking up at her as she arranged a pillow and lay down on her back, knees dangling off the bed right in front of him.

"That might be a problem because your mistress wants to feel your tongue giving her pleasure right about now."

In a flash, he lifted her calves and positioned them over his shoulders, rising up on his knees to press his face deeper between her thighs. He could smell her arousal, and it drew him in. She tensed the muscles to keep him at a distance. "If you'd like to taste me and please me, you need to say, "Please, Domina.""

"Please, Domina" No hesitation this time, and she relaxed and lay back. He took hold of her hips and pulled her closer to the edge of the bed, and nuzzled his lips between her soft folds. He started slow, coaxing with little flicks of his tongue, centering his attention on her clit, even though the heady aroma of her arousal drew him to lick up into her core.

The first time his tongue strayed she let him lick his fill, and then drew his tongue back up to her most sensitive peak. "Stay on target," she urged. Her out of practice lover was learning quickly, and she took a steadying breath. "Can't you feel it, when you get it right? Can't you feel the tension in my thighs, and can't you feel my clitoris swelling?"

"Ummmhmmm," he moaned, not lifting his tongue from its duties. He followed his instinct, licking, angling his tongue over her, knowing he was getting her close to the edge. He felt triumphant when she arched her back and tensed, holding her breath while the pleasure overtook her. His arms flexed around her thighs, cradling her close as she came apart under his mouth. He loved the smell and taste of her passion, and tenderly lapped her one last time before lifting his head and catching her eyes.

"I believe I am learning how to please my mistress," he joked. Her legs slid off his shoulders and she leaned down to kiss him full on the lips before she rose to her feet. He tasted and smelled of her, and she liked it.

"I believe you are," she smiled. "And pussy face looks good on you," she commented as she tugged him to his feet. He opened his mouth to argue, and then laughed instead.

"I'm not even going to let you ruffle my feathers with that one. I'll take that as a compliment."

227

She turned him and faced him in the direction of the bar. "I left my drink in there somewhere. Find and refresh my drink. I'll be in in a moment." Eliza patted his tight buns as he left, admiring them as he walked away. It was amazing to think how lucky she'd gotten. She had first been drawn to his voice and his cologne, and then the seductive way he had caressed her shoulders and helped her into her coat. Had it been instinct? Luck? Whatever it was, if she had noticed his backside first, she would have been sold immediately.

After a quick trip to the bathroom to tame her wild hair, Eliza slipped back into her dress and went in search of her wine, which was thrust into her hand as soon as she was settled on the couch. In her other hand, she picked up the remote.

"Shall we see what's on television?" she asked, surprised to see Frank standing in front of her. He was still wearing the ultra-short toga that didn't really cover his hard on. A little confused, he looked from her to the floor to the seat on the couch next to her. As an afterthought, he dropped to his knees and scooted close to her spot.

"Would it be all right for me to pour myself a glass of that Chardonnay?" he asked.

"Slaves don't socialize and sit around drinking wine," she scoffed, but the look of disappointment on his face made her remember how new he was to role-playing a scene, and he was completely immersed.

"Come here, sexy," she breathed. Eliza lifted her glass, offering him a sip. He only took a taste, but the next time she offered it he took more, deciding it was sweet and sexy, the way she shared with him.

She reclined against the arm of the sofa, one foot curled up under her and the other foot dangling. By subtly shifting her weight her painted toes found his thigh and caressed up under the hem of his toga. She laughed as she nudged his engorged cock this way and that. One minute it was tame, hidden by the white fabric, and the next it poking forward, rising up and lifting the hem.

"Oh my, that cock has been teased a lot tonight," Eliza commented. "It has been so well behaved, but it has to learn never to expect an orgasm." She took a long sip of wine but didn't offer him any afterward, savoring the control. She met his eyes again. "What?" she asked. "Does my new slave have a complaint?"

Frank once again tried not to let his disappointment show. It was a bit of an emotional roller coaster, keeping track of Eliza's moods and discerning what to say. He hesitated and gathered his thoughts, finally replying, "No, Domina." He like the sound of the word 'Domina', given the whole scene she had set up for him. "As you said before, I am here to serve."

He sat back on his heels and brushed the toga down to cover his cock.

To Eliza's eyes he looked gorgeous, kneeling proudly, his chest thrust out. His broad shoulders were bisected by the triangle of white fabric. No one would ever have guessed that beneath the habitual coat and tie of a professor he was hiding a runner's body, lithe and sleek. Eliza took her time looking him over. He did look fine, and under her scrutiny he clasped his hands together behind his back, the move accentuating muscular curves of his arms. Sneaky man, Eliza thought, almost like he was posing in a body-building contest.

"I do believe you're trying to seduce me, Mr. Sutherland," she commented. It was working, too. The gentle flush of his cheeks, the heat in his gaze made her want to pull him to the bedroom for some sweaty lovemaking, but not tonight. She had other plans for tonight, other lessons to teach.

She let her toes do the speaking for her and let them find their way to the dark recesses under his skirt. "Oh!" he panted and looked down. Her toes had found him, eager and swollen, and slightly sticky. She rubbed her instep along the underside of his cock, brushing over the head and then back beneath, feeling his heavy member try to follow along as her touch retreated.

"I think my slave boy likes that," she cooed. She pointed her toes and let her foot drift back down to him. His arms were tense, muscles bunching as he clasped them harder behind his back.

"That's right, stay like that, love. Knees apart." He was so easy to read, so eager to please. Her instep was soon coated with slippery juices, his cock twitching every time her toes took a stroll along his tightly scrunched up ball sack. His lips parted in a low moan, and his hips thrust forward to increase the pressure.

"Oh, my, you seem to have spilled something on my foot!" Suddenly it was up in the air in front of him, inches in front of his slightly befuddled face. "What is that, slave?"

His eyes flicked down, then back up to meet hers. "It's precum, Domina. My cock is so ready for you, sweet lady." Her foot moved closer, hovering in front of his lips.

"Take it in your hands, and hold it steady. Use that tongue of yours to clean up your mess!" His hands cupped her heel gently and his eyes locked on hers as he lifted her foot, gently massaging the arch as his tongue caressed along the top, lapping from toes to instep, inhaling the heady musk and then experiencing the taste for the first time.

Frank didn't want to think about it, about what he was doing. In his world before Eliza, it wasn't something he had ever thought of, he would never have considered. But now, with her here tonight, it seemed like a natural conclusion, and he thought, why not?

He laved her with his tongue in long sweet strokes until she pushed his head back roughly.

"That's enough for now. I grow tired of the way your uniform blocks my view. Remove it please and set it here on the couch."

Almost instantly the toga was whisked over his head and folded. Frank lay it on a cushion and scooted back to sit on his heels again at her feet. Eliza leaned forward and cupped his chin in her hand, pulling him close for a soft sweet kiss. "Time for you to put on a show for me, Boy-o." Her fingers curled around his forearm and lifted it, maneuvering his hand to the base of his dick. Instinctively his hand gripped it, flexing, obviously wanting to give a long hard stroke.

"May I?" he rasped.

"Mmmhmmm," she sighed, watching him intently as his grip tightened and he gave a slow pull. His hips rose and fell with the rhythm of it, pushing his slick cock up into his fist. "Lean back, and let me see how you pleasure yourself."

"Yes, Mistress." His eyes jerked up to hers, noting the intensity of her gaze. She was aroused by this, watching his thumb caress over the head of his member, smearing the clear fluid that seeped from it.

As much as he wanted to race headlong and lose himself in a monstrous orgasm, he also wanted to please her, to keep her entertained. He kept his movements slow, emphasizing the thrust and drag of each stroke. Maximizing the precum flowing, until his shaft was almost twitching out of his hand. It was then he glanced up at her again, eyes bright and cheeks faintly flushed. "I am so close, I could cum at any moment." His hand paused and he leaned back, wanting to arch up and release. "May I? Please?" he added.

"I hope you're as close as you say, slave. It will please me to see the extent of your control." She nodded and his hand started moving again, a bit unsure of where she was going with this.

"Stroke harder, a little faster." And he complied, feeling the pleasure building, unsure if he'd be able to stop. "Five! You better be ready, slut. Four! Clench those ass muscles. Three.... Two!" He stroked madly, wanting to time it perfectly, grunting with the effort of it, his hips pumping as he waited for her to finish the countdown. She hesitated and he felt the eruption starting. "One!... and let me hear you cum, my sexy man..."

"Arrrrgh" he didn't recognize the sounds he was making as his orgasm overtook him, and hot seed surged up out onto the cold tile in front of him. His limbs were shaking at the intensity of it, blowing out guttural moans through his clenched teeth. Frank sagged back down onto his heels when it was over, drawing in ragged breaths. His hands dropped to his sides and he fell forward to rest his head on her thigh.

He felt her touch softly on his hair, caressing it back away from his eyes. "Thank you... thank you," he whispered. They cuddled together until they both started to notice the coolness of the evening.

"I'd say it's time for bed, Frank." He got shakily to his feet and gave her a hand up off the couch. She rose up into his arms and dropped a kiss on his lips. "Get a damp towel and make sure we haven't left anything for the housekeeping ladies to deal with tomorrow, and if I'm asleep when you get into the bed don't wake me, just spoon up behind me.

"Yes, ma'am," he replied with a tired grin.

Chapter 17

Activity out in the hallway woke Eliza, reminding her they were in a busy resort. Other residents were closing their doors and bumping their suitcases down the hallway to check out. It would be so easy to roll over and snuggle back into Frank's embrace. She lifted the sheets up over her head and ducked into the shadowy recess under Frank's chin, pleased when he sighed and pulled her closer.

"Don't they realize we had a big night last night?" he joked. "Did we forget to put the 'Do Not Disturb' sign on the door?

"I wouldn't think it would be necessary in a place like this. And what time is it? 8:30?" She dropped a light kiss on the soft spot between his collar bones and closed her eyes. "I could go either way, hit the snooze button for another half hour or get up and search out some breakfast. I think they serve it til 9."

As far as Frank was concerned, she could sleep curled up against him all day, at least until she wanted him in his sex-toy uniform again. He eased out from under the covers and tucked them up around her chin. "I'll go in search of coffee and let you sleep a while longer," he urged, and wasn't surprised when she rolled over and disappeared under the sheet.

"Key card's in my purse," came her muffled reply, as she drifted back to sleep.

Frank dressed in the dim light of the closet and slipped out of the room. The hallway outside their door was empty and filled with morning sunshine. In contrast, departing guests and hotel employees crisscrossed the lobby, venturing between the reception desk, the breakfast area and what looked to be an exercise room. Frank followed his nose into the breakfast area set up in one corner of the restaurant, a simple buffet with the usual cereal bar, bagels, muffins, juice machines and warmer trays of processed eggs and crispy bacon. Other guests were hunkered down at tables, their faces turned up towards cable morning shows on the flat screens.

He surveyed the breakfast buffet once again, not sure how Eliza would feel about any of the offerings. Finally, he decided to put together an assortment on two plates and poured two large cups of coffee. That, at least, he knew how she liked.

It was at that point he realized he was going to have to make two trips, and he flagged down a hotel worker, managing to convince the young lady to lend him a tray, as well as a decanter for extra coffee.

He got good vibes from the breakfast room manager, Zdenka, according to her name tag. She had a sunny disposition and probably encountered the "We want to have our coffee, pastries and fresh fruit alone in our room" request often. Frank was soon loaded up with a broad tray brimming with plates of food, coffee and an extra cup full of stirrers, sugar packets and creamer.

He balanced the tray on one of the dining tables and fished his wallet from a pocket. He handed some singles to Zdenka, which she tried to refuse. "Please," Frank insisted. "I could really use a hand getting this into my room without making too much noise."

Most of the diners had settled into their seats and all the food warmers were full and after a look around to confirm it, the young server nodded. They could make do without her for a few minutes. She lifted the carafe off the tray and cradled it in her palm. "It is on this floor?" she inquired, and at his nod said, "All right, but only as far as your room."

It was a quick trip, and she keyed open the lock so that Frank could shoulder open the door, and then immediately replaced the decanter and dropped the key card onto the tray.

"Thank you," Frank mouthed the words, and smiled when she whispered back, "You're welcome."

He could hear Eliza stirring as the door closed, and headed straight to her. He drew back the curtain partially, letting the late morning sun in, and arranged the feast around her, carefully putting the coffee on the side table before lowering the tray down onto her lap. She propped herself up against the pillows and patted the space on the bed beside her. "Well look how productive you have been this morning!" she teased, selecting half an English muffin and slathering on the jelly.

He leaned over and kissed her. "You never know what the day might hold. We have to keep up your strength!"

Eliza smiled and offered him a bagel. "You like butter or cream cheese?" And then she looked closer at him. "And I like the new look, Frank. A linen shirt over cargo shorts, a very relaxed look.

Frank plucked the bagel and cream cheese out of her hand and lifted up one foot. "And boat shoes!" He seemed so proud of himself she kissed him again. The change had been happening slowly to both of them and was long overdue. A new summer outfit shouldn't be a big deal, but it was more a sign of change. Each of them taking steps to find common ground, and meet in the middle. As if each of them had taken a step back and decided to pay more attention to their personal lives.

She just had to know. "How in the world did you come by those, Frank? Did you go back to Kohl's with your Kohl's Cash?"

It took him a minute to reply, but finally he shrugged and admitted the truth. "I found them in a box of Benny's stuff that ended up at my place by mistake. I did ask if he wanted his stuff back, but he said he'd come to get it sometime, so voila!"

"Remind me to tell Benny he's got good taste," she chuckled. "So what shall we do today? We can't spend the whole day squirreled up here in our nest." Eliza loved the look of disappointment that crossed over his features and tried hard to hide that she felt the same way.

"I saw some brochures in the hallway," Frank said between bites. "For antique shops, hiking and I believe some kind of water park, but I'm sure my phone could come up with other suggestions if those ideas disappoint."

Eliza stretched over to grab the decanter and top off each of their cups. The breakfast tray slid precariously until Frank steadied it and picked up the plate piled high with scrambled eggs and bacon. "We might be able to find one of those breakfast in bed trays at the antique place, so when I bring breakfast tomorrow you don't have to worry about it sliding off your lap."

She delved a fork into his pile of eggs and stole a bite. "Antiquing it is. A tray like that might turn out to be useful in the future. For all the times my rusty lover fetches me breakfast in bed."

The low humidity and sunny skies formatted the perfect day for getting off the beaten path and finding hidden antique shops, barn sales and even a full-fledged indoor flea market. Once in a while, Frank inquired about prices, but mostly he meandered alongside Eliza letting her hand swing in his. He hadn't furniture shopped in years, even though his new apartment definitely needed it.

One road-side barn sale was littered with old wooden tools and farm equipment, but off to the side, Frank spotted a beautiful wrought-iron standing lamp. "That would fit perfectly beside my desk if the wiring isn't 19th century like the rest of it." He climbed over some wooden barrels and extracted the lamp. The black iron curled in various places, under the bulb and on its three feet. He led it at arm's length and looked it over. The shade needed replacing, and he quirked an eyebrow at Eliza, hoping for her opinion.

She lifted a small tag and laughed. "Three hundred dollars...."

Frank set the lamp back carefully. "I wish I had known that before climbing over all those barrels," he joked.

Eliza caught his hand and pulled him close for a quick kiss. "I don't know," she chuckled. "The view of you bending over was spectacular."

"Quit teasing me," he responded and then gasped when she pulled him down more sharply for a rougher kiss.

"I'll tease you all I want. This excursion is just for fun. Stop taking life so seriously."

She was right, Frank thought. He was comparing prices in a touristy antique shop to shopping for home goods twenty years prior. Even if the prices were outrageous, even if the sellers expected a little haggling, he wasn't seriously shopping here. Maybe good weather on the first weekend in June automatically guaranteed the dealers were doubling their prices.

Eliza seemed unfazed by it all. She looked cool and delicious in a bright floral print sundress and strappy sandals. When he looked at her his pulse picked up a little bit, and he wondered what she was thinking. She always had a mischievous look in her eye that made him wonder if she was remembering the previous night. He felt a familiar tightening in his groin and squeezed her hand.

Frank hadn't had a getaway like this in years. A vacation spent doing something with no purpose. The point of the day was to spend time together and converse, hold hands and discover new places. He didn't mind at all that they never did find anything resembling a breakfast tray, and as they headed back to the hotel empty-handed Eliza joked that she'd just have to be up and presentable before 9, to eat in the breakfast area. "And it will give me a chance to show off my new man."

Eliza might be making light of that, but it made Frank's chest puff up with pride as he followed her into their suite.

Their room looked plainer in the light of day, as Eliza plunked down on the couch. "Was that some kind of gym I saw down off the lobby?"

"Not a very well equipped one, but I think I saw some exercise equipment in there." Frank tried to keep the longing out of his voice. He wouldn't mind spending half an hour down there. He had some extra pent up energy to burn off, even if it was a little-used hotel gym.

But Eliza was his first priority. He found a clean wineglass and poured half a glass for his Mistress. Inside these walls, her power returned and he recollected her words. "Once we walk in this door you are mine, bound to serve the entire weekend. Is this your wish?" And oh yes, he still wished. Even if it meant passing up on his daily workout. He dropped to one knee as he handed her cocktail to her.

She took it gingerly and dismissed him. "I have a few notes to go over, sexy." She double checked the time. "Make us a dinner reservation at the restaurant for 7 pm, and then you're free for an hour to work out in that gym area. Be back here by 5:30, ready for adventure in that tub for two."

"Oh, yes, ma'am!" Frank gave a clumsy bow and hustled off to find his gym shorts. The lines were blurring between what was serious between them and what was roleplay, but he didn't care. The idea of giving a proper bow with a flourish tickled him, and would please Eliza, too. Diving deeper into the role was going to be fun, he decided and palmed his phone just long enough to search Youtube for a how to video.

He bookmarked it for later, and stopped by the restaurant to make the dinner reservation. It was easy, and soon he was hustling his way down the hall to the workout room. The area was small, just a few cardio machines, but Frank intended to try all of them.

As he passed the lobby he caught a glimpse of Zdenka chatting with the desk clerk. Her dark hair was cut bluntly at the shoulders, swaying gently as she gestured animatedly as she spoke. Frank gave her a friendly wave, since she had been so helpful to him earlier, and then he got a bright idea. He caught her eye as she was about to leave for the day and waved her over.

"I need your help again," he began. He was in shorts and a t-shirt, his gym towel hung around his neck. He grasped an end in each hand, somewhat protective of it now that it had become his uniform.

Zdenka stopped and turned back from the exit. It was only then Frank noticed she had her handbag slung over her shoulder. "I can find another staff member to assist you, sir, since I'm off the clock and headed out."

"No… no. I'll just come down to breakfast a little early and work it out then. I was hoping the kitchen might have one of those lap top breakfast trays, that sort of has legs? Is lifted a little?"

Comprehension dawned and she nodded enthusiastically, waving as she turned to leave. "I think we have one or two of those in the back. Come down any time after 6 am and remind me what you need."

Happiness surged in him and he bounced up onto his toes. Eliza had hinted about getting up early enough to breakfast in the cafe area, but he still liked the idea of pampering her, plus he yet had a perfectly wrapped gift to deliver. He had an image of a pretty white tray with a flower on one side and her gift on the other, and a plate of breakfast in the middle.

Ten minutes of his workout time had evaporated by the time Frank finally got to the gym. There was a TV in the far corner showing a baseball game, but Frank ignored it, increasing the pace on the treadmill and letting his thoughts return to Eliza as he ran. Usually, it took very little time to get lost in his own thoughts, but his sexy mistress stayed on his mind.

Clearly, Eliza demonstrated a deep awareness of his needs. On the surface, a couple on a weekend getaway might expect to be joined at the hip and do everything together, but Eliza had the sensibility to give him a mental and psychological break. His admiration for her grew another notch, and he returned to the room wondering how she might befuddle and confound him again tonight.

Eliza was right where he'd left her, working on her phone, comforting an anxious bride that even though she was out of town, her invitations would be ready to be mailed on Monday. He grabbed the wine off the bar and refreshed her glass as covertly as possible, and then stood quietly in front of her, wiping perspiration from his face with the little white towel.

"Oh!" she exclaimed as she set aside her phone. "You're back, and you have an interesting smell to you." Her nose crinkled up. "Best if you get a quick shower. For both you and that little towel. I am sure it's aromatic too."

Eliza swatted his ass playfully as he ducked out of the room and headed through the bedroom. The cool spray of the shower felt wonderful, and he took the time to rinse out his towel and hang it up over the curtain rod. The face he saw looking back at him in the mirror as he ran the electric shaver over his cheeks and patted on aftershave kept smiling back at him. He pulled the toga over his head and then smoothed his hair back into place. He never thought he'd be one for role play or assuming the role of a Roman house slave, but the light fabric rustling over his groin made his cock start to stir.

His mind went into overdrive, fantasizing about everything a Roman house slave might have to do for his mistress as he went to the bathtub for two and set about filling it for her. For a moment his mind dwelt on corny 1950s movies about ancient times where slaves had served wine and grapes as their master or mistress lounged in a pool. Miss

Eliza would be impressed, with his attention to detail and his devotion to his role.

Frank stepped out of the bathroom and set about his duties, making sure her glass was filled and serving up an assortment of tasty hors d'oeuvres.

It was an odd feeling, being next to naked and aroused as he moved through the villa. His lovely domina was still ensconced on the couch making notes. He wanted desperately to settle into the tub with her and share a glass of wine. To hold her in his lap and watch her beautiful breasts float, but she'd been very clear. Slaves didn't sip wine and socialize.

He turned off the faucet and tested the water one last time, glancing around to be sure everything was ready. "Domina," he called, "Whenever you are ready."

She stopped at her suitcase on the way into the bathing area, and pulled one of the thinner pieces of rope out of a side pocket. It dangled loosely from her fingertips as she approached.

"Feet shoulder width apart, Rusty. Fingers laced together behind your neck."

A shudder went through him as he turned and stood, hoping his growing cock wasn't too noticeable. Her fingers were gentle, lifting his balls and looping the thin cord underneath them, bringing the ends up and tying a half knot on the top side of his flag pole of a cock. Within seconds she had looped it around and tied it again. A few more wraps and a final square knot at the top, and his balls were firmly secured. It was tight, but not too tight, as if her hands were encircling his balls with a light squeeze.

Eliza gave his package a final pat and stepped into the tub. Her curls were twisted loosely up on top of her head, and after growing accustomed to the temperature she looked up at Frank. "There's soap and a washcloth on the counter. Come help me bathe."

He washed her carefully, slowly running the cloth over her pale skin, and gave her his hand as she stepped out. It felt like a page out of an erotic novel, toweling her dry with an over-sized towel. He even helped her dress, slipping her feet into black pumps and closing the latch on a strand of white pearls. He left her dabbing on mascara and lipstick and hurried to dress. "Make sure those balls stay nice and snug in that wrapping I gave them!" she chided.

"Yes, Ma'am," he replied, gingerly stepping into his underwear, already worried what might happen if it came unraveled. It might even earn him a whipping. Oh, hell, yes, he hoped it was a whipping!

They dined in the fancy resort restaurant and danced alongside other couples in the bar afterward. Eliza deliberately took her time, wanting the evening to last, not rushing dinner, and definitely not rushing the dancing, She wanted to give that little cord as much time as possible to loosen up and fall off. She was fairly confident it would. It always had with Jim. Although it was entirely possible Jim helped that conclusion along.

Frank's arms surrounded her and kept her close as they slow danced. She chuckled and pointed out that his assumption had been right. Every song in the jukebox was a perfect couples' song. She clasped his hand and lay her head in the crook of his neck, inhaling the scent she'd always associate with him, taking her back to the day they met, talking awkwardly at the downtown Marriott.

"Who would have known two months ago that we'd be nestled together like this, feeling like we have known each other for years?"

"Truly, you rescued me from a night of confusion. I read the pamphlet on how the meet and greet was supposed to be different from speed dating, but it wasn't really very clear. They should have done a better job of matching the daters with potential dates. Done a little questionnaire or something."

Eliza squeezed him close and laughed. "Trust my scientist to want to take a scientific approach. There are web sites online that do that, but it was so daunting." She slapped his ass hard. "And don't you be thinking about trying any of those right now. Even for scientific purposes."

"But how will I know which approach is better?" he joked. "Unless I try both systems and compare results?"

That earned him another spank, and next thing he knew they were headed back to the room for a bout of 'behavior modification'. And it was as mind-blowing as he had hoped. She stripped him as soon as they stepped onto the foyer, of everything except the ball string, which somehow had managed to stay in place. She angrily wrapped one loose end of the string around her finger and led him like a pet on a leash, directly into the bedroom.

"Is my pet ready to make amends with his tongue?" she asked as she kicked out of her heels and pulled her dress up over her head."

"Yes, oh yes, please!" The thought of tasting her, pleasing her would be the perfect way to show her what he was feeling inside but kept drawing back from uttering out loud.

"All right then, Rusty. Let's get you ready then. Reach down, and grab those ankles."

His breath caught in his throat, but it was easy to stand for her, spread for her, feel her teasing fingers, spreading his tight pucker, spreading lube and preparing his passage for whichever latex plug she chose.

Her hands were gentle, her words encouraging as she worked his body, making every muscle tighten with desire. So that when she finally lay back and invited him close to her warmth and slick desire he almost wanted to cry with the strength of the emotions he felt for her. "Oh, God, Eliza, I love you," he breathed as he lifted her hips and pulled her up to his mouth.

Her reply was a sharp tug on his balls. Damn, he had forgotten she had the end of that string in her fist. "Show me, pet. Make me cum with that tongue, and then I want to ride that thick cock of yours."

Frank was still exhausted at 8 the following morning. Eliza had kept him awake most of the night, but his internal clock was reliable enough to get him up at his usual time. He slipped from the covers without waking her and set about orchestrating his surprise breakfast in bed for the woman he was proud to call 'mistress'.

Zdenka was in the breakfast area when he arrived and had the elevated breakfast tray that he had inquired about, plus a rolling tray ready to deliver breakfast for two to their fantasy suite.

"Do you think you might have a little vase or a champagne flute I could put a flower in?"

Zdenka had nodded, impressed at the effort Frank was putting in. "A flute would be perfect for one of those daylilies outside by the walkway." She handed him a pair of scissors and motioned for him to head outside. "Go cut one, or maybe two. I will fill your coffee pot and find your vase."

Frank was grinning from ear to ear as he rolled the breakfast cart back to the room. The flowers were a nice touch and the little gift of books he had brought and not found time to give her balanced out the other side of the tray. Plates were piled high with enough food for 4, and best of all she was going to be able to prop herself up in bed and eat at her leisure.

The door to their room opened almost silently, and Frank pushed the surprisingly pretty cart into position right outside her door. There were sounds coming from inside, blankets rustling like someone was rising from the bed.

"Why didn't you wake me, Frank? We are going to miss breakfast. Get your clothes on."

With more bang and less flourish than he intended, Frank bumped the door fully open and presented the overloaded breakfast cart with a little Ta-da! gesture. "You don't have to rush down for breakfast, my lady. Breakfast has come to you!" He shook out a cloth napkin and draped it over his right arm and gave a little bow.

For a moment she sat there on the edge of the bed, poised to rise, taking in the tableau of the gentleman and the meal and then with a sigh she scooted back towards the headboard and tucked the sheet up under her armpits. "Just to be clear, Rusty. This is not what we discussed."

"Yes, ma'am, I am aware." He levered the tray over, fitting it across her lap, waiting a moment while she took in the special touches. "I am aware there may be… consequences, but I had a special gift, have had it since last Friday, but hadn't found the right time to give it to you."

Eliza palmed the small package, weighing it with her hand. "Feels like a book," she said, pulling on the ribbon.

He was pouring coffee, stirring in the cream and sugar for her. "With a little something extra in the bow," he said. "Something I could use a little help from right about now." He set her mug down beside her plate as the mood ring slid free of the ribbon and clattered down beside the flatware.

"A ring? Isn't it a little soon?" she teased, her mood lightening as he blushed. "Never mind. I'm teasing." In a flash she was adjusting the size, working it down onto her finger. "We used to love these things, Jenny and I. Had to get one every time we went to the boardwalk. She always used to say mine was broken since the stone always stayed black." She held up her hand, wiggling her digits. "See?"

He peered closer, and sure enough, it was pitch black. "What does that mean?"

Her laughter filled the room as she started sipping her coffee. "You were the one who was supposed to bring a card with it. I always figured that black meant my hands were always warm. When we get home you can look it up on the internet." She took a minute to salt the scrambled eggs and nibble a corner of a bacon slice before digging into the fruit.

Now that she was settled, Frank turned back to the cart to fix himself a plate. He was feeling pleased with himself, knowing she had the books spread out on the bed beside her, her fingertips brushing over the covers as she read the titles out loud. He remembered reading the blurbs on each one, picturing her as well as himself in the title roles. Frank felt his cock start to stir.

"Oh, no breakfasting in bed together today, Rusty. Inside this room, you serve. Now if we had gotten dressed and gone to the cafeteria, then we could have sat all morning and chatted. But here, it's best you kneel here beside the bed until I need seconds."

Disappointment hit him hard, but he didn't question it. Already he regretted changing her plans and wished he had spoken to her about it first. He slowly knelt down at the foot of the bed, and caught the small paperback she tossed in his general direction.

"Let's see what kind of an eye you have for erotica, my sexy. Start at the beginning, and let me hear that smooth voice of yours read all about Lady Carmen and the House of Discipline."

Shivers broke out over his skin at the thought of it. He held the book carefully in his hands and opened to the first chapter. At first, he was a little bit hesitant, but after a few pages his cock was rock hard, and the graphic descriptions made the desire audible in his voice. Eliza finished her eggs and buttered her toast, slathering on jelly. He grew more comfortable the longer he read, and soon Eliza was relaxing against the pillows sipping the last of her coffee.

Following that last sip, Eliza lifted the tray and rose up from the bed. She dragged the sheet with her over to the breakfast cart, stopping to spoon some eggs and place two pieces of toast onto a plate.

"This is for you, pet." She held the meal out to him. "I need a few minutes, and when I get back I want you and all the toys on the bed, ready to serve.

Frank took the plate she offered and nodded. "I will be ready,   Domina."

Chapter 18

Eliza knew instinctively this was not how Frank had expected breakfast in bed to go. She noticed the slight crease between his eyebrows and a rigidity to his spine that denoted his disappointment and displeasure. Good, she thought. It was high time he learned that not every situation would turn out the way he wished, and it was time she got to see how he coped with following her desires over his when it really went against his plans. How did he accept her authority when it wasn't something he'd beg for? It appeared that he did so with just the slightest scowl, but no argument or resistance.

Once he got going, he read with inflection, even softening his voice when he read the mistress's words. Sitting in bed all day would not have been a problem, listening to him recount the abduction and training of a male submissive. He was aroused by it, that much was evident in his muscle tone and the shine in his eyes. Even his voice took on an extra sexy timbre.

The story was just starting to get good as she spread jelly on her last triangle of toast, and a stray thought popped into her head. She envisioned him draped over her knee for a paddling, his own legs slightly parted, the warmth and stickiness of his cock pressing down onto her thighs. Suddenly a new plan was forming and making her insides tingle. The appeal of the image made her eager to get started. She washed down the toast with the last sip of coffee, lifting the tray off her lap as she rose from the bed. He needed just a little more discipline, enough reprimand to remind him who was boss.

Frank looked up in surprise and found Eliza was suddenly standing over him, beside the breakfast cart and spooning some food onto a plate. His elbows were still braced on the bed, book forgotten in his hands. He slowly set it down when she handed him the plate where he still knelt. "This is for you, pet." Her gaze pinned him in place while she laid out instructions.

She might not have needed to be so harsh, but her words were tempered by the vision she presented, half wrapped in a white bed sheet with the curve of her ass peeking out in back. She let him have a good look as she made her way into the en suite.

Eliza only needed a few minutes to run a brush through her hair and pull a chocolate-colored nightie over her head. The cool, soft fabric clung to her curves and the lace drew attention to her cleavage. It seemed a bit peculiar to be getting dressed for bed now that she was getting up, but being clothed when her submissive was not amplified her power. She was dressing for a scene, she reminded herself.

The atmosphere in the bedroom was different when she returned. It hummed with anticipation.

She ignored Rusty, going straight to the nightstand to ring the front desk. "Hi, good morning, this is Eliza Hamilton in room 122, would it be possible to change our check out to 1 o'clock? It would? Thank you so much!"

She set the phone in its cradle and turned to Frank. The dishes had all been cleared and the cart removed from the room. Her professor sat on the bed with an anxious look on his face. Eliza was pleased to see he was naked and mused that he looked a bit like the statue of 'the thinker', except she could almost feel the warmth rising his sun-kissed skin. It stood out in stark contrast to the linen sheets. Two steps took her close enough to lay a hand in his hair, tilting his head back so she could lean down for a kiss.

'Mmmm" he sighed.

Eliza pointed to the toys strewn about on the bed. "Find your cuffs, and get them on." She could hear the sounds of him obeying as she checked her handbag and pulled out a worn wooden ping pong paddle. "And look what I just happened to find at the flea market yesterday!" She held it aloft. The green rubber matte was faded and past its prime. "Not much good for ping pong, but perfect for us."

Frank gave a non-committal grunt and continued to slide a leather strap through a buckle.

She traced a pattern over the rough surface. "Have you ever been paddled OTK?" she asked.

Frank swallowed hard, fascinated. "If that means what I think it does, then not since I was about seven."

She laughed and sat down on the edge of the bed, motioning for him to approach. The lace hem slid up to reveal more thigh as she moved. "Even still, you should know this is one of my favorite positions. It may not be the easiest thing to do here, without a wing chair or another sturdy piece of furniture, but it's a position you should get used to."

"I should get used to?" the words trailed off, then he shook his head and his eyes focused on her knees. He pulled himself slowly down across her lap, bracing himself on the floor, feeling her smooth legs underneath him. The mocha satin of her lingerie rode up her thighs, caressing his hip as she arranged him to her satisfaction.

Frank felt so awkward, barely balanced in such a precarious position, totally dependent on Eliza's thighs for support. To thrust up against her would have felt so good, so erotic, but she was still shifting her feet, trying to find a way to balance his weight and position his ass. She finally gave up, setting him back on his knees.

"This won't work. Let's try it like a second breakfast," Eliza joked. She caught his hand and pulled him up onto the bed with her. She scooted back until she was leaning against the headboard once more, and motioned to her lap. "Come take the position your lovely breakfast tray had not too long ago."

It was erotic, the way he slowly crawled over her lap and lowered himself down. He lay carefully across her, arranging himself. Eliza pressed a hand between his thighs and urged them to part slightly. He complied eagerly, obliging immediately. Her right hand reached lower, finding his ball sac, still totally denuded of hair. His cock remained pressed between them, as her left hand took position on the small of his back.

"Head down, Rusty, and hands behind your back."

She could see him remembering he had cuffs on and watched as realization dawned about why he had donned them. "Reach that short piece of rope for me, would you? The one by your knee."

Frank stretched and snagged it, dragging it over the sheets and into her hand without dislodging himself from where she'd carefully positioned him. It wasn't a very long cord, but it was sturdy, and she took her time wrapping it through the D-rings and pulling it tight. The more loops she made, the more leverage she had to draw it tighter.

"How's that, Frank? Not too tight?"

His hands flexed open and closed a few times before he declared, "No, ma'am."

He looked delicious, spread out over her lap. She was even more hungry for this than she had been for the bacon and eggs earlier. She let her gaze roll over him, taking in the broad shoulders, the tension in the muscles of his arms, and the tight clenching of his pert buttocks. She tried to memorize the tableau, and add to it the sensation of his sensitive cock pressing against her.

Her hand cupped one ass cheek. "You look so sexy like this." She caressed him slowly, feeling the strength in his bum. He tried to look back over his shoulder, seeing her beautiful face and the excitement in her eyes, but unable to view what her hands were about.

She caught him staring. "You better close those eyes, Boy-o. It's not too late to find a blindfold."

Instantly his eyes shut.

"Just feel. Relax and give up control. Trust me."

"I do trust you, Miss Eliza. Completely."

Her index finger teased up and down the crease between his cheeks and dipped down further between his thighs to find his heavy balls. He wriggled a little, opening his thighs even more, allowing her better access.

"Such a good pet," she breathed. The cap of the lube popped open in her hand, and he remained completely still while she reached down for the tapered silicone plug, spreading a thick coating of lube over it. He was relaxed and ready when she drizzled more into the valley between his cheeks, ready for her fingers, swirling around, then pressing in, first one and then two, working lubricant around his dusky rosebud, coating him inside and out.

He was so responsive. She loved the feel of his inner muscles gripping her tight, even as he thrust forward, grinding his cock against her thigh. She could feel it oozing, and she wanted to make him feel hotter, wilder. His hips moved in time with her fingers, thrusting deep, then withdrawing. "Oh, yes, please, more," he sighed and moaned.

He was so ready, open, quivering with excitement. The silicone plug slipped home easily as she pressed the tip slowly in, allowing him time to get used to the feel, even though he had taken it easily the night before. His inner muscles gripped it and pulled it in the last few centimeters, and it settled into place.

"Mmmmm," he sighed, still smiling.

Not wanting him to get too confident, Eliza took hold of the base and tugged, pulling it back out an inch before letting it sink back into position. Now the area around his cock head was slick with precum and it slipped easily between them as he moved. "Get used to it, slave. Your ass is mine to fill and tease."

"Oh, God, yes, thank you. Yes."

She spanked his ass hard, but it barely left a mark. "Thank you, Miss Eliza," she instructed.

"Thank you, Miss Eliza." She spanked with her bare hand again and then again before deciding it was time for something more.

She picked up the paddle and rubbed it in circles over his buttocks before giving him a swat. It was a little awkward to use sitting up in the bed, but after a few strokes, she found the best way to get a full swing in. "Grip down tight on that plug, pet," her voice was firm. The way his hips bounced and swayed was adorable, half the time trying to evade the paddle and the other half trying to find it. His hands were balled into fists behind his back, and his eyes were squeezed shut.

"You are doing so well, Rusty. Your cock feels so good grinding on my leg. It makes me wet to think about whipping you and then fucking you."

"Oh, God," he whispered.

"Feel how slick your cock has made the space between us, I know when the plug or my fingers rub deep inside you it opens the flood gates and you ooze for me."

"Yesss," he thrust harder against her.

Eliza swatted his taut buttocks determinedly, both sides, top and bottom. He writhed and moaned beneath her as she stoked the fires of his passion. His hindquarters turned pink, and then a deeper rose. Sometimes Eliza would stop to tease fingers down between his legs, or shift his ass up higher across her lap. She wanted him elevated and bent, ass up, head down.

Trembling, he held the position. Eliza wanted him vulnerable. Her left hand delved into the space below the apex his hips made and wrapped around his throbbing cock. He thrust his hips forward uncontrollably, garnering himself a sudden swat from the paddle.

"No one gave you permission to lie flat again!"

"No, mistress, no, I know. But fuck... it feels so good..."

That earned him another swat and made him jerk with the intensity of it. "I want you to keep your ass up, and hips still, so I stroke this dangling appendage you have here." She gave a playful yank, drawing a desperate moan from him.

"Oh, God, yes, I will..." Swat! "Yes, mistress, I will...."

It wasn't easy for him, and she felt a certain pride in his determination to maintain the position. The hand she had wrapped around the length of his shaft had little room to move, but even the slightest pump got a reaction. He was lost in the intensity of it, his body taut as a strung bow. She played him perfectly, knowing he was trapped between his desire to please her, feeling every intense sensation she wanted to heap on him and fighting his desire to surrender to the roaring orgasm that was about erupt from his aching balls.

The paddle fell from her hand as she caressed the curve of his backside, feeling the heat. It was hot against her hand, and he moaned softly at her touch.

"Such a good pet, Rusty," she coaxed. His cock in her hand oozed as she milked it, setting a slow rhythm. His face glistened under a fine sheen of sweat, and he gazed up at her from one eye, the rest of his face obscured by the tangle of bed sheets under him.

"I'm so close," he gasped.

"Not yet!" Her hand stilled for half a minute and resumed the slow, sensual stroking. Her paddle hand, now free, found the base of the plug nestled between his cheeks. She pushed on it, feeling him fight to maintain his pose as he sucked in a sudden breath. She loved how hot he got, this man of hers.

"You like it when I press this into you? Does it make you want to cum?"

"God, yes, please?"

"Oh yes, my rusty boy," Her hand stroked faster, and her fingers teased the plug back and forth. "As long as you clench down tight on that plug and feel it wriggling into that..."

"Fuck, yes. Yesssss......" he groaned and came hard, gasping and moaning as his hips pushed forward into her grasp, coating her hand and thighs. She marveled at the joy of it, having this sexy man come apart in a way she could feel it and control it and command it.

He lay still across her lap as she untied the knots and slipped his wrists free of the cuffs. He lifted himself off her slowly, turning to wrap his arms around her hips. "I don't know how you do it, my lady." He dropped a kiss onto the curve of her waist and lay for a long while pressing his body into the warmth hers.

At noon he stretched and then pulled her up from the bed. "How you get all of me wrapped up in the moment like that. It's so…"

"Intense?" She took his hand and pulled him behind her, naked, into the elegant bathroom. The shower stall was huge, obviously designed for two, and filled the small room with steam almost immediately. Within seconds she had pulled the silk nightie over her head and stepped into the shower. She caught his eye and crooked a finger at him. He didn't need any further invitation.

The over-sized stall had spray jets from above as well as from the side. "So no one has to stand and freeze while their other half hogs all the water," Eliza joked. "Poor Jim used to always insist I get the warm part of the spray."

"He sounds like he was always good to you. Always put you first." Frank lathered up the soap in his hands and spread the foam over her shoulders and down her back, drawing a subtle sigh from her as she relaxed into the massage.

"He did. Oh, he did. And seeing this shower, I'm inclined to take out that tub in my house and see about putting in one like this. I have a feeling we'd use it a lot. Would you like that, Frank?" Eliza half turned to look at him as she posed her question.

"Any shower with you, my lady." He whipped up more bubbles and started washing her chest. "I'd stand in the cold, back half of the tub, or under warm jets like these, to be naked and in the shower with you." His hands made slow circles over her breasts, and he could feel the taut little peaks under his palms. He couldn't believe his body would be reacting again so soon, but it was. His eager cock was starting to swell with arousal, and he suddenly felt Eliza's hand cupping him, her thumb grazing back and forth over the tip as she was inclined to do.

"Better get those hands soapy again, Professor, and take care of washing your own pelvic region. No more sneaking a feel of me!" She traded spaces with him, urging him beneath the densest part of the spray and supervised while he soaped himself. Satisfied he had the job well in hand, she slid the door open and stepped out, drying herself hurriedly with a surprisingly fluffy hotel towel. "We have to get a move on. There's not much time left before our late checkout."

Her whole head disappeared into the soft gray fabric as Eliza toweled her hair vigorously and then peeked back into the shower. "And we have a mess to clean up." She waggled her eyebrows at him, and he laughed. "In fact, Frank, I think you better leave a twenty as a tip for the chambermaid. We wouldn't want them to go uncompensated in the event they find something... nefarious."

He laughed again. "No, ma'am."

Frank drove on the way home and saw just how far into the Poconos they had come. The sight of the resort disappearing in his rearview mirror made him want to plan a return trip in the fall, maybe when he could accept a real collar, one with an owner's tag with Eliza's name on it.

He stretched back into his seat and concentrated on the road, letting the miles roll behind them, but all the while wishing the weekend wasn't ending so soon.

They pulled in for a late lunch at a shiny chrome diner on the side of Route 100. Walking in was like taking a step into the past. The rail car facade held a long Formica counter along the back wall and rows of vinyl and chrome booths pushed up against the front windows. To Frank's delight, each booth had its own personal diner table jukebox. As soon as they were settled he gripped the round turn handle at the top, twisting and making the pages flip. "Anything special my lady wants to hear?"

Eliza looked up from her menu and fished a pair of quarters from the depths of her purse. "Go ahead and put those in while you search. All those boxes are linked, and we can hear whatever other diners have selected."

Frank dropped the coins in with a heavy clink, and sure enough, strains of Billy Joel's "Always a Woman" filled their booth. "Sometimes," she chuckled, "You can wait the whole time you're in here and never hear your own song choice." He studied his menu for a minute and then looked over at Eliza, reading glasses perched on her nose as she frowned down at hers.

"See anything you like?" he prompted.

Her dark eyes flashed at him. "Look at you, fishing for compliments." Her manicured hand stretched out over the retro-looking table and clasped his, the pad of her thumb tenderly grazing back and forth over his knuckles.

She went back to looking over the lunch selections until a cheerful waitress stepped up for their order. Pen and pad were held at the ready. "Good afternoon, I'm Hailey, what can I get for you two?"

Eliza pointed to a a picture of a chicken salad sandwich on a croissant. "I'll take that, but no fries. Have you got chips?" The waitress bobbed her head and looked expectantly at Frank who pointed to the identical photo on his side.

"I'll have what the lady's having, same way. And iced tea for both of us." Their server looked young enough to be in high school, with her dyed black hair and heavy coating of eyeliner. She scribbled down their order and muttered something about putting it in right away before whisking away their menus.

They watched as she disappeared into the back. "Want to lay odds we get something other than chicken salad?" Frank joked. "I am very familiar with students that age and know when they aren't paying one bit of attention.

"Oh..." Eliza looked at him blankly. "Were you saying something?" And then she laughed at the outrage on his face. "You are so easy, my love."

That caused a hiccup in the conversation, both of them sitting like fools, smiling at each other. Both wondering if any more needed to be said. And after a moment the familiar guitar chords of Simon and Garfunkle's 'Cecelia' floated up from the jukebox.

Eliza went on like she hadn't just used the L word, even as part of a joke. "I have always wondered this song is about a domme." They both listened for a moment to the iconic refrain.

'Oh Cecelia, I'm down on my knees,

I'm begging you please, to come home...'

Frank pursed his lips and half sang along. "I think it's definitely about a woman who is wielding her own personal power. Not sure that makes her a domme, though."

They listened intently to the lyrics. "But that bit, right there. 'I got up to wash my face'" Eliza let that thought hang in the air. "Just what was he doing that his face needs washed?" she giggled.

"Oh, I see," said Frank, sipping his iced tea. "She seems like a woman who takes what she wants and moves on. Like she doesn't have much respect for men. Is that what makes her seem like a domme?"

Eliza slapped the back of his hand. "Shame on you!" She leaned out over the table and looked him right in the eyes. "A domme isn't a woman who doesn't respect men! It isn't about respect or lack of it. It's about recognizing that wearing the cuffs or letting the lady lead is a huge turn on to some men. I never thought I would find such a thing again, a man with the emotional confidence and the devotion to put my desires first. That's so rare, and to have it arouse him the way it does me, that's like a gift from the gods."

"Oh...." Was all Frank could manage, and then they both heard a small cough. Hailey had returned and looked down at them, pen and pad still in hand. "We're out of chips, I'm afraid, but I could substitute a cup of soup or the fries."

"Fries!" both Eliza and Frank responded in unison.

Chapter 19

The heat wave that had settled down over the area dragged on through the last week of June and continued on, broken only by swift moving thunderstorms that swept the region at dusk. Frank got back into his routine, mornings at the Atlas gym, afternoons split between grading assignments and sprucing up his former home for showings. Both he and the realtor were eager to get it sold.

The Fourth of July rolled around as another hazy, hot and humid day. Just walking from the front door to the car was enough to make sweat bead on Frank's forehead as he loaded up a cooler full of the most refreshing wines and beers he could think of, because damn, it was hot. His linen shirt was starting to cling, and he hadn't been outside ten minutes.

He lifted a large picnic basket and wedged it next to the cooler so it wouldn't slide. As if meeting all of Eliza's family at once wasn't difficult enough, he was going to be a sweaty mess when he did it. According to her, this shindig was always held outdoors in her Aunt's back yard, and everyone brought drinks and something to grill. Every other year it was probably a perfect barbecue, but this year, the heat and humidity would force anyone sane to remain indoors.

Eliza fluttered out of the house and down the steps in a purple and black floral sundress, holding a wide brimmed hat down on her head with one hand. "Are we all ready?" she asked.

Frank slammed the trunk and let her pull him into her arms, lowering his head to meet her lips. "Oh, ummmm" she sighed, dropping one last kiss on his cheek. "You smell delicious."

"I'll take any advantage I can get, milady, considering it feels like we're inside the laboratory oven. Let's hit the road and try to get the AC blowing before I have to walk the gauntlet." He settled her into her seat and backed down the drive, happy when cooler air flowed from the dash vents. Eliza appeared cool and collected, as always. She plugged her cell into the car charger, and as an afterthought sent a short text to each of her offspring to let them know they were on their way.

"I have a feeling each of those two will be on time today. They are eager to meet you," she quipped.

"The feeling is mutual, but, I'm just not sure this feels right, Eliza. I mean you and me, together, that feels amazingly right, but your family, do they know I'm still technically married?"

She lay her hand on his thigh and gave a gentle squeeze. "Those who need to know, do, and no one is going to bring it up." She waited for him to protest, but he didn't. "Just like all those times when you thought about asking your wife for some kind of leadership in the bedroom and didn't, whenever you think about discussing your most private details, I want you to remember how you just couldn't bring it up. Your marriage is over, but you don't even have to say anything."

"But your mom...?"

"My mom has impeccable manners and would never ask, and if you bring it up yourself I will punish you severely." That stern edge was back in her voice.

"Oooh," he was sounding breathless again. "Will you whip me, mistress?"

She plucked at a curly hair on his thigh, yanking it out. "That wouldn't be punishment, Rusty. More like you'd be banned from my pussy for a week or more. No licking, no fucking..."

He put on a sad puppy face, and she almost laughed.

"And definitely no cumming for you."

Frank gripped the wheel even tighter and made the last few turns. Damned if she hadn't just woken his dick up, like she was planning on having him flying at half mast when they walked into the party. He swung into the driveway and parked on the grass. They were in a very nice part of town. The wide, tree-lined streets were lined by large manicured lawns. Not at all what he expected, after Eliza's tiny rancher.

He unloaded the trunk and looked around. The tranquility of the well-kept front yard and perfectly trimmed topiaries ended abruptly at a white picket fence that outlined the rear garden. Murmuring conversations and the sounds of happy children grew louder as they headed around back.

The heavy white gate swung open easily when Frank leaned on it, and he stepped aside to allow Eliza through first. He had to quickly let the gate bang shut as a pair of dogs bounded for the gap only to be called back by a clamor of voices from around the corner under the shelter of the back porch.

The yard was not large, and he followed along as Eliza wound her way between some tables, past a small crowd assembling a tent pavilion of some kind and dropped the cooler in a row of others beside the grill. It was no ordinary grill, but part of a built-in outdoor cooking area, complete with a vibrant trellis overhead loaded with purple blooms. He only had a moment to take it all in. Eliza gripped him tightly by the hand and swung him around.

A young woman bearing a striking resemblance to Eliza rushed up, laughing and sweeping her mother into her arms. Frank knew he would have recognized Jenny anywhere, and grinned as the two embraced.

Eliza's daughter had the same dark curls and even the same sunglasses. She looked comfortable in khaki shorts and a pale pink polo that perfectly matched her flip flops. She turned to greet Frank but kept her arm linked through Eliza's in a proprietary manner.

"So I finally get to meet the new man!" she exclaimed, eyeing Frank up and down before reaching out her hand. Frank kept a smile on his face, waiting to see if he passed the test, returning the handshake absently. Jenny nodded in his general direction as another twenty something appeared. "Come meet Frank, Tyler. Oh, and mom, you're right! He does smell good!"

Jenny put him instantly at ease with her banter and her charm that was so reminiscent of Eliza. He shook hands with

Tyler, Jenny's clean-cut boyfriend and scanned the yard, trying to figure out who was who. He soon realized he hadn't a clue. It seemed most of the older generation were either in the house or ensconced on the back porch, and all the cousins and in-laws were chaperoning kids in the yard.

Frank thought he heard a faint hum in the air and guessed there was a ceiling fan over the back veranda. No wonder the adults were hiding up there. One cluster of parents supervised while the small children braved the sunshine, running around shrieking, tossing water balloons and arguing over a blue plastic kiddie pool. The porch was cooler than the back yard, and would stay that way until sunset.

A steady stream of guests passed through the white gate. Hydrangeas blossomed around the perimeter of garden, and the air was heavy with the scent of their blooms. Frank marveled a little at them, since the flowers were bright pink and white, instead of the customary blue and white he usually encountered.

"Stay here with Jenny, Frank, while I go find Aunt Lucinda and mom. I have a feeling they'll be together up in the kitchen, and I'd rather bring them out here than let them corner us inside." He watched her go, admiring the sway of her hips as she climbed the porch stairs. He fervently hoped that her caution about the hostess was a joke, or maybe something she had conjured up in her mind.

He glanced around, and studied Jenny as she watched the new arrivals lugging a pair of coolers to the cooking area and returning to their chosen tables to claim seats.

"I never would have taken this family," he muttered. "For a "Dibs, this one is mine" kind of crowd." He wasn't sure if he should be setting up something, or staking a claim on a table himself. Eliza's daughter had the same unruly hair slung back in a scrunchy and the same coffee colored eyes. She waved towards the gate, and Frank studied a couple as they stopped at the first folding table.

The girl looked young, barely out of high school, and her beau could have been one of his students. The boy was lanky and tall, his board shorts looked as if they might fall off at any moment, and his mismatched Hawaiian shirt was open to reveal skin that was already deeply tanned. He needed a haircut, badly, and tossed his head trying to clear his vision by flipping his blond bangs off to the side.

Realization struck Frank. He had seen Eliza do that exact same maneuver. "Is that Josh?" he asked, astounded that Josh could be so different from his mom and sister.

The young man in question abandoned his picnic basket on the table and ran over towards the kiddie pool, snatching the hose from a giggling child. The whole jumble of kids had been awaiting this moment. They shrieked and scattered in circles, flinging balls and water balloons at Josh as he twisted the nozzle. With great flair Josh took aim at the oldest of the preschoolers. He squirted each in turn, until they joined forces to rush back, wrestling the hose away from him.

"Yep, that's him." Jenny laughed. "Hero to small children everywhere." The noise level was drawing concerned looks from the parents, and the screen door banged as Eliza hurried back out onto the porch. She glanced briefly at Frank, happy to see him still chatting with Jenny and headed down the steps to rescue Josh from the army of toddlers. With great reluctance they surrendered him, nodding as Eliza made his excuses.

"Come on kids, you know he's got to go say hi to Grandma and Aunt Lucinda first! I promise he'll be back to play later, so fill some more water balloons!"

Josh followed his mom inside to make his obligatory hellos to the hostess and soon reappeared to collect his girlfriend, Lauren, and stride over to the crowd around Frank. Jenny was holding court and chatting with everyone who stopped nearby to meet Frank, who hadn't done much talking yet. Jenny was all smiles and hugs, motioning to Frank and introducing him as her mother's guest. She was so like her mother, welcoming her curious aunts and cousins and then sending them on their way.

"Yes, this is Frank, mom's friend. He teaches Chemistry." Frank couldn't keep up with the names.

Frank had a suspicion he knew where Jenny got her determination and confidence. She was able to work through most of the awkward moments of cousins, nephews and nieces wanting to shake his hand and take his measure. Each relative had a brief introduction and a chance to say a few words before Jenny whisked them away from the table. One elegantly-dressed lady about his age eyed him with interest, shaking hands longer than necessary, inquiring about where he worked and his academic aspirations.

"Now, now, Aunt Marjorie," Jenny broke into the conversation. "Frank and mom are relatively new acquaintances. Let's not scare him away!"

Josh and his girlfriend even managed to get their table set up while she did it.

Soon they had staked a claim on a table and dressed it up with a pretty white table cloth and a small vase of purple flowers situated in the center. Frank arranged a tray of veggies and dip and had several bottles of wine set up with glasses beside them. He thought he had done well, bringing a White Zinfandel, a Reisling and a little-known rosé from the south of France. They were in the shade of a tall magnolia tree, and Frank felt good as he settled Eliza in one of the chairs and remained standing beside her, warmly shaking hands with her mother, Jane Carlton, who wasn't as imposing as he had feared.

Aunt Lucinda, however, was overly direct and a bit intimidating despite her small size. She looked charming in her cherry blossom dress and low heels. Her silver white hair was cut short and perfectly coiffed. She smiled warmly at Frank as she shook his hand and accepted his thanks for the invitation to join her family gathering, and then pulled him down firmly before releasing his hand. Her voice was low, and laced with venom as she whispered. "Our Eliza is a special girl. She deserves only the best. We expect you to take the best care of her. The best!"

It was a little frightening, for such a small elderly woman to be so forceful. "Yes, ma'am," he answered quickly. "You don't have to tell me, I know she is a treasure."

He was a little relieved when she stepped back. He grabbed the tray of burgers off the table and gestured to Tyler, Jenny's beau, to follow him to the grill. "Tyler and I will get these burgers on while you all get caught up." He bowed slightly as he eased himself away from the table, breathing a sigh of relief as he reached the outdoor kitchen. Grilling burgers he could handle, and Tyler was a pleasant surprise, offering up a mature take on the family dynamics. "It's all about the kids," Tyler informed him. "The birthday parties and the holidays, until the kids grow up and it's like they have a dozen parents all telling them what to do."

Tyler was almost smirking. Until today he had been the newest pledge at what he called the "family fraternity." His grin was infectious as he symbolically passed the torch to Frank. "All the adults will frown at you and ask about your background, all the kids will shriek and run away when you come near, and Jenny's grandmother will probably ask you to sit beside her at dinner and grill you with a thousand questions."

Frank wasn't really surprised, he had known this whole introduction would be uncomfortable. "Oh my God, really? Is that what she did to you? Eliza said it's bring your own burgers, grab your own table." Tyler had a sheepish grin on his face. He winked at Jenny, "We really shouldn't tease the new guy, but it's so tempting."

Eliza's mother didn't end up sitting next to him. She moved from table to table in her role as hostess and spoke with everyone. As the afternoon waned, Jane Carlton pulled up a chair beside her daughter's surprise guest at the family cookout and studied the body language between the two, before finally nodding at Frank. "Lizzie has seemed a little… understated since Jim died. But now," she added, "Now I am happy to see her blooming again." Her words made Frank grin.

"Good work," she whispered, before moving on.

After that it wasn't really hard for Frank to fit in. He had no idea who anyone was, or how they were related. He was generous offering glasses of wine and found many ladies had taste similar to Eliza's. Everything he brought was refreshing and accompanied the standard cook out fare.

He found a safe place behind the grill, replenishing potato salads and bowls of mixed fruit, and discerned that the majority of Eliza's family members were a bit intense about their work. He shook hands and listened to their tales of work as lawyers, account managers and medical researchers. His career as a professor of chemistry seemed to impress them. "I bet you'll be good for Eliza, and help her get started on a serious career," her brother Christian mentioned. He stood about the same height as Frank, with his graying hair and businessman's air. As if almost daring anyone to question his authority.

Frank wondered again how Eliza could have come from this family. Christian had little respect for Eliza's company, High End Design. "It's time for her to stop playing with her postcards and do something meaningful," he commented.

Rendered momentarily speechless, Frank cast around for something to occupy is hands and his mind before he said something rash. But he couldn't help himself. He squared his shoulders and raised himself up to his full height. "She has raised two wonderful children who genuinely love her and her business means everything to the young women who hire her to make their weddings perfect."

"She barely makes ends meet! And her house. It needs to be gutted and redone, or better yet sold."

Over the counter and across the grass, Eliza was trying to catch his eye, waving her wine glass at him. If he had to guess, her sixth sense was kicking in that trouble was brewing in the outdoor kitchen. Frank grabbed the wine bottle he'd brought for Eliza and gave Christian a terse nod. "More likely she is sentimental about the house, since she and Jim had been talking about downsizing to that little town once the kids were gone."

"They were?" Christian asked blankly.

"Yes," Frank went on. "They were going to get a rancher or a Cape Cod there and fix it up together. Walk into town on Sundays to pick up donuts and the morning paper. Only Jim was gone before the time came." He sensed Jim had been old fashioned, and deep down he admired Jim's plans for retirement, enjoying a quiet life with Eliza.

Fearing he had said too much, Frank ducked away and used the last of the rosé to fill glasses around the table. Eliza pulled him into an empty chair next to her and sent Josh back to the buffet to fill up some plates. Happy for her nearness, Frank scooted his chair close enough that their thighs touched and wrapped his arm around the back of her chair. He was still angry about her family's attitude about success. Not just Christian's comments but from the offers from others to help him jump into the big leagues, whether it was high-priced colleges or giant pharmaceutical companies. Having Eliza tucked under his arm reminded him that his work made a difference and helped him relax.

"What were you and Chris talking about?" Eliza asked. "Was he offering to get you a job at a big Pharma company or introduce you to the head of the science department at some big wig university?"

The noise level around their table dimmed, as Eliza and her kids awaited his answer. "Yes, him and also a few others. But, really, we barely talked about me." Frank pulled her close and kissed her temple. "He wanted to talk about you, but…"

"But what?"

"I don't think he understands you at all!"

Laughter and cheers of agreement broke out around the table, plus a few glasses raised in his direction from the rest of the Hamilton table. "Oh, most of them don't!" Eliza added, and Frank thought he distinctly heard Jenny say, "Oh yes, he's a keeper, Mom."

As dusk started to deepen into night, the adults ferried leftovers and dirty pans into the kitchen. Someone had found a box of sparklers for the little ones, and had crowded them around the kiddie pool to dance within safe distance of the water. The sparklers themselves were larger than the usual variety, and gave off a cloud of smoke and a low crackling rumble much to everyone's delight. Frank stood silently beside Eliza, softly cupping her elbow as they peered over shoulders at the spectacle.

Frank felt a faint vibration in his shorts pocket. He had felt it earlier and ignored it, but now that the evening was winding down her wondered if maybe Benny was trying to wish him a Happy Fourth. He excused himself and jogged through the gate and out into the darkness and quiet of the side yard.

He pulled out his phone and swiped a finger across it.

Benny sounded frantic. "I have been trying to get a hold of you all evening, Dad. Where are you? Mom says she's been expecting you all afternoon, and now she's worried you were in a car wreck somewhere."

Frank had no idea what was going on. "Wait a minute, Benny. Just wait. First of all, I never had any plans to spend today with your mother. If there was something with the house, I haven't heard of it. I don't go over there at all if I can avoid it, only to cut grass before a showing.

I have been at a barbecue with Eliza all afternoon. So slow down, and tell me what's going on. You know I wouldn't plan anything with your mom these days."

"Well I don't know what's going on. I'm at the house now, and mom's not here anymore." The silence stretched. "It's like she's been living here. The sink is full of dishes. There are papers all over the dining room table, and there were messages on the answering machine scheduling showings for tomorrow."

Of course there were. A heavy sigh escaped Frank and he pinched the bridge of his nose, trying to ease the ache that started behind his eyes. "Give me ten minutes to say goodnight here," he breathed. "And I'll head over there to help get the house straightened up."

He hated to quit the party early, but he knew Eliza would understand. He heard Benny say goodnight as he lowered his phone, and then jerked it back up to his ear. "Do you think she's deliberately trying to sabotage this? Really?"

"I don't know, dad." Benny was quiet. His voice thoughtful. "There are a whole lot of bills in the dining room from a Dr. Cohen. I think he's part of the counseling group mom sees sometimes."

Frank headed back to find Eliza and pack up the cooler for her. "I probably shouldn't look at any of that, kiddo. Maybe you could contact him and see if we can do some kind of group session, maybe next week when we meet to talk about the house? He should probably be around on that, since it looks like he's the one encouraging her to fight for it."

"Yeah, I can handle that. And thanks dad, I know it isn't easy for you to give up your time with Eliza."

"She'll understand, and don't sweat it, there's always tomorrow."

Benny chuckled as he hung up the phone. "It's been a while since I heard you so optimistic. See you soon."

It was almost midnight when he locked up his old house and headed back to his apartment. He could see the light was on in the kitchen as he parked, and he knew it couldn't be Benny. He pulled himself up the stairs and leaned tiredly against the door while he let himself in. The kitchen light was the only one on, and he spied Eliza's purse on the love seat. Oh! That was unexpected.

All sense of exhaustion left him as he tip toed down the hall. She was curled up in his bed. He washed up as quietly as possible and spooned up behind her, doing his best not to wake her.

"Hmmm took you long enough," she sounded sleepy, and sighed into the sheets. "What did you think of my family?"

"As far as families go, they're pretty typical," Frank responded, trying to keep it light. He pulled her back against his chest and kissed her hair. "And your mom calls you Lizzie!"

She chuckled and wrapped his arm more tightly around her shoulder. "I know, like I am five." She relaxed in his embrace, drifting off. "And I never even got my present... and you never got yours either. I'll have to make sure you get it in the morning."

"My present? What was I supposed to get?"

Eliza chuckled and snuggled into the pillow. "Pussy face."

Chapter 20

Frank spent the next day following the party organizing his documents, everything from pay stubs and bank accounts to contractor's receipts for home improvement. He bought binders and a three-hole punch, setting income statements, tax returns, and amortization schedules in order.

He spoke at length with Kaitlyn, one of the human resource managers at the college and got the paperwork rolling to withdraw a large sum from his 401(k). It would be a setback for his retirement plans, but it might clear his conscience to have Abby settled.

It still burned him a little, that the woman who had walked out on him so bitterly and taken every valuable belonging they had was about to get more. But he was so ready to have this divorce agreement finalized. He wanted there to be no excuses for why every financial question couldn't be answered. Since his online class was rolling, he didn't have to leave the house much, just be available for office hours and monitor the discussions. So he worked out in the early morning, prepared a little bit for his classes in the fall, and spent the rest of his time re-examining his past life.

Emptying their safety deposit box yielded the deed to the house, the title to his car and Benny's birth certificate. Any jewelry that had been there was long gone, though he did find an envelope with some savings bonds. He sighed and tossed those into the bag too.

The remnants of his past life didn't add up to much. The best things he had to show for it were his career and Benny. When he examined the rest, he wondered what he'd been doing. Or maybe it was just Eliza that made him comprehend his heart could feel so much more. Life hadn't been bad, it had been secure, and accomplished what he needed, to provide a home and raise a child. Now, however, he wanted more, and it was finally within reach!

The final meeting with the mediator couldn't come soon enough for him. He dressed up in a suit and stowed his binders into his briefcase. He felt well armored, and even figured he had a way to help Abby keep the house if she wanted it so damn bad.

The drive to the mediator's office was a nightmare of traffic, and even so Frank still managed to walk into the waiting room early. He took a seat and tried to calm his pounding heart. It would all be over soon.

His phone buzzed in his inside coat pocket, and he checked it, smiling when he saw Eliza's quick text. "Good Luck this afternoon. Thinking of you." He typed back a quick, "Thx" and tried to relax in his chair.

At first, he thought he was the first to arrive since all the doors were closed and even the receptionist had looked annoyed when he arrived, but other professionals were arriving and being ushered into a back room. The noise of voices from the conference room grew. And he thought he heard his name. And then Abby's voice. And then Benny's.

He rose and strode to the meeting room, pushing the door open and taking in the group that all stopped talking when he entered the room. None of the group had taken a seat yet. Abby and Benny were on one side with Paul Charleston, the mediator. Two others stood on the far side of the table, Abby's lawyer, Adam Perkins, and a polished man in a sky blue linen suit that Frank assumed was Dr. Cohen.

It was very apparent that all the occupants of the room were working together.

This wasn't a final ironing out of the financial details. This was an ambush. As Frank stepped into the room and set his briefcase on the table, Abby broke away from Benny and flew into his arms. "Oh my God, Frank. Thank God you're here." He held her, feeling her shaking. She seemed more fragile than usual. She had lost that healthy glow she had had for the first few months after she flipped him off and walked out. That was ingrained in his memory, the flush in her cheeks and the anger in her eyes as she had said, "Sionara, Frank."

He stood in the meeting room and wondered what the hell was going on. He met Benny's eyes across the room, but his son looked away almost immediately.

Something definitely was not right. Getting a hold of himself, Frank got Abby seated at the table and waited as the others arranged themselves, all except Dr. Cohen who stepped forward to shake his hand. "Sorry about the circumstances, Frank. I'm Dr. Stanley Cohen."

Frank nodded, feeling his anger rise. "Of Family therapy? A little late for therapy, isn't it?"

"Oh, no. No. Not of Family Therapy. Director of Main Line Oncology." He paused a moment to let that sink in. "I have been treating Abby for about four months now."

Frank dropped down into his chair, feeling the world drop out from under his feet. "Tell me all the details," he croaked. And between Benny and the oncologist, the full disaster was revealed. Abby had cancer. She had been dealing with the diagnosis for almost a year, but putting off treatment while she worked out her new life, and never once thought to inform him of it.

Dammit, she'd had a tumor in her brain, and hadn't told anyone for months. She had been driving to the center for radiation treatment by herself. That asshole Kendrick had been all supportive at the start and when treatment got difficult and it came to driving her down to the cancer center he had cut and run.

Voices were droning on around him, discussing the prognosis, the treatment, and the changes that would need to be made once the memory loss got worse.

Abby was patting his hand and apologizing. "I should never have taken you for granted, Frank. I want to go back to the way things were before. Back when we were happy, the three of us in the house."

Frank pulled away from her, astonished. "You can't be serious. It's been two years. The house is almost sold! We've spent thousands of dollars on lawyers. What is it you think is going to happen here? I thought we were setting the court date to sign the final paperwork."

Abby pushed back her chair and started to stand, covering her face to hide the tears, but Dr. Cohen held up his palm to stop her. "It's all right, Abby, this is a lot for him to take in. Sit down."

Then the doctor turned to Frank and explained. "I highly recommend she stay in the house she's most familiar with, as her short term memory has been eroded. Staying with people she's most familiar with and places where she feels secure will keep the stress to a minimum and allow her to remain independent as long as possible. We have a plan for treatment of this tumor, and there's medication to stem the progression of the memory loss, but she's not going to be able to work, and in time not able to care for herself."

"So I am the best candidate? Good old Frank will drop everything and come home?" he bit out angrily.

"Dad!" Benny interjected, but the mediator cut him off.

"There are alternatives. She could continue to try to work to keep up her health insurance and probably make the disease progress much faster. Adding COBRA coverage to your divorce decree will provide her with 36 months of health insurance, but after that, it will get expensive, if she can even find coverage."

Adam Perkins, Esq. Was incredibly direct. "Or you could sign over care of her and make her a ward of the state. She'll be fine for a while, but the treatment would be unreliable."

"Please, Frank," Abby begged, "You swore it. You promised for better, for worse!"

He felt blindsided. He had sensed the ambush when he walked in, but nothing could have prepared him for this. All the little things were starting to make sense now though. The confusion over what items had been divided or sold. Why she wanted the house so badly, and why she suddenly wanted to stay on his health insurance. The community college offered a damn good policy.

He stared at Abby in disbelief. "Maybe you don't remember hiring movers to come load up all our valuables while I was at work." Frank bit out a laugh. "I don't know why I was surprised. You made it clear that Kendrick was way cooler and more ambitious than I ever was."

"I did not!" Abby gasped.

"You said it to my face! That I was going nowhere, and I dragged you down, being so boring."

"I can't believe I ever said anything like that. You're making that up!"

A soft cough broke into their conversation. "I hate to say it, Mom, but you did," Benny said guiltily. "I was there. But none of that matters, really. We need to settle on a plan to help you, mom. Laying blame and arguing is wasting time."

Frank ran his fingers through his hair and sighed. "What, exactly are you asking of me," he bit out. "And for how long?" He turned and looked at Abby. She looked tired, dark circles ringed her eyes. Her usual high-energy polished look was gone. She looked older. Sadder. "Are you sure you've been to the best cancer center? The best one for your type of tumor?"

She looked confused for a minute, like she didn't know, but both the lawyer and the oncologist replied in unison. "She has."

Frank felt like he was drowning. His future with Eliza was fast disappearing, and it made his heart start to clench. He wasn't sure how she'd react. Would she understand if he took on this responsibility?

Abby was crying again. "Don't you love me anymore?" God, he could see the confusion in her eyes. How had he missed it before? "Why don't you want to stay married to me?" she pleaded. "We always agreed that marriage was forever. No excuses."

Frank grimaced. His estranged wife wanted 'forever' now that her plans for independence were crumbling. He sat and struggled to find a way out.

Paul Charleston, the mediator, clasped a sympathetic hand on his shoulder. "You can't abandon her, Frank."

It was hours later that Frank left the building and wandered blindly to his car. He tossed the briefcase into the backseat and sank down behind the wheel. Anger burned its way through his chest. He had listened for hours to the treatment plans, the prognosis, the amount of care Abby would eventually need. Half the time she had looked at him with hope in her eyes, and the other half her eyes shot daggers, only when she noticed him looking it went back to a dull stare.

Benny had sat beside him and listened too, agreeing with the outline and volunteering to do his best for his mom. They had torn up the divorce papers and agreed to take the house off the market. His real estate agent had been shocked and angry now that she'd gotten word of a couple offers that might be in the pipeline. However, she had agreed to remove the property from the listings.

He felt shell shocked and taken advantage of. Angry that his whole life seemed planned for him, just when he had found out how to really live. And holy crap, what was Eliza going to say? She'd kick him to the curb and never forgive him. He pulled out his phone and sent her a text. "On my way to your house. We need to talk. Things got BAD."

He could barely concentrate on the road, his inner monologue trying to work out how he was going to explain all this to Eliza. He realized how much he hated the words they'd been throwing at him all afternoon, words like Can't and Must. "You can't abandon her, Frank. You must do what's right and take care of her!"

Eliza knew something had to be very wrong. Frank sounded upset in his last text, and he hadn't answered any of the messages she had sent since. She told Shelly she was leaving for the day and headed home, only to end up pacing in her front hallway as she waited for Frank. Today was the day they were finally supposed to know when they were getting their freedom. But Frank hadn't exactly sounded free.

She met him in the doorway after she watched him sprint down the walkway and leap up the steps. He stepped inside and the look on his face… he looked devastated.

"Come in, Frank. What is it?" Eliza let him pull her over to the sofa and they sat down together. He reached out and held her hands, unable to look up at her. Eliza started to get a very bad feeling. She squeezed his hands. "Whatever it is… tell me. I can't help if I don't know."

Frank sank down onto the floor in front of her, going onto his knees and burying his face in her lap. His arms wrapped around her legs and held her close. She could barely hear his voice, it was so muffled at first.

Her hand moved to his hair, stroking softly, and his shoulders started to shake.

"It was all of them, five on one," he began. "Her, Benny, the doctor, the mediator, and the lawyer."

"Wait, the doctor? The therapist?"

He shook his head against her thighs. "A real doctor. An oncologist. She's got some kind of tumor in her brain, slowly eating away at her memories and language ability. She wants the house because any major change would be difficult. The doctors are saying she needs the familiarity."

"Ok. I am sure we can come up with some way to afford to keep it. Get your name off it and set up some kind of trust."

Frank let out a small moan of anguish and held her tighter. "She needs expensive treatment. It's going to be too much for her to handle, especially if she can't work. The options… and poor Benny. I can't dump this on him. He can't make enough to handle all this."

"What is it you are trying to tell me? That you don't think the two of us can oversee all this?" Eliza's heart was starting to pound. The whole situation was crazy. "And take a step back, Frank. Think about it. Exactly who is it that set up this mediation appointment? Who was it who led you into that ambush? Was is her, Abby? Giving you no escape and no backup?"

"It doesn't matter if it was Benny or Abby." He sounded defeated. "They are my family, and they need me."

She could feel her insides shriveling up, praying he wasn't going to say what she didn't think any man in his right mind would be thinking.

"She wants to stay married. She begged me not to divorce her. She can't remember all that's gone on for the last twelve months. She's devastated that I would abandon her, leave her as a ward of the state."

Eliza wanted to shake him. He had to know Abby was using him. "You are her best option, Frank. She needs a nursemaid. She needs health insurance. She needs your old house. You are forgetting she was moving on to greener pastures long before she got sick. She wanted some hot shot stock trader, and she dumped you, good old dependable Frank. But now that she's got nothing else, who does she turn to? Dependable Frank."

"But you knew how I felt about marriage. How I never wanted to divorce."

It was then she actually got it. He was going to stay in the marriage. He was going to move back into the house and provide what that stupid bitch wanted and needed, because she had gotten to him first. A woman who would never love him or desire him again, who hadn't loved or desired him in years. And now Eliza was going to lose him. He was choosing another over her.

Eliza squeezed her eyes shut as the hot burn of tears flooded them. The sting of them burned through her nasal passages and took her breath away. She tried to swallow, but it felt like someone had taken a knife and slashed it across her throat. It had closed up so tight that she couldn't breathe. She remembered the feeling well.

Her mind raced back to the night six years prior when she had gotten a stumbling phone call from one of the local cops, telling her there had been some kind of accident, and she needed to get down to the emergency room at St. Mary's. She would never forget that night. The bright lights of the emergency room, the nurses behind the desk who didn't seem able to tell her anything, just directing her to a crowded waiting area.

At first she had sat patiently, wondering how it was her husband could have been in an accident so far from home. Jim had been out golfing all day, but as evening fell, she had gotten a worried feeling in the pit of her stomach. No messages from him, no offers to pick up milk on the way home had appeared on her cell. And then that phone call had come.

She made it to the hospital in record time, only to be shown a seat on the fringe of the busy ER. Staff was hurrying everywhere, but after half an hour she couldn't take not knowing anymore, and she had waited in line to speak to the nurse at the desk again. "He's still in surgery, Mrs. Hamilton. He's in good hands. I will let you know when we hear something."

It had become a revolving scene, Eliza fretting in her seat in the corner, watching the activity of the busy ER. Ambulances arriving, and patients being wheeled in on gurneys.

As the evening wore on, volunteers had stopped by occasionally, offering to fetch her water or fruit, but she hadn't been able to eat. She tried to read the out of date magazines on the side table, but eventually, she had gotten up to inquire again, only the nurse had been less happy at her interruption. "I know it's hard to wait, but we are doing everything we can."

"Could I maybe know what room he will be headed to, so I could wait there, out of everyone's way?"

The nurse had at least checked the computer and her clipboard before responding, "I don't have any information about that yet, either. We haven't assigned a room number yet."

Eliza had turned to go back to her seat, resigned to more waiting when she'd noticed the emergency doors slide open and realized it was her mom and Jenny hurrying through the double doors. The pair had their arms wrapped around each other, which was odd. They hesitated in the vestibule, scanning, and then zeroed in on Eliza. The look on Jenny's face said it all, and Eliza stood frozen while realization dawned.

The nurse's words were code. "We're doing everything we can" really meant "We are doing everything we can to find your next of kin to get them down here."

"He's in good hands" really meant "He's in God's hands." And "We haven't assigned a room number yet" meant "We haven't assigned a room number yet because he isn't going to a room, he's going to the morgue."

The tears had started burning their way out of her eyes and they hadn't stopped flowing, just run harder as Jenny ran to her mother and held her when her legs would have given out. Eliza's throat felt closed off, like an icy hand held it in an unrelenting grip. And then her mind had blanked. Jenny had somehow stood strong when her mother and grandmother had fallen apart.

The three of them huddled there in the bright lights. Jane had tears streaming down her face and her arms wrapped around her daughter, patting her head like she was a toddler and saying "Aw, honey" over and over.

Eliza knew that pain well, her heart constricting, making it painful to breathe. Her throat muscles clamped down so hard she couldn't swallow or speak. She felt it, her world closing in on herself as she felt Frank get ripped from her life. Wait, as he elected to walk out of her life in favor of an ex who would have thrown him in the trash if he didn't come with health benefits and couldn't act as a home health aide.

Her fingers clenched and unclenched in his hair as she repeated the line in her head, "He's all right. He's ok. He's not dead…"

She tried to blink away the tears, but that only seemed to blur her vision more. The searing sting in her sinuses eased and she found her voice.

"You know she is using you."

Frank moaned and rubbed his face against her leg. "I know." Eliza could feel the dampness of his tears on her slacks. It burned her ego that he would knowingly allow himself to be taken advantage of in this manner. But then he wouldn't be Frank if he would toss aside a woman he had devoted himself to so easily. She had picked him for that quality. She had even pointed it out to him, "You have the potential for that kind of fidelity." Those were her exact words.

If she managed to change him he wouldn't be the old-fashioned honorable gentleman he was. She couldn't expect him to change and not lose some part of himself.

Her grip tightened in his hair and pulled his head up. "You have to go, Frank. We can't be together like this. Not anymore. Not when you're a married man."

"But she and I, we won't be together really, in the sense of a marriage. It won't be a sexual thing. I can't. She can't..." his voice trailed off hopefully.

Eliza pushed him away and stood up. "And what kind of a woman would that make me? The kind to step out with another woman's husband? An adulterer?" God, she hated that word, because given half a chance, she would end up one if she didn't get Frank out soon. Out of her house, out of her life. She should have known he was too good to be true.

Frank rose up and wiped the tears from his cheeks with the back of his hand. "I am so sorry, Eliza. I don't know what to say. I thought maybe you and I could, you know, have dinner sometime?"

Tears rolled over her spiky lashes and dripped down her cheeks, eventually falling down to stain her blouse. She tried to blink them away, and she knew she must look a fright as her mascara ran. She had gotten used to the look in the weeks after Jim's death, but she didn't want Frank to see her this way. "Just go away, Frank. There's nothing left of us. Go home."

Frank wasn't budging. He wanted to take her in his arms again, but refrained. "Wait, Eliza, what can I do?"

"Nothing. Leave." Her decision was final. Eliza sat back down on the couch and covered her face with her hands. Her voice was muffled as she whispered, "I want Jenny."

Frank let himself out and drove home in a daze. After he parked he got out his phone and texted Jenny. "Your mom needs you, right now."

Her reply was a single word. "Blocked."

Chapter 21

The days and nights started to drag by. The nights were the worst, lying awake so long that she would finally get up and turn on the television for company. Only weeks before she had been scheming to get the house to herself, and now, she wanted to be alone and yet the solitude just felt depressing.

Eliza avoided anything that involved leaving her house except work. And even that was by rote, getting up and getting herself off to the office every day, but she mostly stared at the computer screen and played solitaire or Sudoku. Eliza tried to shake herself free of her funk, aware she was neglecting her business even as she sensed Shelly quietly picking up the slack.

Dealing with bubbly and sometimes spoiled brides now turned out to be harder than she thought. Why did it seem that everyone else was entitled to a happily ever after when she wasn't?

She finally convinced herself to remove all the bookmarks that had anything to do with Frank, the little clip of him at the college first and foremost. She removed him from her phone and from her emails. It was hard. Just seeing his name made her want to cry, but she held herself together.

She had had many years of practice. Any time the wrong song came on the radio or she thought of something that made her realize what she had lost, the tears started to flow and she had to redirect her mind. Sometimes long moments of not blinking were a way of not giving in to the tears.

The atmosphere seemed to agree with her. The humidity rose and the water in the air could almost be felt the instant the door opened, but there was only condensation, never any actual rain falling. It was like the sky was trying to hold back its tears in commiseration.

Initially, Frank had tried to text her and repeat, "I'm sorry" so often that Eliza had her finger on the block button. She needed to do it. She really did, but her heart hurt just thinking about it. It proved impossible to ignore him so she finally texted back. "I need you to stop texting me. I NEED this."

July rolled around into August and then August into September, and gradually Eliza exorcised him from her thoughts and her life. The veil of tears pulled back a little. She had more breathing room, and didn't feel like the wrong song on the radio or the wrong aftershave on the man next to her in line at the grocery store would bring that familiar sting to her eyes.

Eliza didn't know what to tell her family, so she said nothing. But no one asked her about it, and she suspected it was Jenny who had handled it for her. She kept her focus on work and bad summertime TV, going to bed early and thankful when she managed to sleep until five. To alleviate some of the tension she joined a gym. Or rather, she started going regularly to the one she already belonged to, for once.

As one week turned into two, she began to really believe it. He was going to let what they had die because he somehow felt honor bound. The more she thought about it, the more a knot of anger started in her stomach and wouldn't go away. She convinced Jenny to set up another account for her on Match.com and spent her days swiping through pictures and sending flirts. They all looked nice, and had fantastic profiles, but they were all so predictable. And none of them had the same spark she'd found with Frank. There was no way to tell if any of them had the right chemistry, and oh, God, the word chemistry even had the power to make her cry.

Appearing normal took more and more effort, and Eliza allowed her children to distract her with movie nights and surprise visits. Her mother was back to offering subtle hints about nice men she'd met at the senior center. The senior center!? Had she gone back to being old? The idea infuriated her.

She put him out of her mind, repeating the mantra "He's all right. He's not dead... " But he might as well be. Eliza finally felt the need to have a conversation with her mother about it, but couldn't bring herself to go into the details. She only said, "It's over. I told him it was over and sent him home. There's no fixing it." Thankfully, Jane didn't press.

The evenings were the hardest now that Josh was spending more and more time at Lauren's place. Eliza sat in the big rocker in the living room, distracting herself with mindless television and playing solitaire on her tablet. Out of habit, she swiped over to check her current challenges in Words with Friends. She had purposely deleted the game with Frank, but his name still popped up as a suggestion for a challenge now and then. She wished she were smarter about computer logistics; that she could go in there and delete him from her game history.

Her finger froze above his name on the list. The little green icon was filled in. He was online. This time Eliza couldn't stop the tears filling her eyes. Her eyes ached almost immediately as she squeezed them shut. Why did she do this to herself?

She opened a game. Not to actually challenge him. Just to confirm he was online. Her finger touched the chat box, bringing up the keyboard. "Hi." She typed. It was dumb to get her hopes up, but within a minute the answer came back.

"Hi."

Her vision started to blur. She blinked furiously, trying to see as she typed, "I miss you." Part of her wanted to throw the tablet across the room, while the other part waited breathlessly for his reply.

"I miss you, too." And a moment later, "I am so lost. I can't even put it into words."

She just sat there and cried. She wanted to type something scorching and angry. Why had she done this? She couldn't see the letters anymore, and her nose was running. She grabbed a tissue and wiped angrily. "I understand. I hate it, but I understand."

"Are you home next Friday? In the evening? I have some things to return. I can arrange the delivery for then."

Eliza didn't know whether to be insulted, angry, or suspicious. "I don't think you have anything I need."

The screen showed him typing for a long time, but finally, the response was only one word. "Please?"

She knew it was a mistake. That it would get her heart expecting something or her hopes rising, wondering what he was sending. Oh, God. She was insane to consider it. "I'll try. But I make no promises."

She thought about it all week. Tried to tell her stomach not to do backflips thinking about it. She stayed in the back of the house, away from the vestibule, but there was nothing she could do to stop her ears from perking up every time a thump sounded outside. And then she'd check for a delivery.

It was almost seven when a soft tap came at the door. Eliza hurried out, thinking the driver might need a signature. "What the hell could he be sending, anyway?"

She swung open the door and froze. Not a box on the stoop. Not a delivery man. It was Frank himself. He had his hands jammed into his pockets and his shoulders were slumped forward, like a dog expecting a kick. She almost slammed the door in his face, but the look in his eyes stopped her. He looked haggard, dark circles beneath his eyes, and they glistened with unshed tears.

Too bad, she thought. This is all his doing. His choice. She started to swing the door shut, but he yanked a hand out and braced his palm on the door. "Please, Eliza, just 5 minutes, please. I know you are home alone."

"Why do you say that? Josh may not be home, but he isn't far away."

Frank stared at her, his mouth set in a firm line. "I know because I called him, and begged him to help me catch you alone. So we can talk."

Josh was in on this? Her heart stuttered. "Can't you see how hard it is for me to see you and want what I can't have?" She thought about closing the door.

"Please?" Frank asked quietly.

He stood there on the stoop in his quiet way until she gave in.

"There's really nothing to talk about," she replied, but she swung the door open and stood back, not wanting to have this personal discussion in front of the neighborhood.

Standing there in the front hallway, where they had been so intimate was hard. Frank swallowed past the lump in his throat and finally got the words out. "I know this is wrong, being here with you. Hurting you more. I know... I know I can't be what you need. But I think I have finally figured it out, Eliza. Figured out what it was you were talking about when you said 'There is one more way a slave can show his complete submission.'"

Eliza had to look away. Up at the ceiling, feeling her eyes fill. "No, Frank. There will be no contract. No way for you to still belong to me, when you belong to someone else. There is nothing you could put in a contract that would show you put me first."

He was retreating even more into himself, shoving his hands back into his front pockets. "No, at first I thought that was what you meant, but then I remembered. You were specific. You said, 'a male submissive' and it got me thinking. About what might be different for a male as opposed to a female. And then it hit me." His hands moved to his waist and flicked open the button on his slacks. Before Eliza knew it he was undoing the zipper.

"What the hell are you doing?" Eliza bit out, angry at herself for softening.

"Look, or give me your hand. You can feel it through my jockeys, I promise."

And it was all too much for her. She held out a hand and let trembling fingers caress down his cock, feeling the hard plastic ridges and bars, the small metal lock of a chastity cage. She couldn't help it, she reached down and palmed him, feeling the whole package, locked down snug and tight. And suddenly he was Rusty again, his eyes bright with passion, his expression belying the arousal she could sense in him.

He reached up and pulled a long gold chain over his head, showing her the shiny key dangling at the end. He held it out to her. "I am offering you this freely, and asking nothing in return, except that maybe once in a while you might permit me to take it off and find some kind of relief. But I want you to know, there's nothing for me with anyone but you. I have nothing at home, having it caged won't be a hardship. Until I walked up to your door there hadn't been any life in it."

Eliza held the chain tight in her fist, pulled up close against her chest. The thought of this was so intriguing. She wanted it so badly, this hope. The hope for the future. For someday. But it wasn't fair to either of them.

"I can't take this, Rusty. I can't put my life on hold. Sooner or later I might find someone who could be a good match, a good companion. I can't ask you to wear that showing me obedience and devotion every day. It could be years before Abby needs hospitalization or loses memory of your marriage, and Benny certainly won't. We have no way of knowing if or when you might actually ever be free."

The tears were back in his eyes. "I know. I have no right. All I know is I need to have something for myself. Some little connection with you. And this was the only thing I thought might work. We could try it. For a few weeks, or a few months. You hold the key. I can get away on weekends, to help you rake the leaves or pull weeds or trim hedges, whatever."

God help her, she was considering this. "Wouldn't you just love it, every weekend." She pulled the chain over her head and felt the key settle into place between her breasts. "We can start with a six-month agreement. We are not dating, and if I encounter anyone on eHarmony or Match I am going on a date."

Frank nodded, buttoning up his pants and zipping up his fly. He wouldn't like it, but to have her back in his life, he could accept it. Eliza took his hand and squeezed it, looking at the floor. After a moment's hesitation, he dropped to his knees. "Let's say 4 pm on the last Friday of the month. You will arrive here and help me out with yard work or whatever chores I might need assistance with, and I will unlock that cage for an hour. It goes back on before you leave, no exceptions. I am not going to be your lover or your girlfriend. I am your key holder, and this is about you making atonement to me for breaking my heart."

Frank was so relieved he nodded enthusiastically. "Yes, mistress." He loved the steel that was back in her voice. But he wouldn't have come and made the offer if he wasn't serious about it.

"You have tried sleeping with that on? I don't want to hear whining that it keeps you awake at night."

He had a self-satisfied grin on his face. "No, ma'am. I have been wearing it for 48 hours already. As an experiment to be sure there wouldn't be any problems."

"Of course. My scientist." Now it was her turn for the self-satisfied grin. "Very well. We are agreed. You can write up a short document for us both to sign when you come back in a week for the last weekend in September. You will also need to bring the small duffle that holds your adult toys when you come, also."

His breath caught, but he was nodding, smiling, a little dumbfounded that somehow this plan had worked. He headed for the door, wanting to get to work on her hedges while it was still light.

The edge was back in her voice when she stopped him. "And Frank, I know those cage locks come with a set of two keys. I expect you to bring me the other when you bring the contract."

"What? Oh yes, I thought it would be safer to have it on hand at my place, in case of emergencies, or doctor's appointments." He looked at her hopefully. "I wouldn't use it without telling you," he insisted.

There was a trace of anger in her voice. "I can't do this halfway, Frank. It's all or nothing. I am not unreasonable, you will have plenty of time when you schedule doctor's appointments to let me know of your needs. In case of emergencies, nine times out of ten I'll be available, although I can't imagine what kind of emergency might lead to inspection of your pelvic region."

She waited, patiently as the minutes stretched out while he mulled it over, and, finally, he acquiesced. "You are correct, as usual, Miss Eliza." He reached into his back pocket and pulled out a blue velvet bag, pulling open the drawstring. He fished with a finger and pulled out a little key that matched the one on her chain. She accepted it gracefully and had him unclasp the chain so she could add it on. His hands lingered on her shoulders as they had all those months ago when they first met. This time Eliza leaned back against his warmth and sighed, allowing herself a small taste of his comfort.

He savored the feel of her lush body against him, breathing in the floral scent of her shampoo. The two of them fit together so perfectly, and it felt so right. He hated to let her go when she finally she stepped away.

"Ok, Rusty, get some work done before night falls." She showed him the out and then leaned against the door as he went down the steps and around to find shears in the garage.

The world had changed in the space of an hour. She never would have guessed that this wild relationship with

Frank would take her someplace totally new. But it meant they had a relationship, even if it wasn't really the usual romantic kind. Trust Frank in his earnest way to come up with a plan to give them some bit of hope. Eliza peeked out the window at him, snipping away at her overgrown hedges. There was no one like him, her rusty lover. He had her in uncharted territory, had somehow convinced her his devotion was still there, still serious. She didn't really know where it all would lead, but she couldn't wait to find out.